# A Social
# AFFAIR

## Dear Reader:

Collaboration novels are always a real treat. You get to witness two prolific voices do their magic together and such is the case with *A Social Affair*, penned by seasoned novelists Earl Sewell and Pat Tucker. I get thousands of advice emails a month and at least twenty-five percent of them deal with relationship drama after two people met on the Internet. They meet complete strangers in cyberspace, get caught up in the fantasy that allows them to escape their dismal reality, and eventually start to catch feelings. It gets even worse when they take the inter-action offline; that's when it becomes authentic. That is also when it can become careless, immoral and even dangerous. People do things that they never imagined themselves doing and start behaving in ways that almost makes it seem like they are having an out-of-body experience. Sure, the Internet can be a major cure for being bored, but some people need to stick to online games and steer away from online dating. Not everyone is prepared for the consequences and people are rarely every-thing that they make themselves out to be.

In *A Social Affair*, two married people that are unhappy with their respective spouses find something in each other that they feel is lacking at home. But like everything you do in the dark, you cannot hide it forever and they both learn the hard way that sometimes home is where the heart truly should remain. Sewell and Tucker tackle this modern-day topic with humanity, sexiness, and compassion.

As always, thanks for supporting Strebor Books, where we strive to bring you the most groundbreaking, out-of-the-box literature in today's market. If you would like to contact me directly, feel free to email me at Zane@eroticanoir.com. You can also find me on Facebook @AuthorZane and on Twitter @planetzane.

Blessings,

*Zane*

Zane
Publisher
Strebor Books International
www.simonandschuster.com/streborbooks

ZANE PRESENTS

# A Social AFFAIR

# PAT TUCKER & EARL SEWELL

STREBOR BOOKS

NEW YORK  LONDON  TORONTO  SYDNEY

Strebor Books
P.O. Box 6505
Largo, MD 20792
http://www.streborbooks.com

ISBN 978-1-59309-449-2
ISBN 978-1-4516-8671-5 (ebook)
LCCN 2012951343

First Strebor Books trade paperback edition February 2013

Cover design: www.mariondesigns.com
Cover photograph: © Keith Saunders/Marion Designs

10  9  8  7  6  5  4  3  2  1

Manufactured in the United States of America

For information regarding special discounts for bulk purchases, please contact Simon & Schuster Special Sales at 1-866-506-1949 or business@simonandschuster.com

The Simon & Schuster Speakers Bureau can bring authors to your live event. For more information or to book an event, contact the Simon & Schuster Speakers Bureau at 1-866-248-3049 or visit our website at www.simonspeakers.com.

# CHAPTER 1

*Codi*

"I *hate* being married! I mean H.A.T.E. hate it!"

There. I said it and I didn't give a rat's ass who heard me. A part of me wished my husband, Larry Bernard Johnson, was here to hear, but he was at work. It was not him really. It was me. He was your typical husband, I guess. He worked, came home, and thought I should wait on him like a lowly slave instead of being his marital equal.

I could have bigger problems. He could be a male ho, he could be an alcoholic like his mama, he could beat me or skip out on us, but still, this married life was for the birds. And by that I meant, the dead birds. It was so damn boring! We did the same thing day in, day out, and it was wearing me out.

When I heard single women yearning for a husband, I wanted to tell them they could take mine! Seriously, what was there to want? Who wanted a controlling man constantly monitoring their every move, checking each red dime they spent, and judging their friends? Most times, I felt more like an inmate than a wife.

I stepped over Larry's pile of dirty clothes, including his streaked boxers, and walked to the kitchen. It was like he believed I was his personal maid. Who would walk in, strip, and leave their clothes in the middle of the bedroom floor like they'd magically make it to the hamper on their own?

I rolled my eyes as I thought about his stinky, lazy, triflin' behind.

Seven years ago when I was single, I was free. I wasn't stressed out all the time. I could come and go whenever I pleased. I partied when I wanted and didn't have to worry about checking in with anyone!

Back in the day, after being out all night, I could sleep until midafternoon the next day and it wouldn't be anybody's business but mine. I might not have had the latest designer clothes, but I always dressed well. I kept my hair and nails looking nice at all times. Now, I couldn't remember what the inside of a beauty salon looked like.

Back then my bills didn't exceed my income, I didn't have a slave master, and I didn't have a snotty-nosed kid constantly working my very last damn nerves.

All those damn studies that claimed married life was better were lying! They said your combined incomes meant less financial stress, monogamous sex combined with love was safer and more enjoyable, and your overall life expectancy was supposed to be longer. I said bullshit! Bullshit! Bullshit!

I've sat here at home and flipped through the channels, bored out of my mind. The problem with being unemployed was you were stuck at home watching TV while everyone else was at work. Working friends didn't have time to sit up on the phone with you, or check out the newest posts on Facebook.

In all honesty, I wished I could be more like my girl, Katina. Unlike our other girlfriends, she didn't work, but she didn't care. Katina always had nice things, tons of money, and she kept her man under control instead of the other way around. Well, when she had a man.

Larry couldn't stand Katina. He said she was trouble, but the more I looked at her, the more I liked what I saw. Take our situation, for instance. While he was sitting up hating on Katina, our household was in a constant state of chaos, so I didn't see how he could complain about her and her household.

Our bills kept piling up, my unemployment was running out fast, and I was tired of robbing Peter to pay Paul. We were behind on everything—the mortgage, car notes, and the light bill. Often-times, I was so stressed and frustrated I didn't even want him to touch me, much less give him some.

"Chile, you betta sex your husband anytime he wants it! You know what you won't do, some other woman will!" That was my mama's voice ringing in my ear. She worked my nerves, too.

The only reason I thought about her now was because of this Social Security commercial on TV. My mom was a widow who thought she could write the book on marriage.

"You young girls don't know how to treat a man. Back in my day, we used to..."

"Urrrghhh!"

I rolled my eyes as I thought about her unwanted *tips* she offered every chance she got. That's why I started avoiding her calls. Who wanted to hear all that foolishness? This was not *back* in her day, times were different now, and I wasn't trying to be submissive to no man. I didn't care how many rings I had on my finger!

I had other issues to think about, like being unemployed.

I had survived three rounds of layoffs at Davis-Pinch, a company that manufactured, sold, and serviced equipment for the offshore oil and gas industry. But they got me in that fourth round.

I was an executive administrative assistant at DP. I swear I wished that moratorium on offshore drilling had never happened. I would've never lost my job in the first doggone place. But it did, and I did, and because of that things were tight and our situation kept getting worse.

The phone rang, but I ignored it. Thoughts of my mother and

my lack of a job always left me feeling some kind of way. My sour mood didn't change until I saw Katina's number pop up on the caller ID. I tossed the remote to the side and picked up my cell phone. I was always glad to hear from Katina.

"Hey, gurrrl," Katina sang the moment I answered.

"Hey, gurrrl," I sang back. That was our customary greeting.

"What's up? What you know good?"

Talking to her always made me feel good no matter what. She lived a life I only dreamed about. She. Was. Single.

"Same ol' same ol'."

"Why you sounding so broken down?" Katina asked.

"You know the drill. Money woes, girl, money woes," I said.

"Yeah, I feel you on that. Things are kind of tight over here, too, but that's okay 'cause I'm about to supersize my side hustle," Katina sang. I could see her doing that played-out cabbage patch dance she did when she thought she had a bomb-ass idea.

I didn't want to ask what she meant by that because in order to have a side hustle, you first needed a job. And since Katina didn't work I couldn't see a side hustle, but who was I to talk? At the moment, unemployment was sustaining me.

"That's why I'm calling you," she said.

My interest was instantly piqued. When Katina had a plan, that plan usually translated into money. She wasn't selfish, so usually if I wanted in, she was willing to share.

"Okay, I'm all ears."

Katina Dawson was a free spirit who lived life to the very fullest, but you had to get to know her to really like her. She found something to celebrate every day and that was what I liked most about her. She spent a little too much time on the Internet in chat rooms for my taste, but I didn't judge.

You could say I lived my life vicariously through her to a certain extent. When she met a new man online or had a blind date, we walked through the process step by step like we were preparing for battle. Katina and I got along really well because she was always quick on her feet and always offered an angle I hadn't considered. We complemented each other.

Sometimes when things got too rough around here, I'd think, *Now what would Katina do?*

"No, girl. This is the type of proposal that requires face-to-face discussion 'cause I'ma have to explain a few things," she said.

I wanted to laugh, but I knew Katina well enough to realize she was dead serious about whatever plan she'd come up with this time.

"Well, you know the baby is sick." I was talking about my three-year-old son, Taylor, who couldn't go to daycare because of a fever. "So I had to keep him home today. I can't come meet you anywhere."

"Don't trip. I can come to you. When do you want me to come through?"

"Let's see..." I was stalling as I tried to determine how long it would take for me to get the house *company* ready.

Katina was like family, but because I stayed home all day, I didn't need her thinking I was nasty and lazy. The reason I didn't clean as diligently as I should was because I was always trying to teach Larry's lazy, ungrateful, chauvinistic ass a lesson!

Uuggh! He made me so sick.

"Uumm, it's ten now. How about around one? That way I have time to feed Taylor and get him settled back down again."

"Okay. I'll be there sometime around one," Katina said.

"Cool."

"Codi!" she yelled as I was about to hang up.

"Yeah?"

"Just promise me you'll have an open mind."

That really made me curious. An open mind?

"Ah, okay, I guess," I replied.

She laughed and I hung up. Great! Now I was gonna drive myself crazy for hours, wondering why I needed to have an open mind about Katina's next side hustle, and what in the world it possibly meant for me.

# CHAPTER 2

## *Quinn*

I f I had a dollar for every time I heard someone say, "Count your blessings because someone in the world has it worse than you," I'd be wealthier than Bill Gates and Oprah. The thing about that saying was I really didn't give a rat's hairy ass about everyone else's issues. I had enough drama to create my own reality television series. My show would be the bomb. All a television network would have had to do was bring the cameras into my house and watch pure bullshit in action.

My sister-in-law, LaQeeta, had temporarily moved into my house. She was thirty-seven and liked dating guys in their twenties. She thought she was the finest woman to ever have had the pleasure of walking around on God's green earth. She'd been unemployed for longer than I could remember; she was waiting on her big payday from a workman's compensation lawsuit she had against UPS. LaQeeta claimed that she had dislocated her spine lifting heavy boxes, but from I could tell, she was strong as an ox. LaQeeta was always boasting and grandstanding about her big payday.

"You just wait, Quinn. When my ship comes in, I'm going to set everyone straight. I'm gonna throw a big-ass party and then buy myself a new car, a new house, some new clothes, some new jewelry, and maybe get myself some even younger dick. Like a nice nineteen-year-old!"

I said to her, "If you go any younger, you'll end up in jail for corrupting a minor."

"Hell, I'm not the one doing the corrupting. They are. You should see the way young boys are always trying to get some of my juicy loving. Truth be told, I wouldn't have to dip back into the twenties if men my own age could keep it up." She turned her behind toward me and smacked her ass.

My wife, Tameecia, has been to jail. Twice. Once for drug possession, the second time for assault. The first incident occurred when the police pulled her over for a traffic violation. When the officer walked up to the car window, the song "Mary Jane" by Rick James was blaring, and she stupidly continued puffing on the joint she was smoking. She was even bold enough to offer the cop a chance to hit it. She explained that she had full authority to smoke weed because of medical reasons, but the officer nailed her because she was driving under the influence and the kids were in the backseat inhaling just as much as she was. So, that led to charges of endangering minor children.

The assault charge came as a result of a fight she got into one night when we went to a club. We decided to dance and some woman, who ironically was wearing the same dress as Tameecia, stepped on her foot several times without apologizing. The woman once again inadvertently made contact with Tameecia, this time spilling a drink all over Tameecia's clothes.

Before the woman could offer an apology, Tameecia slapped her, grabbed a fistful of her hair and slung her to the floor. It was the most ignorant and embarrassing crap I'd ever witnessed. When the police arrived Tameecia had taken the incident to another level. She really showed her ignorant side that night.

"Arrest that bitch, too!" she yelled as the cops were handcuffing her. "I've got bruises from where she dug her heel into my foot! She assaulted me first!"

"That's not what the witnesses said, honey," commented the female officer who was escorting Tameecia out the door.

"Quinn, are you going to let them do this shit to me?" she began barking at me.

I asked, "Why did you have to jump on the woman?"

"That bitch knew what she was doing. I look better than she does in this dress. I'm a real damn woman! I'm from the streets and that's how I handle my business when someone disrespects me!"

I let the law haul her drunken ass to jail. I fully intended to bail her out, but I needed over one thousand dollars to do it. Since I didn't have that type of money, she had to stay in jail until her court date. She was locked up for nearly two months because of the backlog of court cases. As a result, she lost her job. She pleaded guilty to the assault charge and did community service for the crime.

Sometimes, I sat back and thought about all of the foolish decisions I'd made in my life. I often wished I could travel back in time, see my younger self and say, "If you do this dumb shit, you're going to regret it later on." Since there was no way I could ever turn back the hands of time, I had to play the cards I'd been dealt. The problem was, I'd been given a really crappy hand.

I've told everyone that I was a regular motherfucker. In high school my gym teacher would select two team captains and instruct the boys to pick their teammates. I was always the last kid standing. I was the first to admit that I looked like Steve Urkel. Big-ass glasses with a string attached. Pants held up by suspenders and all of my shirts were in some ungodly pattern of plaid.

My mother, God rest her soul, had absolutely no sense of fashion. In fact, her two best girlfriends were Polly and Ester. My father, ironically, was a sharp-dressed man. He always wore designer suits and expensive shoes. He had swagger that made women turn their heads. He couldn't even pump gas or pick up his dry cleaning without some woman smiling at him. He once said to me, "When you get old enough I'll let you in on my secret to attracting women."

I idolized him and wanted to be just as charismatic. My mother, on the other hand, wanted me to be nothing like him, especially after she received a videotape of him having sex with another woman. Apparently my dad's lover forwarded the tape after she caught him cheating on her. My mother always knew she never truly had him all to herself. From what I understood of their relationship, he only married her because she became pregnant with me.

My life was average. I lived in an average house, located in an average neighborhood and I worked an average job as a used car salesman. Hell, I even looked average. My life, in my opinion, was pathetic on every level.

My best friend was my cousin, Calvin. My father and his father were brothers. I would have loved to trade places with him, even if only for a day. Calvin Hamilton was born with the handsome looks and charm that my father had. He was tall, well-built, and had wavy hair and gray eyes. In high school, girls would take one look at him and their legs would fly open. He was the captain of the basketball team. He was such a gifted athlete that he earned a full-ride basketball scholarship to the University of South Carolina.

During Calvin's senior year his team made it all the way to the NCAA Championship game. Although they lost that year, it was still great to watch him play. He went pro and played for the L.A. Clippers for six seasons before an injury ended his career. During those six years he dated some of the prettiest and most expensive women on the planet. He was living the ultimate bachelor life.

He was young, wealthy, and didn't have any nappy-headed kids fucking up his flow.

After his pro career ended Calvin got married, settled down, and had three kids. He owned a chain of fast food restaurants throughout the city. He'd picked up weight and was out of basketball shape, but he still had those pretty boy looks and plenty of money. He crept around on his wife on a regular basis. Last time I spoke with him we were having lunch at Ruby Tuesday. He said, "Man, social networking is the bomb. I have to tip my hat to all of the computer geeks of the world. I've hooked up with so many freaky women, my big-ass dick needs to be arrested for breaking and entering."

I laughed so hard when he said that, the beer I was drinking nearly backwashed out of my nostrils.

"I'm serious, man," he boasted.

"You haven't changed one bit. In high school, college, and during your career, you screwed everything that moved," I said jokingly.

"That's what a man's dick is for. Fucking. Did you miss the memo on that one?" he asked sarcastically.

"No, man. I've just never been as blessed as you," I answered earnestly.

"What do you mean, blessed?" he asked.

I explained what should have been obvious. "You've got the looks. You had the body and the money."

"You think my looks and my money are how I'm getting over on women?" He leaned back in his seat.

"I've always assumed that's what it was."

"Well, I'm not going to lie. That is part of it, but a lot of the guys in the league had the money and looks and still couldn't pull women."

"I don't believe that one." I smiled at him.

"No, I'm serious. Money and looks help, don't get me wrong. But you have to know how to get inside a woman's head. If you can get past all of her mental defenses, you can have any female you want. Your father taught me that one. You must've missed that lesson, too," he teased me.

"Whatever, man. One of these days you're going to run into some crazy woman who is going to go Lorena Bobbitt on you and cut your nuts off."

"That will never happen because I don't deal with crazy chicks like the one you married." He chuckled as he took a sip of his drink.

"What's that supposed to mean?" I asked defensively. My response was really a knee-jerk reaction. We'd had several conversations about how unhappy I was at home.

"Tameecia's the kind of woman who will stab you in your sleep. Tell me I'm wrong." He dared me to challenge the truthfulness of his words.

"No, you're right," I conceded.

"I've told you time and again to leave her crazy ass, but you're a sucker for punishment," he badgered me.

"She's not that bad." I attempted to protect my ego, which was clearly unhappy with the marital choice my logic had made.

"Shit. She's bad enough," he disagreed. "Anyway, enough about all of that. Guess how many women I have in rotation?"

The number of women Calvin bedded was directly linked to his manhood. The higher the number, the more of a man he was. That's the way my father viewed manhood as well. For other men, their manhood was linked to how much alcohol they could consume or how much money they made.

"I have no idea," I said.

"Come on, take a guess," he insisted.

"Two or three," I ventured to say.

"Nah, fool. Seven." He was, without question, grandstanding. "I'm trying to beat Wilt Chamberlain's record." He laughed obnoxiously.

"How many women have you been with?" he boldly asked me.

"I don't know," I said, waving off the question as being a silly one.

"Seriously. Think about it. How many chicks have you nailed? How many pairs of panties have you pulled down?"

Shrugging my shoulders, I said, "Three."

"Damn. That's all? You're still a damn virgin, man," he said, absolutely convinced of his proclamation.

"So you're saying that I should've been like you?"

"I'm saying the more experience you have, the better lover you become. Women love an experienced man. That's why a lot of young girls hook up with older men. That's also the same reason these young boys are lurking around screwing cougars. Again, that was a lesson your father taught me. Did you miss that lesson as well?"

"No, I didn't miss that lesson. I never had enough time or opportunity to chase after women the way you have, that's all."

Popping his fingers, Calvin said, "You know what? I should take you to Nevada."

"Where, Las Vegas?"

"No, to the Moonlite Bunny Ranch," he said. "Just so that you can be with a different woman and add a few more notches to your belt."

"Calvin, there is no way in hell I'm going to allow you to take me to a brothel to fuck a prostitute."

"Hey, don't knock it until you try it." He laughed again. "There's nothing like a woman who knows how to make your toes curl into fists."

I was about to respond to his last comment, but paused in

thought. I sat there feeling as if I'd missed out on some secret male rite of passage. In my heart I realized that I longed for the same types of lustful adventures Calvin had experienced. In reality, if I even dreamed of attempting to become a playboy, Tameecia would shoot first and ask questions later.

# CHAPTER 3

## Codi

I had no idea how dirty my house was until I started trying to clean. When I opened the dishwasher it was full of dirty dishes. Shit! Feeling overwhelmed, I leaned against the counter and wondered what the hell to do with all the dirty dishes. I didn't even realize we had these many dishes.

"Shit!"

I sighed hard. There was no way I could clean the kitchen, the living room, and the guest bathroom before Katina got here. I thought about waking my son now to give him another dose of cough syrup, but if I did that I really wouldn't be able to clean.

Looking around the kitchen again, I said, "Fuck it," and walked out. I'd make sure Katina stayed in the living room. I figured the chances of her having to use the bathroom were better, so I decided to tackle that first.

After looking in on my son, who was still fast asleep, I cleaned all the visible spots in the bathroom. I didn't do a deep cleaning or anything like that, but just enough so Katina wouldn't think I was lazy and nasty.

It was a good thing I switched focus because as soon as I finished straightening up the living room there was a knock at the door.

"Damn. Was it one already?"

It was. And Katina had arrived. I shoved a couple of Larry's dirty socks under the couch cushions and rushed to the front door.

I pulled the door open and stood in stunned silence, staring at Katina. She looked damn good!

Girlfriend was rocking an extra-long, bone-straight, waist-length weave with a part down the middle. It looked so good, like each strand of hair was literally spouting up from her very own roots. Her fitted T-shirt had rhinestone letters that read, *Warning: Bad Bitch Walking!*

Katina had on a tight pair of True Religion jeans that were rolled a couple of inches above her ankles. When I glanced down to step aside and saw the bad-ass pair of gold stack-heeled Christian Louboutin wedges she was wearing, I thought I was gonna be sick.

At that moment I realized I didn't give a damn what this business plan was. I needed to be a part of it. Thank God she was blabbing away on her Bluetooth and didn't notice the envy seeping from my eyes. I was too through.

Katina wiggled her fingers, saying hello, and strutted into my house. I listened as she wrapped up her phone call and plopped down on my sofa. She dropped her Donna Karan leather hobo on the floor and eased back.

"I'm about to walk into a meeting now, so I'm gonna need to holla back at you later," she said.

From the false lashes adorning her eyes to her French-tipped nails and toes, the girl looked fabulous! Suddenly, I started to feel very self-conscious about my own appearance. How did she get blessed with my life?

I had been so busy worrying about the way the house looked, I hadn't even thought about how *I* looked. My ratty oversized T-shirt was stained with crusty peanut butter and dried throw-up. When I sat and crossed my legs, I noticed a stain on the old sweats I was wearing and I felt completely inadequate.

"Guuurrrl!" Katina blew out an exaggerated breath and rolled her eyes. "Men are really a trip. I mean, you give 'em a lil taste and next thing you know, they wanna be wifing you and shit!" she huffed. "I swear, if I get another man tryna propose to me I'm just gonna have to shut down my damn Facebook page."

"Are you still meeting men online?" I felt dirty sitting across from her. My hair probably looked like a bird's nest. Nothing on me had seen any kind of professional attention and sitting in the same room with her, it showed.

"Girl, I don't see how you live without Facebook. I mean, I love it. I met my last two sponsors on there and every time I turn around, a new man is tryna holla. Whew!" She sighed and fanned her face, using her flashy ice-laced fingers as an imaginary fan.

The bling was blinding. I told myself they weren't real diamonds.

"Must be nice," I said. I didn't even try to hide the envy in my voice.

"It is, girl, it is, but sometimes the shit is just too damn much!"

I couldn't relate, so I merely sat and let her get it out. Again, for someone who was unemployed, Katina looked better than a lot of working people I knew.

"Sooo," she began.

I was so eager to hear about this plan that I wanted to beg her to get to it quick, but I controlled myself because *desperate* wasn't a good look on anyone.

"Oohh weee! I almost forgot." She bent over and reached into her bag. "I brought some goodies for us to enjoy. You know, since you don't really get out much I wanted to share a cocktail with you. Sort of like an early happy hour." She smiled and jumped from the couch. She had a large bottle of Nuvo in one hand and a small bottle of Courvoisier in the other.

I panicked, jumped up, and stopped short of tackling her.

"Wait!" I screamed.

She suddenly turned and looked at me with wide, scared eyes.

"What's the matter?" Katina shuddered.

"Girl, you've had me going crazy about this new business of yours! Sit your butt down and let me go get us some glasses. You just keep talking." The last thing I needed was her walking into the kitchen. It looked like a war zone in there.

"Oh, okay. Well, we don't need any ice, but I like drinking out of pretty glasses!" she yelled.

That I could do. I only had three fancy glasses and since I never had any reason to drink socially at home, those were clean.

Rushing into the kitchen, I grabbed them from the top shelf of the cabinet and cursed because the second one had a massive crack running down one side. *I swear! I can't have shit!* Larry's simple ass did that and didn't tell me.

I inspected the other glass, rinsed them quickly and rushed back to the living room where Katina was waiting patiently.

"I love drinking Nuvo during the day. It's the perfect light cocktail," Katina said.

I couldn't remember the last time I drank this early, but I figured all traces would be gone by the time Larry got home.

"Okay, here are the glasses. Now seriously, spill it! I wanna hear everything about this new business of yours."

Katina started giggling. "Okay, remember what I said," she began.

"That's the problem, you haven't *said* shit! Not about the business anyway. Now c'mon, spit it out!" I urged. I was so excited.

"Well, remember you agreed to have an open mind. Just hear me out." She looked me dead in the eyes. "I've started a new webcam business!" she said in slow and dramatic fashion.

"A what?" I frowned. I felt defeated.

I waited all this time to hear about some Internet mess? For the first time since she arrived, I was disappointed. I rushed to clean my house for this? I thought she had a real hustle, a true money-maker. She could've told me about this mess over the damn phone.

"See, that's why I had to explain this in person. My new online business is basically a series of web cameras set up in my bedroom. Not my real bedroom of course, but for business purposes it will be my bedroom. Anyway, men subscribe and pay to tune in and watch me."

Now if this wasn't the craziest thing I'd ever heard. She could tell I wasn't impressed because she stopped talking and picked up her purse. When she opened it and shoved it toward me, I screamed.

"Where'd you get all that damn money from?"

"You don't hear me when I talk. I told you this shit is a bona fide moneymaker! I work a few hours a day either in the evening or in the morning, sometimes both, and I charge five dollars an hour. So far, I have ninety-eight clients."

I blinked. I couldn't wrap my mind around what she was saying. Would it be tacky for me to ask for a loan? I wanted to wear True Religion jeans and rhinestone T-shirts.

"So just to give you an example, last week I made a little more than four thousand dollars. That's with me working only three hours a day, three days last week."

I couldn't believe my ears. Her words replayed in my head over and over again.

*...last week I made a little more than four thousand dollars. That's with me working only three hours a day, three days...*

*...last week I made a little more than four thousand dollars. That's with me working only three hours a day, three days...*

"You're trying to tell me you made close to five thousand dollars working three hours a day?" It was simply unbelievable.

She shoved her bag back toward me. I couldn't remember a time when I'd ever seen that much money!

"Well, what exactly are you doing on this web camera?"

"That's the crazy thing." Katina laughed. Were her teeth whiter?

"It's not like I'm playing with my coochie or anything like that. I'm getting dressed or undressing. One day I was painting my toes. Now I had a T-shirt and some panties on, but all I was doing was painting my toes. It's so crazy. These men are just horny freaks. Horny freaks with money, and I'm getting rich, biiitch!" she yelled.

She started cracking up, and I couldn't help it, so I started laughing, too. I had to. If I didn't laugh, I was scared I'd burst out crying.

# CHAPTER 4

## Quinn

I awoke to the sound of a loud crash. I remained in bed, blinking rapidly as my eyes struggled to bring the ceiling fan into focus. For a moment, I thought the earsplitting sound I'd heard was carried over into reality from a dream that I couldn't remember the details of. I craned my neck to the right and listened to Tameecia's ruckus snoring. She was resting on her back, roaring louder than a lion. She had some type of medical condition, which I couldn't remember the name of that caused her to growl the way she did. Her hair was wrapped up in a black scarf that had the scent of hair chemicals embedded in it. I lifted the covers to see if she was naked. I was hoping I could wake her up by caressing her breasts and kissing her nipples. Unfortunately, she was wearing a one-size-fits-all, red and black flannel housedress that my grandmother wouldn't have been caught dead wearing. Tameecia was always cold. It could be one hundred degrees in the shade and the woman would insist that it was chilly. Last weekend the weather people on TV were warning residents about excessive exposure to the heat and she walked out of the house wearing a sweater. I said to her, "Your ass is going to pass the hell out in the middle of the street, wearing that sweater."

"No, I'm not. It's not ninety-six degrees yet. The day still has to warm up to that temperature. Right now it's cool outside. Can't you feel it?"

I remember swiveling my head disapprovingly and thinking she must have had a mental condition she didn't warn me about.

Although Tameecia's current appearance and sound weren't even remotely close to sexy, I was horny and erect and needed a good release. I positioned my hand over the neckline of the beastly nightgown she was wearing and tried to reach one of her tits. The moment she realized I was touching her, she snatched my hand away as if she was backhanding a child, turned her back to me, and continued snoring.

Frustrated, I positioned myself on my back and glared at the blades of the ceiling fan whirling. I realized that if I wanted any type of pleasure I was going to have to do it my damn self. I guided my hands beneath the covers and down my stomach until I reached my own firmness. I closed my eyes and tried to visualize myself having sex with one of the teachers at my kids' school.

It was the English teacher, Miss Rosemoore. I had met her during the open house a few weeks ago. She was about twenty-six years old and had an ass so round and delicious that I could've gotten down on my knees and kissed it as I thanked Jesus. I imagined myself walking into her classroom after school. She was standing at the blackboard, naked as the day she was born. Her body was perfect. No stretch marks, no drooping breasts and no unsightly body scars, just flawless silky skin that I wanted to devour. She met my gaze and smiled at me.

"Do you know the meaning of the word *cunnilingus*?" she asked as she moved away from the blackboard.

I could see her beautiful perky, chocolate breasts, her sexy flat stomach and her hourglass-shaped black pubic hair. I licked my lips at the thought of my tongue sweeping across her inner thigh while my fingers teased her pubic hair.

"No." I played dumb.

"Do you want me to teach you its meaning?" she asked.

"Oh yeah," I whispered to myself as I enjoyed the fantasy that was taking place in my mind's eye. I imagined her gently resting her ass atop her desk and spreading her legs open as wide as the horizon. I walked over to her, squatted down and rested each one of her legs on my shoulders.

Just as I was about to savor the taste of her, I heard, "Quinn! What the fuck are you doing?" Tameecia's annoying voice snapped me out of my fantasy.

"Trying to concentrate," I barked back as I opened my eyes and lost the image of Miss Rosemoore and her beautiful pussy.

"If you shot that crap on my sheets, you're going to pull them off and do a load of laundry." Tameecia shot daggers of disgust at me with her eyes.

"Why are you waking up in a foul mood?" I complained.

"Because I can and it doesn't cost me a damn thing," she fired back.

"Hell, I was trying to give this to you this morning." I tossed back the covers and showed off my *pride*, which was standing tall and strong. I was hoping she'd put aside her evilness, shut up and perform her wifely duty. It wouldn't have mattered if she had because, at that moment, the loud clanging of pots smashing against the floor got both of our attention.

"Go see what those damned kids of yours are doing," she said, motioning for me to go and investigate.

Reluctantly, I got out of bed, slipped into my pajamas and robe and walked out of the room to find out what happened. Tameecia and I had two children, twin boys who were ten years old and rough. They fought about everything and blamed each other when something came up broken or missing.

During her pregnancy, I insisted on giving the boys normal

names and not one of those jacked-up ghetto names like my sister-in-law, LaQeeta. However, Tameecia was offended by my lack of creativity and loved the idea of giving the boys unique names that no one else would have. I cringed at some of the whack choices she came up with. Names like Wiconia, Leviticus, Lexinacious, and Crisconia.

We ended up having to settle on each one of us picking a name for one of the boys. I named one of the boys Michael and she named the other one Cerius, pronounced like the word *serious*.

I walked down the corridor, past the spare room where LaQeeta slept and into the family room. When I got there, Cerius and Michael were hurriedly trying to sweep up busted drywall along with the pots and pans they'd knocked down from the ceiling rack.

"What the hell?" I asked as I looked at a large hole in the wall that separated the family room from the kitchen. It was then that I realized the loud sound that had woke me up was the sound of drywall busting.

"I didn't do it, Daddy. Cerius did!" said Michael, pointing a finger at his brother.

"Daddy, it was Michael. He's the one who threw me into the wall." Cerius turned around and blamed his brother.

"You can't be serious. How in the hell did you guys bust through the damn wall?" I asked, but really didn't expect to get a logical answer from two ten year olds.

"We were playing fighting, right," Michael began, talking fast. Whenever he got nervous, his mouth ran a mile a minute. "And Cerius hit me in my eye. He hit me so hard I saw this white light flash and I thought he killed me. And then I told him to stop, but he wouldn't. And then, and then, and then he hit me in my other eye, so I pushed him real soft, like this. And he fell through the wall." Michael looked me directly in the eye and expected me to believe every word he'd just said.

"That's not what had happened." Cerius began giving his version of events. I could always tell when he was lying because his eyes would blink rapidly.

"Michael tried to bite me and I told him not to. And then he bit me on my elbow and it hurt so bad that I jerked and that's how he got hit in the eye."

Not wanting to hear any more, I said, "I'm going to go get my belt." As I walked away, they began fussing at each other.

"What's going on?" Tameecia came out of the bedroom and asked.

"They've knocked a damn hole in the wall," I said, utterly disgusted.

"What are you about to do?" Tameecia questioned my haste.

"Whup their asses!" I said with absolute resolve.

"No you're not. You know that I don't believe in hitting kids," Tameecia disagreed with me.

"Well, I do," I said, unwilling to change my mindset.

"Well, I don't, so it's settled." Tameecia spoke to me as if I had no authority in my own house.

"How in the hell are you going to tell me how to discipline the kids?" I raised my voice at her.

"I know one damn thing, you'd better lower your voice and watch what you say to me," Tameecia warned me.

"You know what?" I pointed my finger at her.

"Get your finger out of my face, Quinn." Tameecia slapped my hand away.

"You're lucky I'm not the type of man who hits women," I barked at her.

"But you'll go and hit little kids, right? That's not any better," she argued.

"Hitting kids is different. They have to learn right from wrong." I couldn't believe I was having such a dumb debate with her.

"No one is going to hit my kids." Tameecia turned her back to me and headed toward the boys.

"You go deal with it then! And don't say shit else to me about a goddamn thing!" I shouted out behind her.

Turning and looking at me, she said, "They're boys, Quinn. They roughhouse. Didn't you horse around when you were a kid?" Before I could answer she hit me with a low blow. "Never mind. I forgot. You were a sickly child."

"What's that supposed to mean?" I was beyond pissed off by that point.

"It's true. You know that up until your mid-twenties, you weren't healthy. If it wasn't for me nursing you back to health you'd still be someplace struggling."

"That was a long time ago, Tameecia. I'm no longer that guy," I reminded her.

"Whatever, Quinn. Go lay back down and do what you were doing earlier. You'll feel better," she said and continued toward the living room to deal with the boys.

I stepped back into the bedroom, slammed the door and locked it. I opened and closed my right fist several times to prove to myself that I was strong and not weak.

Sometimes I felt like the character Forrest Gump. Most of my life I was a sickly kid. I'd had childhood cancer. The cancer took a lot of my strength and left my body defenseless to fight off other illnesses. I missed a lot of days at school, but it wasn't because I didn't want to go. I struggled with health issues through junior high and high school. The doctors finally found a combination of medications that worked well with my body after I'd gone through a series of radiation treatments to kill my cancerous cells. I was finally allowed to go back to high school on a regular basis, even though the class I began with had already graduated.

Then, just before my twentieth birthday, I'd finally earned enough credit hours to become a senior. However, I was told that I'd aged out of the system and couldn't come back. My only alternative was to study for the GED exam. Then on the morning of my twentieth birthday, my mother passed away and my life spun woefully out of control.

I became depressed, stopped taking the medicine that was keeping me healthy and became sick again. I lived with my dad and his girlfriend for a little while, but that didn't work out. By the time I was twenty-two I still stupidly refused to take medicine. I'd do okay for a while, and then I'd get sick again. I was able to work as a security guard and keep a small kitchenette apartment for myself. The place wasn't much. A stove, a refrigerator, a bed and a toilet. Yeah, it was a real pathetic existence.

During those years my cousin, Calvin, graduated from college and went pro. I watched every game he played in and wished I was as gifted as he was. He encouraged me to study for and take the GED exam because I'd pretty much given up on myself. When I passed the exam, my confidence was boosted, but not by much because of my health.

Then one day while hanging around at a neighborhood block party, I connected with Tameecia. At the time I suppose subconsciously I was searching for a mother figure to replace the one I'd lost. I was searching for someone who was strong enough to nurse me back to full health.

Tameecia filled that void and helped me to get strong again. Then one evening after leaving a Boyz II Men concert, I made the biggest mistake of my life. I asked Tameecia to marry me. In my heart, I realized I was only doing it because she'd been nagging me about marriage since she stuck around and helped me get out of my slump and onto my feet.

But the naked truth was I didn't love her. I agreed to it out of a sense of guilt. I wanted to go off and date other women and live the playboy lifestyle like Calvin. The last thing I wanted was to settle down.

From the moment I got married and had children, my life turned into one fucked-up situation that I could hardly bear. I tried my best to lay in the bed I'd made, but I didn't know how much more misery I could take.

# CHAPTER 5

*Codi*

I'd be lying if I said I hadn't been thinking about Katina's new business non-stop. The shit was driving me mad. Actually, it was all I could think about, so much so that I started making excuses for what she was doing.

*It ain't like she's selling porn or anything like that. She probably doesn't even have viewers in this state. What's wrong with what she's doing, really?*

The truth was I wanted it to be an option for me, but there was a part of me that knew better. The things I could do with that kind of money. For starters, I'd get us caught up on some of our damn bills! Larry didn't seem the least bit worried about them anymore. We kept *paying on* the cable bill, *paying on* the water bill, and *paying on* everything else. I couldn't remember the last time we paid anything either in full or before the due date. What I hated most was the fact that Larry seemed comfortable living like this. He made me so sick I often wondered why I stayed married to his simple behind.

Katina's life looked more and more appealing to me. It had been more than a week since the new and improved Katina came floating in here, but everything about her new business had my mind spinning. I looked around the dirty house and wondered how my life went so wrong so fast. When did I fall from pretty into this? Before I had the chance to answer any of my own questions, the front door swung open and Larry came strolling in.

Larry was about 5'11" with a regular build. There was nothing enticing about his body. As a matter of fact, he was even developing a budding beer belly. He wore his hair in a close-cropped fade and his facial hair consisted of a thin beard that ran into a goatee. Larry wasn't handsome and he probably wouldn't turn any heads. He had a face that would blend into any crowd, but back in the day, I used to think he was all of that and then some! His brown skin seemed so nice and flawless to me. Boy, did love have a way of making you blind! I must've been one of those very desperate women I always thought about.

"Codi, whatchu cook today? I'm starving like shit!"

I rolled my eyes. He didn't say hello or anything, just wanted to know what was for dinner. I did a silent count to ten as he rushed into our bedroom. Larry worked for the city as a sanitation worker. That meant he always smelled like shit! And when he didn't smell like shit he was talking shit!

Just as I was getting up from the sofa, he came back into the living room wearing a dingy wifebeater undershirt and a pair of basketball shorts. Larry ain't never touched a ball in all the years I'd known him. What ticked me off even more was that he didn't even bother taking a shower! How nasty! Who worked around trash and shit all damn day and didn't wash their ass afterward?

I walked into the kitchen, shaking my head. He still smelled like the trash he worked with all damn day and he didn't even care.

"Oh, I forgot to tell you. Sam and a couple of the homies are coming through to watch the game," Larry said.

*Homies?* I frowned.

But before I could respond Larry had rushed back out of the front door. As quickly as he was gone, he came back in with two cases of beer secured under each arm.

At the sight of all that damn beer I was hot!

"You seen my cooler?" he asked.

I hadn't moved from my spot in the kitchen. Either he didn't notice my hands on my hips or he just didn't give a damn. Knowing Larry, it was the latter.

"Since you ain't cooked shit, can you at least call and order a few pizzas? Oh, I told Sam I'd go half on the wings he bringing, but we gonna need more than just them little damn hot wings," he said.

When had I become a part of the damn planning committee?

Larry pulled his cooler out from somewhere I didn't see, then started dumping his beers inside.

"Damn, Codi. Can you try to straighten up a little? The fellas are gonna be here in about an hour!" He sounded exasperated.

Did I look like Martha Fucking Stewart? Here I'd been trapped in this house all damn day long with his screaming brat, and he came waltzing in here with plans to throw an impromptu party! I was fit to be tied.

"Umm, where's the money coming from for this party?" I finally spoke.

Larry froze where he stood. He'd found the socks I slipped behind the sofa's pillows.

"Party?" He looked like he didn't understand my question. "Damn, Codi. I work hard all damn day while you sittin' up in here on your ass! If I wanna have a few brews and chill with my boys, why you gotta piss all over my plans?"

"I'm not pissing on anything. You came up in here throwing orders around, I'm wondering where you get money for cases of beer, pizzas, and hot wings when your son needs Pampers!" I shouted.

"Pampers! Damn, he still ain't potty trained? What the hell

you do all damn day around this mug? Look, I ain't got time to be arguing with you. Are you gonna order the pizzas or what? I'm tired as hell, but gotta be up in here cleaning shit up. Damn!" His face twisted like the answer to his question was really baffling.

I wanted to throw a butcher knife at his head, but that probably wouldn't be the best way to handle this situation. I shook thoughts of him dying from cyanide poisoning from my mind and turned my attention to the sink full of dirty dishes.

I was pissed for several reasons. Not only was cash too tight for him to be throwing some damn party, but I felt like he didn't tell me about it because he didn't want me making plans to go hang with Katina. He knew if he would've said something I'd be on my way up outta here. Instead, I'd be stuck here waiting on him and his obnoxious loser friends like the hired help.

"You ordering the pizzas or what?" He repeated his question like he was talking to our infant instead of a grown-ass woman.

"I don't have any money to order a damn pizza," I barked.

He blew out a breath as if it was all he could do to deal with me, then he gathered up some more pieces of clothes and stomped back into our bedroom. He was muttering something under his breath, but I really didn't give a damn. When Larry came back out and tossed three twenties at me, I was stunned.

We barely had any damn food, were behind on every single bill, and he had sixty dollars to order pizzas for a damn party?

"Order the damn pizzas," he demanded.

I rolled my eyes at his back as he stood there surveying the living room. I didn't give a damn what the place looked like. I was pissed over how we could afford a damn party, but not some of the other stuff we needed. I hated my life with such a passion.

As I sat on hold with Pizza Hut I told myself it made no sense for me to be living this way. At that moment I decided I'd have to talk with Katina again. Why should I have to suffer? Wasn't it enough that I was married to this loser? I didn't have a job, I was two steps above a live-in maid, and my future seemed bleak.

When the teenager asked for my order through the phone, I quickly said, "I need to order some pizzas."

The pizzas came up to fifty-six dollars! That pissed me off even more. That sixty dollars could go on the cable bill, the water bill, or hell, in the refrigerator.

"How many you order?" Larry had the nerve to ask.

"I ordered five," I said.

"Damn. That's it?"

I wanted to spit on him.

Nearly two hours later my living room looked more like the inside of a rowdy frat house. Larry and his friends were sprawled all across the furniture, throwing back beers like they were going out of style.

The big screen TV was blaring loudly and they were louder and more rambunctious. As they sat around having a good time drinking and eating pizza and wings, I tried to stay out of dodge, but with little luck. I eased into the bedroom, but before I could close the door, I heard him.

"Codi!"

I was frustrated because I couldn't reach Katina by phone and my mind was spinning with thoughts about the wonderful things she was probably doing.

"Yo, Codi!" Larry called out to me again.

I couldn't ignore him for long, but I was tired of running back and forth between the bedroom, the kitchen, and the living room. These guys were pigs who looked and smelled worse than Larry himself.

When I walked out of the room, Larry looked over at one of

the guys who had the nerve to have his socked-foot propped up on the coffee table.

"Aeey, Kevin here wants some crushed red pepper. We got any?"

I looked at him, then looked at Kevin. The pizza boxes were spread out between them on the sofa, the floor, and the coffee table.

When I noticed a few bones and empty beer cans on the floor, I wanted to bolt up out of there as fast as I could. Instead I walked to the kitchen, opened one of the cabinet doors and stopped when something caught my eye. Right there on the counter, next to two empty pizza boxes, were small packets of crushed red pepper.

I looked toward the living room where the guys were laid out, screaming at the TV, laughing, exchanging daps, and fist bumps, and I stormed back into the bedroom, and slammed the door shut.

"Codi!" Larry screamed louder.

He really got me messed up. If I wasn't putting beers in the freezer, then walking out to retrieve them, it was like he kept thinking of reasons to bother me.

"Ugghh! I wish Katina would answer her damn phone!" I said.

"Why?"

Larry's voice startled me! I turned around to see him standing in the doorway with an attitude stretched across his plain features. I didn't even hear him sneak up on me.

"You know you heard me calling you," he said. Did his words slur a bit? Was he already drunk? "Why you tryna embarrass me in front of my boys?"

I sat there staring up at him, thinking quite surely he wasn't serious, but I realized he was!

"Embarrass you?"

"Yeah. You heard me calling your ass! What the hell you doing up in here that you can't come see about me? Kevin had to get up and get his own damn pepper. What kind of shit is that? You tryna make my boys feel unwelcomed over here or what?"

He was drunk. I should have ignored his simple behind. "Larry, what do you need?" I asked calmly.

His head tilted just so. I couldn't tell if he was trying to figure out the answer to my question or was really perplexed.

When the belly-wrenching belch erupted from him I wanted to vomit. He didn't even bother to excuse himself.

"I'm the man of this house! I work my ass off. If I wanna come home and kick it with the fellas, I don't need you walking around here looking pissed off and shit! If they wanna see that type of shit they'd stay they asses at home with they own ol' ladies," he said.

"Dawg, it's cool," someone said from the other side of the door.

Larry waved his arm as if swatting away the words. "Nah, she needs to hear this shit!" he stuttered.

I sat staring up at him, thinking how lucky he was. Here he was hanging out, partying with his friends and showing out for them. Meanwhile, I had to sit and take his shit because I had nothing else to do. That sixty dollars could've taken me out to happy hour with Katina or someplace else—anywhere but here.

Except Larry didn't like when I drank. He had the nerve to say it wasn't ladylike. I knew that was because of thoughts of his mama, but what to do? Oh, I had my ways of getting my drink on without tipping him off.

"Dude, you missing the game. Quit trippin'," someone else screamed.

I wanted him to listen to his friends and leave me the hell alone. It was bad enough that my only friend wasn't picking up her phone. That thought took me back to what she was probably doing. She was working, making five dollars an hour times ninety-eight! She was working and making money while I was sitting here dealing with drunk-ass Larry and his sorry friends.

As he turned and stumbled beyond my view, I wondered just who in the world I had pissed off! Quite surely this life was punishment for some scandalous stuff I had done in a previous life.

When my phone rang and I saw Katina's number flash across the screen, I could've cried tears of joy.

"Heeey, gurrrrl! What's up?" she said the moment I answered.

"Heeey, gurrrrl! Nothing! What have you been doing? I've been calling you non-stop for the past two hours," I hissed.

I had to check myself. It wasn't her fault I was stuck in this miserable excuse for a life.

"I was busy, but what's up?"

Suddenly, I felt a bit stupid. I looked toward the door and listened to the laughter, loud game and chatter going on in the next room. I took a deep breath and blew it out. My throat felt dry, like it was closing in on me and my heart started racing a little, too.

"Ummm, hellllo?" Katina sang. "You blowing me up like crazy and now cat got your tongue?"

"Uh, no," I said.

"Well, what is it? What's so important? What do you want?"

"I was thinking maybe we could talk about your business again," I stammered.

*Silence.*

"Um, I mean, you know, me working with you," I said.

# CHAPTER 6

# Quinn

I grabbed the car key and walked out onto the sales lot the moment I saw a man taking a look at a 2003 Lexus four-door sedan. The man appeared to be in his mid-to-late twenties. He had scraggly blond hair, thick black eyebrows and lobster-red skin from too many hours of baking in the sun. I spread an easygoing smile across my face as I approached him.

"It's a really nice car," I said, placing my hand on the door handle. I opened it up so he could take a look at the interior of the vehicle.

"Yes, it looks very nice," he agreed as I stepped out of his way, allowing him to take a seat. "How many miles on it?"

"Take a look." I handed him the key so he could turn the ignition switch and read the odometer.

"Seventy thousand. Not bad for a two thousand three," he said, poking out his bottom lip and nodding his head approvingly.

"Would you like to take it for a test drive?"

"I'd like that." He smiled and I thought that I was going to have an easy sale and make me a few thousand bucks really quickly.

"Follow me inside. I'll need to make a copy of your driver's license." I felt confident that I'd be able to talk the guy into buying the car.

"So, where do you work?" I asked, probing for information to try and assess how much money he could afford to spend.

"I work at Midway Airport," he said.

"Oh, yeah?" I asked, wondering what exactly he did. "Are you one of those TSA Agents?"

"No. I hate those bozos. I'm a baggage loader for Southwest Airlines," he answered as we walked in the door of the dealership.

"A working man," I said in a complimentary tone of voice as I patted him on his back. The guy gave me his driver's license and I took a look at it so that I could get his name.

"Nathan. It's nice to meet you. I'm Quinn," I said, extending my hand for a handshake.

"Same to you," he said, taking a look at the other cars in the showroom.

"Take a moment to see if there is anything else in here you like. I'm going to go make a copy. I'll be right back," I said, heading toward the owner's office, which was where the Xerox machine was located. No sooner than I'd walked into the office, Big Sam, the owner, greeted me. Big Sam only cared about two things—money and more money. If you weren't making money for him and his shabby dealership, he was going to let you know about it.

"Which car is he interested in?" Big Sam asked as I lifted up the lid on the Xerox machine. "I saw you on the lot talking to him."

"The Lexus," I answered.

"Yeah, make sure you sell him that. I picked it up at the police auction. It's got a rebuilt transmission in it."

"How long is that going to last?" I asked.

"Who gives a fuck? Once he signs the papers and drives off of the lot, the car is his headache, not mine."

"You really shouldn't screw people over, Sam," I griped, feeling somewhat guilty. Selling crappy cars was nothing new to me. I'd been doing it for a while, but for some reason that I couldn't explain, I'd suddenly gotten a conscience.

"What the hell has gotten into you?" Big Sam glared at me, completely perplexed. His breathing was labored and sweat beads were covering his forehead and nose. Sam was one of those guys who'd sweat if he talked too long.

"Aren't you afraid that one day you're going to screw over the wrong customer?" I don't even know why I'd asked that question because I already knew the answer he was going to give.

"Screwing people is the American way. Everyone is fucking over someone else. I just happened to be the one who likes to do the fucking and not the one getting fucked. If you have a problem with the ethics here, you can walk out the door right now." That was another thing about Big Sam. He didn't mind firing sales reps who didn't produce. Big Sam was the bloated and crotchety Ebenezer Scrooge of used car dealers.

"When was the last time you had a sale anyway, Quinn?" he asked.

"Two months," I said.

"Shit, man. You're becoming a goddamn liability. You'd better go on out there and sell that car or start looking for a new job."

"Whatever, man," I mumbled as I turned my back and walked out of the office. In my mind, I could hear Big Sam mutter the words "bah humbug." The last thing I needed was to get fired, especially since the job market was rather bleak.

"Nathan, are you ready to take your new Lexus for a test drive?" I asked, handing him back his driver's license.

"Absolutely," he said. We walked back out onto the lot, got into the car and drove off.

"She rides smoothly, doesn't she?" I mentioned as I sat in the passenger seat.

"Yeah. I've always wanted this car," Nathan admitted as he turned a corner. We drove about two miles up the road, across a set of railroad tracks, and came to the next intersection.

"Why don't you do a quick U-turn and head back? You can go ahead and punch it so that you can see how much power the car has. The police rarely come down this road." I encouraged him to do a little speeding.

"Yeah." Nathan smiled, agreeing. A young guy like him would love the idea of bending the traffic rules. Making sure the road was clear, Nathan swung the car back around, pinned the gas pedal to the floor and we were off. The engine roared as the car picked up speed. I glanced over at the speedometer and noticed that we were doing 70 miles per hour in a 30 mph zone.

"It has some power, don't you think?" I asked.

"Oh yeah." He smiled as we approached the railroad tracks. Nathan tapped the brakes and slowed the vehicle down before crossing the tracks.

"This is the car for you. You look fantastic in it. Why don't we go back so that I can do some paperwork for you? I'm sure we can work out a great monthly payment plan."

"Cool, man. I take the bus past this dealership on my way to work every day and I've been looking at this car for a long time. I've just gotten my income tax check, so we can certainly do something today."

Seeing dollar signs in my mind, I said, "Then let's make sure you drive away with it today so that you'll be the envy of all your friends."

We were less than a mile away from the dealership when Nathan said, "Something is wrong."

"What?" I asked, chuckling and thinking that nothing could possibly go wrong now that I'd pretty much nailed the sale of the car.

"The car isn't accelerating anymore," he said as he kept pinning the gas pedal to the floor. The Lexus began shaking violently, then bucked hard like a bull trying to throw a cowboy off of his back and then finally stopped.

"I'm sure it's nothing," I said as a distressed smile spread across my face.

"Oh no, it's something, man. This thing is a piece of shit." Nathan was clearly not satisfied.

"It's probably just a sensor or something simple like that. We can get it fixed today." I attempted to downplay the fact that the car had rolled to a complete stop. Nathan tried to start the car up again, but it was completely dead.

Looking at me, Nathan said, "Good-bye," and got out of the car.

"Hey, man, can you at least help me push it out of the street?" I asked as I got out on the passenger side.

"Hell no!" Nathan yelled as he walked away.

"Damn," I growled through clenched teeth. I called Big Sam to tell him that the car stopped and he needed to send out a tow truck. I knew the moment I informed him of the news, his grumpy ass would blame the breakdown and loss of the sale on me.

Later that evening when I arrived home, I was exhausted and wasn't in the mood for bullshit. I didn't want to hear any noise from the twins, and I didn't want to hear LaQeeta's loud mouth, or any of Tameecia's complaints. In fact, if I could've had one wish at that moment, it would have been to escape to someplace other than where I lived. As I was pulling up to my house, I noticed a brand-new black and red Dodge Challenger parked in my driveway. I didn't recognize the car and had no clue as to who was visiting. I parked on the street, got out of my car and shut the door. As I walked toward the house, I saw a man coming out of my front door. He was as dark as charcoal, had a perm like Kat

Williams and was wearing a very loud peach suit. He had jewelry on all of his fingers and was checking out my property as if he were looking to either buy it or move in. He looked like a cheap pimp from a bad 70s movie.

"Who are you?" I asked, pinching my eyebrows together.

"What's up, baby?" He chuckled. "No need for hostility." He reached out to shake my hand.

"And you are?" I asked once again.

"I'm nobody, baby. I'm just a figment of your imagination." He wiggled his fingers as if he were a magician about to mystify my mind with an illusion.

"Okay, Mr. Nobody. What are you doing in my house?" My tone of voice wasn't pleasant.

"Oh, this is your place?" he asked, pointing to my house. "LaQeeta said this was her spot."

I exhaled loudly. "LaQeeta is just staying for a little while."

"No problem, baby." He popped his collar. "LaQeeta and I have a little business arrangement. I'm going to roll through every so often and put some of this pipe in her and then roll out," he said, grabbing his crotch. I immediately realized that I had to communicate with the man on a completely different level. Telling him to stay the hell out of my house would be too direct for him to comprehend.

"Look here, playa. Pimp to pimp, man to man. You can stick the pipe to LaQeeta until hell freezes over, but you can't do it in my backyard."

"No disrespect, baby. We got off on the wrong foot, that's all. I'm sure we can set this thing straight," he said as he moved toward his car. He opened the door, then paused. He met my gaze, and said, "By the way, my name is Smokey Love. I run the gentlemen's club off of Interstate fifty-seven. If you ever find yourself in the mood for some adult entertainment, come take a walk on my side of the street for a little while. Before you come, hit me up on Facebook. Just type in my name, Smokey Love. Inbox me and I'll make sure that you have a life-altering experience at no charge." Smokey winked at me before he got in his car and pulled off.

Feeling insulted, I marched inside to confront LaQeeta about having men in my house.

"LaQeeta!" I shouted out her name. I wanted her to jump with fear when she heard the tone of my voice.

"Why the hell are you shouting out my damn name like you're the police?" LaQeeta asked as she stepped out into the archway that separated the kitchen from the living room. She was wearing a black camisole that was snuggling her full-sized figure tightly. It was obvious the lingerie was too small.

"I don't appreciate you having Smokey the Clown in my house," I said, folding my arms across my chest while standing with my legs shoulder width apart.

"Smokey is harmless. I've known him for a long time. Besides, my little young boyfriend pissed me off. He never has any money," she explained.

"I don't care how long you've known him, and I damn sure don't care about your broke-ass twenty-one-year-old. I don't want Smokey in my damn house." I raised my voice so she'd understand how serious I was.

"Look, Tameecia said I could have all of the company that I wanted and it wouldn't be a problem. My young boyfriend has been over here countless times and there hasn't been an issue. I try to do my personal business when everyone is out of the house. A woman as sexy as me has needs. Tameecia took the kids to see a movie, so I figured it would be a good time to get my freak on. I'm sorry that you ran into Smokey, but I'm not going to stop inviting him or my young guy over unless Tameecia tells me differently," LaQeeta snapped back at me as she scratched her sagging left breast. I glanced down at her chunky chocolate thighs, which had unattractive cellulite ripples, and curled my lips into a sour expression. I'd passed judgment on her and in my mind was thinking that she needed to lose weight.

"Have you forgotten that you don't pay a damn thing up in here, including the food that you eat? Where do you get off telling me what you're going to do in my home?" I decided that I wasn't going to hold back my anger. "And you need to go on a damn diet!"

"Oh, you want to go there with me? Are you sure you want to go down that road?" LaQeeta asked unapologetically as she pointed her chubby index finger at me.

"All I know is I'd better not see any other men coming up in here or there will be hell to pay! You need to have your boyfriends take you to a hotel," I said, standing my ground.

"No, I don't. Me and my sister are close and nothing will come between us, not even you. And in case you haven't figured this out yet, which I know you haven't, my sister runs this house and not you. You never have, Quinn. She's the woman and the man in your marriage and the sooner you realize that, the better off everyone will be."

With flames of resentment smoldering in my eyes I opened and closed my fists. I was done talking and wanted to whip some ass.

"What? You feeling like you want to do something?" LaQeeta read the rage in my eyes. She opened up a nearby drawer and removed a butcher's knife. "Come on if you feeling like you want to take it there. You know that I don't mind getting into it!"

"You will not threaten me in my own damn house!" I fired angry words at her.

"Come shut me up then." She called me out. She thought I was a complete punk.

"Hang on, I've got something for your big ass! You'd better call nine-one-one right now," I said as I turned toward the front door. I walked back down the driveway and opened the trunk of my car. I lifted up the floor covering and removed the tire rod. As I was heading back up the driveway, Tameecia honked her horn.

"Where are you going with that?" she asked as she turned into the driveway.

"To crack your sister's skull," I growled as she brought her car to a halt.

"What? Wait a minute," Tameecia said as she got out. She rushed over to me and placed the palms of her hands on my chest to stop me.

"I'm tired of being treated like I'm a damn child around here. The only way I'm going to get some respect is to crack open someone's head. Today is ass-whipping day for your freeloading sister," I yelled. I momentarily glanced at the boys, who were watching the drama from the safety of the car.

"Quinn, you need to calm down." Tameecia chuckled, not taking me seriously.

"Let him go. I've already dialed nine-one and I'm just itching to press the other one." LaQeeta had come to the front door to aggravate me more. She had the butcher's knife in one hand and the phone in the other.

"LaQeeta, let me handle this, please." Tameecia glanced at her sister and motioned for her to go back inside. Without saying anything more, LaQeeta went about her way.

"Now put that tire rod down before you hurt yourself. You know good and well you don't have the strength of a flea."

"I'm not a fragile man," I snapped at Tameecia.

"Well, you're certainly no thug either," she said with a chuckle. I looked at her with disbelief. I didn't want to accept the fact that she viewed me as a weak man.

"Be careful of what you say to me, Tameecia," I warned her.

"Or what?" She had a silly smirk on her face that I wanted to slap off.

"Fuck it, Tameecia," I said as I backed away from her. I walked over to my car and got back in.

"Quinn, stop being such a baby." Tameecia didn't get it and I didn't know how much more I could take. I fired up my car and drove away.

# CHAPTER 7

*Codi*

The sun wasn't even up yet, and already my day was off to a pissy start. I had to be strategic. Usually, Larry was out the door before I could focus my sleep-encrusted eyes on the digital clock next to our bed, but today it seemed like just because I had plans, he was moving slower than a lethargic drunk. I tried to be patient because I didn't want to make him suspicious. The last thing I needed was a barrage of questions from him.

By the time I saw 6:00 on the digital clock, I wanted to shove his half-naked behind out the damn door! Why was he moving so slowly? Didn't he have a garbage truck to hang off right about now?

"Aren't you gonna be late?" I asked. I tried to hide the irritation from my voice and he didn't see me rolling my eyes.

"Oh, we staying in the yard today," he said, almost bragging.

By the yard he meant the city landfill, and that meant my house would smell like a massive pile of shit for at least the next three days when he finally came home later. I was fuming on the inside, but I struggled to keep a straight face. I wasn't upset about the funk he was sure to bring home with him later, but more for the fact that he was moving so damn slow. I had things to do!

He sat on the edge of the bed, putting on his socks and moving slower than molasses. I needed him gone! I rolled over onto my left side in hopes of discouraging any conversation, but that didn't mean a thing because he started up anyway.

"So whatchu doin' today? Lemme guess, kicking up your feet and eating bon-bons." He laughed like he was ready for *The Original Kings of Comedy* tour.

"I got stuff to do," I said. Again, I was trying my best not to engage him in conversation. I turned my head to see what he was doing, but his back was to me.

"Shhhiiiit, this place is always a shitty mess. You fix shit like Hamburger Helper for dinner and shit, and you expect me to think you got shit to do?" He hunched his shoulders. "Shhhhiiiit, you don't do shit around here and we bof know it!"

I just needed him gone. Usually, when he got on my nerves like this I'd ride him about using the word *shit* as a noun, an adjective, and a verb and that the right word was *both*, not *bof*! But I figured that might slow his nimble behind down even more, so I kept my mouth shut.

The minute Larry finally left the house I picked up the phone and quickly called for a cab. After that I had the pleasure of spending the next thirty minutes explaining to Larry's mom, Linda, why an unemployed woman like myself needed someone to watch my kid. Of course she was the one who asked him if I sat around eating bon-bons all damn day in the first place. Linda didn't like me because I wasn't her idea of the perfect daughter-in-law. If she had her choice she would've chosen Larry's ex, Darlisa Walters, who lived two rows over in the same trailer park. If I had not entered the picture, the three of them would probably be holding court right over there in that trailer park.

On the night before my wedding, Linda snuck Darlisa into Larry's bachelor party to make sure he understood what he was about to do!

At that moment I didn't know who I hated more, Larry or his sorry-ass mama! Finally, I decided it was a tossup.

Linda was a drunk who made my life miserable in ways she didn't even know. Her favorite color was orange, so everything in her house was orange. She even had her kitchen appliances spray-painted orange! Her doublewide was painted orange, she decorated with plastic oranges, and her carpet, sheets, curtains, and furniture were orange.

She had even been featured on the local news because of her odd obsession with the color and the fruit. It had been the highlight of her life!

"Linda, I have an important doctor's appointment and I can't be late. Can I bring him over in about thirty minutes or what?"

"What kinda appointment you got this doggone early? Oh, Laaawwwd! Jesus be the glory! Please don't tell me you expectin' again! Whew! Chile, I don't know how y'all gon' feed another mouth!"

Linda acted like Larry and I had a house full of kids and we needed her to help us feed them. I could hear the swooshing sound of the orange liquor she used to start her day.

"Linda, I'll be there in thirty," I finally said and hung up the phone. That conversation with her could've gone on for hours.

I took Taylor over to Linda's, which was more drama than I needed, but I had to do what I had to do.

"I got an interview," I said as I tried to ease out of the door.

"An interview?" Her face twisted up as she brought the orange mug to her lips and took a healthy gulp. The way she cringed told me she was sipping on something way stronger than a latte.

"You said you had a doctor's appointment over the phone," she said. Her comment stopped me cold.

I blew out a frustrated breath and was at a loss for words temporarily. I still had to get back to the house and get ready before going to Katina's. I didn't need the third degree.

She was wearing one of her many orange housedresses. It matched the carpet, the curtains, and the recliner.

"Uh, it's an interview at a doctor's office," I said and slammed the door shut.

Unable to decide who was worse, Larry or his sloppy alcoholic mom, I rushed back to the cab I had waiting and prayed she hadn't moved from her La-Z-Boy in front of the *Today* show.

When the cab took off, I looked out the back window and saw Darlisa standing there looking toward the cab. She was probably headed to Linda's so they could hold a bitch-fest about me. I didn't care. I eased down into the seat when I didn't see Linda standing at her orange front door.

Later, when the driver pulled up in front of my house, I dug into my purse and grabbed some cash.

"Hey, where are you gonna be in about two hours?" I asked him as I waited on my change.

"Working, why?" the cabbie asked. He never looked up.

"Um, I'm gonna need a ride in about two to three hours. You think you could swing back by?"

That's when he looked up. He flicked a card in my direction with three one-dollar bills.

"You call me fifteen minutes before you're ready," he said.

As I walked into the house I made a mental note of everything I still had to do. My tampons had been soaking in my secret hiding place, so I needed to remember those. I grabbed the skimpiest club gear I could find and grabbed my makeup bag.

Even though Katina and I agreed I'd watch her for today to see how she did things, I still wanted to be ready in case I needed to jump right in.

I was not prepared for what I saw when I made it to Katina's house. Draped in a big fluffy robe, I could tell the girl meant business. Her face was fully made up as if she was getting ready for a Glamour Shots photo shoot. She showed me the cameras and the outfits she had lined up.

Although she said she didn't use them, she had sex toys and porn magazines placed throughout the room that was outfitted with cameras.

Katina ran through a quick list of *dos* and *don'ts* as she touched up her makeup and fidgeted with her hair.

"Okay, that's everything. Now I just need to get busy," she said.

There was no way I could, but I felt like I needed to take notes.

"Oh, and I need you to get on Twitter and Facebook, like today. I'll send you some friend suggestions and before you leave I'll take some pictures of you for your profile. Oh, and whatever you do," her eyebrows bunched together, "don't tell your husband. As a matter of fact, on Facebook we need to call you Candi," she said.

"Okay, so I'm Candi now," I said. She was throwing so much information my way so quickly that I could hardly keep up.

"Remember the key to this is moving around like you don't know cameras are watching," Katina said. She darted around the room, turned on the radio, and pulled off the big robe she had on.

I tried not to stare as she stood in front of me wearing a French maid's outfit. She had on fishnet stockings and even had a feather duster to boot!

"Ummm," I began, but she quickly shushed me with a finger over her pouty glossy lips. She nodded toward the camera, then smiled and winked.

All of a sudden, much to my astonishment, Katina started gyrating and moving to the music. With that feather duster she was doing things I didn't even want to think about. A freakin' feather duster! I'd never look at one the same again.

I was dumbstruck!

I wanted to scream, "What happened to painting your toes? When are you gonna sit on your bed and read a book?" Instead I stood there looking on in sheer horror as Katina nearly masturbated with the feather duster.

For the next hour, I diverted my eyes when Katina's routine became a bit too risqué for me. That's when I realized, once again, that if and when something sounded too good to be true, it usually was.

By the end of the hour I had seen far too much of Katina's body, and she was damn near naked! When she signed off and flopped down next to me, I felt somewhat embarrassed for her. I didn't realize she was selling soft porn!

"I'll bet I made a killing," she said.

"When did you um, start, I mean, when did you change things up?" I asked.

"Girl, when I realized I was making chump change with what I was doing." Her eyes lit up as she talked. "I realized I needed to step up my game after watching some of those other skeezers out there. Would you believe some of those tramps are choreographing their routines? I swear I saw at least three of 'em biting off Beyoncé, especially this one who calls herself DeeLish! So, I had to up my game."

I wasn't feeling this as much anymore and she could tell I was changing my mind.

"You know what? You can do the old stuff, but me, I'm sticking to my upgrades. We got about thirty minutes left. Why don't you change into one of your outfits and let's put you on for this next hour?"

"I'm not ready," I stammered.

"Girl, you're not doing anything, seriously. Just get up and walk around every few minutes or so." Katina shrugged like it was nothing.

I felt hot and nervous at the same time. I went into the bathroom, switched out tampons, and changed into a pair of boy shorts and a fitted T-shirt. Believing that painting my toes would be enough, that was what I planned to do. My tampon was working; it didn't take long for me to start feeling the effects I wanted and that worked just fine for me.

"When you walk, make sure you twist extra hard," Katina whispered. "Put a hand on your hip. That'll help you amp it up."

I took a deep breath.

"Okay, now," Katina coached.

On her cue, and with one hand on my hip, I strutted into the room wearing stacked heels with my boy shorts and T-shirt. My heart was racing faster than a NASCAR motor. I pranced around the room, ignored the sudden rush of perspiration and flopped down on the ottoman.

I eased off my shoes and pulled out my polish. Everything I did was over exaggerated, but Katina said that's what the customers liked.

Although I had several bottles of polish, I struggled to decide on a color. And by struggled, I meant, a finger hanging out of the corner of my pouty mouth as if that might help me figure it out. For the next hour I licked my lips, shimmied my shoulders and painted my toes.

Having always been extra lithe, when I pulled one leg up and puckered my lips to blow air on my toes, Katina sat off in the shadows mimicking claps, blowing me kisses, and giving me an enthusiastic thumbs-up.

At the end of the hour she was all smiles.

"Girl, you are a natural! O.M.G.! You did so good!" She giggled.

I was feeling real good.

"Did I make some money?" I slurred a bit.

"Girl, did you! I'm sure you did." Katina was grinning extra hard.

I was nearly more excited about the money I needed than air.

"Oh, but I have a few tips. Remember," Katina got up to demonstrate, "when you bend down, always get up with your booty up first."

I watched as she bent down, eased to the floor, and then got up while extending her butt outward. She even made it pop as she stood straight. "Always remember, booty out and up first! Here, come give it a try."

It took a couple tries before I got the hang of it. Who knew there was a sexy way to get up? I did it a few more times.

"Girl, you're gonna be rich before you know it! That's good. Now, let me show you how to crawl."

"Crawl?"

"I know, right! But trust, it drives them nuts. Don't ask me why, but it does. You can crawl on top of the bed or on the floor." Katina got down on all fours. As she stretched her spine she put her right elbow forward, extended her slender fingers, and moved her left knee.

"The key is moving in sync—right elbow, left knee, left elbow, right knee. And look at my butt while I'm doing this," she said. "You see how it makes me look like I'm wiggling my hips and my butt is very pronounced? They love it!" she squealed as I watched.

"You wanna give it a try?"

I didn't catch on to the crawl as quickly as I did the booty up.

"This is harder than it looks," I said. I felt like a person with no rhythm trying to dance.

"Just practice. It takes some getting used to," she said. I had no idea Katina was such a sex kitten. A few hours with her, and I was doing things I didn't know I could. After practicing the crawl and getting up seductively, I was spent.

Still, she wouldn't let me leave until I sat at the computer and set up a new Facebook page and Twitter account.

"Just watch. If you do what I tell you, Candi, you're gonna be rolling in the dough before you know it."

Within minutes of setting up the Facebook page and adding a profile picture that showed me from my neck to my hips, I had nearly 100 friend requests. Many of them were from men.

"See, girl, I'm telling you! We don' struck gold!" Katina sang.

# CHAPTER 8

*Quinn*

As I drove down the interstate I gave Calvin a call on my cell phone. Even though it was a weeknight, I wanted him to meet me at a bar so we could talk. I needed to blow off some steam. I needed someone who'd listen to me and who understood misery from a man's point of view. Calvin was the only person who'd be able to sympathize with me.

"Yo." Calvin answered his phone after several rings.

"It's me, Quinn," I answered.

"I see." His voiced sounded rushed as if he was really busy.

"What are you doing right now?"

"I'm at the bank making a deposit from one of my restaurants. Why, what's up?"

"I just had a fight with Tameecia," I admitted as I sped up and switched lanes.

"That's nothing new," Calvin joked.

"I'm tired of her and her sister's bullshit, man." I didn't want to sound as if I were overwhelmed because I wasn't. I felt emasculated and it wasn't an emotion I wished on my worst enemy.

"Quinn Hamilton, I told your ass to drop her a long time ago, even before you had kids. Now look at you. You're trapped in a fucked-up marriage with a bossy woman who thinks her assertive nature and opinioned mouth make her a phenomenal woman. I can't be with a woman who thinks she knows what's best for me."

"Thanks for making me feel better," I said with sarcasm. I was about to hang up the phone.

"Sorry about that," Calvin apologized, but then remained silent.

"Look, I realize you're busy, but I was wondering if you'd like to hit a bar for a quick drink." I'd put him on the spot, but I didn't care.

Exhaling loudly, he gave in to my request. "Where do you want to go?"

"I don't know; anywhere." I was open to any suggestion he may have had. Calvin was more social than I was and he was familiar with all of the local hot spots.

"Tell you what. Why don't you meet me over at this new joint called The Factory? It's on Interstate fifty-seven near One Hundred Thirtieth Street."

"The Factory is that new strip club, right?" I asked, feeling twinges of excitement pumping through my veins.

"Yeah, and they have some fine-looking women up in there. For the right price you can get your dick sucked." The moment he shared that, I knew he was a regular customer.

"Well, my money isn't as long as yours, but one day it will be." I was, without question, envious of his financial success.

"Yeah, yeah, yeah. You've been saying that for years. I'll meet you there in about twenty minutes," he said before ending our conversation.

I arrived at The Factory before Calvin. I went inside and took a seat near the stage. A topless waitress wearing high heels, a red thong and a construction worker's utility belt approached me and squatted down directly in front of me. Her submissive posture made me like her immediately.

"Can I get you something to drink, baby?" she asked with a pleasant tone. She had a cute smile and innocent eyes that made me feel instantly at ease.

Smiling and gazing into her bright eyes, I said, "Do you know how to mix a Dirty Shirley?"

"That's cherry vodka with three olives." She winked at me.

"My girl." I chuckled.

"Let me go and get that for you, baby." She wrote down my order and then headed in the direction of the bar. As she walked away I admired her scrumptious ass. I'd be lying to myself if I said that I didn't want to bend her over one of the seats, spread her legs apart and get in her so deeply that she'd feel me in her stomach. The thought of fucking her hard and blasting her pussy with my essence caused goose bumps to form on my skin. I forced myself to come back to reality before I ended up looking like a total creep.

Since it was the first time I'd ever been in the place, I took a moment to take in the décor. The stage had two poles that the dancers could work. The bar was along a back wall, and to the right of it was the DJ booth. On the opposite side of the room was comfortable seating where the ladies gave out lap dances. Just to the left of the seating was a corridor with a posted sign that read, *VIP Rooms*. At any given moment, the lighting in the room would change colors. When I walked in, the place was lit up with red lighting, then it switched to blue and now it was green. I glanced over at the bar again and noticed a man in a bright lime-green suit. He was counting the money in the cash register. I'd seen the man before, but I couldn't remember where. After glaring for a long moment, I realized it was Smokey Love, LaQeeta's fuck-buddy. I didn't really give a shit about him and I damn sure wasn't going to be cordial toward him.

The waitress returned with my drink. I paid and gave her a generous tip, figuring that Smokey Love wasn't paying her what she was worth.

"Would you like some company, baby?" she asked as she sat

her ass on the arm of my seat. I casually slipped my arm around her waist, resting my hand on her bare hip. It was beyond exciting to feel smooth flesh I'd never touched before.

"Are you going to hang out with me?" I asked.

"No, baby. I have to work, but I could have one or two of my girlfriends come join you."

"Now that's what I'm talking about." I gave her a high-five.

"Smack my ass, too." She repositioned herself, aimed her delicious-looking buttocks at my face, and I gleefully spanked them.

"What's happening, Ginger?" I heard Calvin's voice. "Are you taking good care of my cousin?"

Ginger looked at Calvin, then me, and said, "Of course I am, honey." She gave Calvin a brief hug.

"You have a pretty smile," Ginger said to me.

"Thank you," I said, feeling much better than I had earlier that day.

"Would you still like for me to bring you some girls to keep you company?" Ginger asked.

"Hold that thought. I'll let you know when I'm ready," I said.

"Will you have your usual drink, Calvin?" Ginger asked him.

"Of course," he said. Ginger winked at him and headed back to the bar. I took another glance at her ass and stored an image of it in my memory to use later whenever I got around to having sex with Tameecia.

"So they know you by name up in here, huh?" I didn't want him to think that I hadn't noticed he knew Ginger personally.

"Oh yeah. This is the ultimate place where a man can come, enjoy viewing a healthy selection of girl parts and be treated like a king." Calvin repositioned himself in his seat.

"You're right, man. I do feel like I'm royalty in here. I wish I could go home and receive the kind of respect I got from Ginger."

"Wouldn't it be great to go home and have a woman greet you by asking, 'Who will you be fucking tonight, me or the Wednesday girl'?" Calvin and I both laughed obnoxiously.

"That's what I'm talking about. It would be even cooler if a man could have a woman for each night of the week," I said and waited for Calvin to agree with me.

"Even better, have a different woman six days a week and on the seventh day, you could sit and watch sports completely uninterrupted. Then on Monday morning, six new women would show up. Variety truly is the spice of life."

"I'd be the happiest motherfucker on the planet if I had a life like that. I'll bet Hugh Hefner lives that way. Lucky bastard. Anyway, if I had it going on like that, you'd see me walking around with a smile spread across my face like this. I'd look like the fucking Joker. Shit, people would look at me and say, 'Why the hell is he so goddamn happy'?" I laughed as I took a sip of my drink.

"I've always wanted to be the ultimate adventurous playboy. If I could have one definitive fantasy fulfilled, I'd be a black James Bond. I'd be the coolest double-o-seven ever." Calvin and I both laughed loudly.

"If I had the same fantasy, I'd come out looking like a black version of Austin Powers," I said.

"Whoa! You lost me there, playa. You've just fucked up the vision," Calvin said unapologetically.

"Shit, I couldn't think of anyone else," I said, taking another drink.

"Hell, you could've said Undercover Brother." Calvin playfully pushed my shoulder. At that moment Ginger returned with his drink. Calvin paid her and she moved on to help another guy who'd just arrived.

Taking a gulp of his drink, Calvin asked, "So what did Tameecia do now?"

"I'm just tired of her mouth. Her and her sister, LaQeeta, don't respect me as the man of my house. Tameecia treats me like a sickly child, and I don't how to get her to take me seriously. I want absolute and unquestionable respect."

"I can tell you right now, you married the wrong woman for that. Tameecia has that hood in her and no matter what you do or where you take her, she'll always be hood."

"So you're saying that she'll never be the sweet, easygoing, docile woman that I long for?" I needed to hear his honest opinion.

"I'm not saying she can't be tamed, but I don't think you have what it takes to calm her bossy ass down."

"To be honest with you, man, I really don't want to tame her. I've been doing some soul-searching and I've come to the conclusion that the only reason I hooked up with her was out of guilt. I should've never settled down with her."

"Well, you can't change the past, so there is no sense in crying over spilled milk. And if you leave her, your ass is going to be in the poor house because of child support," Calvin said.

"Man, you know," I glanced around the room at all of the beautiful women walking around nearly naked, "sometimes I wish I could be someone else."

"What do you want to do? Live a double life?" Calvin asked.

I paused, then said, "I wouldn't object to it."

"So, what kind of life would your alter ego have?" Calvin asked.

After thinking about it for a moment, I answered, "I'd be a suave and charismatic man. I'd know how to seduce any woman my heart desired."

"So you'd be a gigolo?" Calvin assumed that's what I wanted.

"No, but I'd know my way around a woman's body the way a gigolo would," I clarified.

"You know a lot of those guys are pretty well-educated," Calvin said.

"How do you know that?" I wondered if he knew any real gigolos.

"When I was playing in the league, a lot of the basketball wives hired gigolos. One player, who shall remain nameless, lost his wife to one of them. The gigolo was some guy from Amsterdam who spoke four languages fluently."

"Well then, my alter ego would also be smart," I said, adding that skill to my growing list of qualities.

"What about money?" Calvin asked.

"I'd be rich like Donald Trump. I'd have an obscene amount of wealth." I chuckled as I took another sip of my drink. Sighing deeply, I said, "Yeah, I really wish I could have a different life."

"What if I told you that I know of a way to make your fantasy a reality?" I paused and looked directly into Calvin's eyes. "Why are you looking confused?"

"I'm trying to figure out what the hell you're talking about," I said bluntly.

"I'm talking about letting the dog out of the yard. I'm offering you a chance to breathe life into your alter ego."

I studied Calvin for a moment to make sure his drink hadn't gone to his head. Since I'd known him all of my life and had seen him drunk on numerous occasions, I quickly concluded he was completely sober. "Well, you're not Houdini or David Copperfield, and you're damn sure not Jesus, so how in the world are you going to work a miracle like that?" I asked, expecting to receive a really stupid answer.

Holding up his drink to toast, Calvin said, "Cuzzo, I'm going to introduce you to alternate reality and the limitless possibilities of cyberspace."

# CHAPTER 9

*Codi*

The cab ride back to my mother-in-law's house was probably one of the best I'd had in a long while. I felt like *that* chick! The way I shook my ass and made love to those damn cameras, I felt so good about myself you couldn't tell me I wasn't a dime piece.

"Girl, you're gonna make a grip doing this." Katina's words haunted me before she called on the new cell phone she let me hold.

When it vibrated in my purse I nearly freaked out, but there she was, singing my praises the moment I answered.

"I hope you're right," I said.

"See, that's what I wanted to tell you about. You need to keep that confidence level going. I'm not sure if you were sleepy when you got here, but I could tell when you got your mojo. Once you got it, you started working your jelly and it was on like popcorn! I need you to bring that kind of energy the moment you walk in the door," she said.

As Katina talked, I could see how this could go to your head. Who knew I'd get off at the thought of being watched? All I could think about was the many ways Larry would kill me if he ever found out.

"I'll be ready tomorrow," I said. She had gassed me up so much I wanted to tell the driver to turn the car around so I could go for round two.

"Good. Oh, and your Facebook page is filling up quickly. You need to make sure you reach out to your fans," she said.

Fans? Me? I couldn't help but think how great my new life was going to be. Imagine being paid to be someone else. That thought alone made me want to think about all of the things I could do as Candi.

"Oh okay. I probably need to buy a laptop or something," I said.

"That's a great idea, but you should consider an iPad. Whatever you get make sure Larry doesn't find it," she said and chuckled a little.

Because I was still floating on what was left of my cloud nine, I didn't even trip off what she was saying. I wasn't worried about Larry. I just wanted to get my son from his mama and get to the house. I needed to get home before Larry did, so he wouldn't hassle me about where I'd been and what I'd been doing.

"Okay, look, girl, I'm here to get Taylor. I'll get with you tomorrow."

"Cool," Katina said, then hung up.

As the cab pulled up outside Linda's house, I momentarily wished I had another tampon.

"Can you wait?" I asked the driver.

"Sure, but I gotta keep the meter running," he said.

"No problem. I'll be back in less than ten and I'll leave my stuff here." I hopped out and rushed up the walkway leading to Linda's doublewide.

Outside the orange door, I sucked in as much air as my lungs could hold and knocked on the door.

"Who is it?" Linda yelled.

"It's me, here to get Taylor," I said.

"Oh, girl, it's open. Come on in," Linda said.

It could be cloudy and dark outside, but Linda's house was always bright. It would be one thing if the walls were one shade and the carpet and furniture were another, but that would be too much like right. Linda's orange house looked like someone got stupid drunk, sick and then threw up multiple shades of orange all over the place.

The moment my son saw me he charged me like his little life depended on being in my arms. He was ready to go.

"Hey, big boy! You ready to go?" I sang.

"Umph!" Linda huffed. I wasn't in the mood and I was pissed that she had his stuff scattered all over the place, even though I'd called to tell her I was on my way.

"One of my neighbors wants to show me something on the computer. You got time to wait?" Linda asked.

I wanted to ask why I needed to see what her neighbor wanted to show her, but I didn't feel like being bothered. I needed to grab my son so we could go.

"I don't have time. I can't even change him before we go," I said.

"Chile, I had no idea this big ol' man wasn't even potty trained!" she hissed. She looked like she hadn't moved from the orange recliner I found her in earlier.

I rolled my eyes. *He'll be back tomorrow, so no need to worry about gathering his things.*

"Linda, I need to bring him back in the morning, so I'm gonna leave his things here."

Before she could remove the mug from her lips and protest, I was out the door. She wasn't about to get up from her seat, so I had made a quick, clean break. I didn't want to be there when her neighbor, friend or whoever this person was, showed up.

As I played with my son in the backseat of the cab I started to get sad at the thought of going back home. I wanted to run back to Katina's house so badly, but I couldn't do that.

Taylor was crazy about his daddy and there was nothing I could do about that. Even when Larry's triflin' behind came home and didn't shower, our son wanted to be all up under him! I couldn't understand how the stench didn't affect his little senses, but it didn't.

When the cab pulled up in front of our house I wanted to tell the driver to take off and keep going. Larry's car was already there! He had beaten us home.

I knew *Shitty* would be talking more shit! But I also knew there was nothing I could do about that now.

Once inside, I heard Larry before I saw him.

"Oh, here she is now," he yelled. I didn't have to guess who he was talking to on the phone. "Yeah, she and the baby just came waltzing up in here."

I rolled my eyes. I wasn't in the mood for any drama.

Once I put my son down he ran to his daddy's open arms. That allowed me to go into the bathroom where I pulled a fresh tampon out of my stash. If I had to listen to Larry's endless bitching, I might as well be under the influence.

Larry hated the idea of me drinking. Years of watching his mother drink like it was going out of style and getting sloppy drunk made him that way. I could never drink around him, and if he smelled traces of alcohol on me, that was all she wrote. What a hypocrite!

Even when we were out and he saw other women drinking, he bitched and complained about it. Oftentimes, he did this while guzzling one beer after another, but I had come up with a win-win for us both.

I washed my hands and peered at my reflection in the mirror. My eyes were cool. My breath was still fresh, but I needed my secret weapon to kick in real fast.

The moment I walked out of the bathroom Larry was waiting for me. He nearly startled me to death, jumping all in my face like he had lost his ever-loving mind.

"What the hell, Codi?" he screamed.

When I saw two of him all in my face, I tried to focus on walking straight.

"How you gon' tell my mama you got a damn interview and dump my boy on her like that?"

I was starting to feel like I might've overdone it. Nothing he said really mattered to me.

"What the hell?" Larry looked at me kind of cross-eyed. "Wha—" He moved closer. "You been drinking and shit?"

I shoved him out of my way. "Don't start," I warned.

Larry got close enough and I could tell he was trying to sniff my breath, but he wasn't gonna smell anything. If anything, he would've been better off trying to administer his version of a sobriety test.

"Look, Larry, I ain't got time for your shit today," I said and heard myself slur a bit.

"I get home early and you and my boy were nowhere to be found, then my mama telling me some shit about you and a damn job interview. What's up with that?"

I wanted him to shut the hell up! I didn't want to fight, I didn't want to scream and I didn't want to have this conversation.

"What the hell you doin'? Hanging out with that tramp friend of yours?"

He couldn't be serious!

"Next thing you know, you'll be out in the streets trampin' with her ass while I'm breakin' my damn back puttin' a roof over your head!"

I didn't know how much longer I could take this.

"Bring my ass home after a hard day of work and ain't shit to eat up in here! Then you out in the streets while my mama watchin' my boy. I don' already told you, my mama don't be feelin' good!"

*Yeah, 'cause she's always drunk!*

"Some shit's gotta change around here!" Larry yelled.

By now my head was throbbing. I wanted him to shut the hell up! Every time I looked at him it reminded me of how much of a mistake I made when I married his ass. I wanted to tell his ass to go pay a bill or take a shower, but I held my tongue.

The moment he eased up off me, I walked into the kitchen and pulled the refrigerator open.

"Ain't shit up in there," he yelled.

I rolled my eyes at his constant nagging.

For the next three hours, I zoned out while Larry found every little thing to bitch and moan about. He didn't know what he was doing to my image of us. I warmed up frozen lasagna and thought about all the things I wanted to do at Katina's house the next day. I also couldn't wait to find out how much money I had made, and then I thought about all the things I'd buy right away.

"So you not gon' tell me where the hell you been today?" Larry asked. His mouth was stuffed with food. He was so gross.

"I went to Katina's. She was helping me get ready for this interview," I lied.

When Larry's cell phone rang, I was relieved. The baby and I finished eating and I took him to the back for a bath. Larry was in his spot. He had finished his food and was on the phone with the game on and a beer nearby. He wouldn't think of me again until his game was over or he was off the phone and a commercial was on.

Once I took Taylor out of the tub and was helping him into his pajamas, Katina called. I got up and eased the bedroom door shut.

When I didn't hear Larry complaining, I got back on the phone with Katina.

"What's up?"

"Girl, you made five hundred dollars," she said.

*Silence.*

I was trying to gauge her reaction. I wasn't sure whether she felt like that was good enough, so I tried to wait on her.

"Ummm, Candi," she sang. That brought a smile to my face and I cautiously looked toward the door. I didn't need Larry sneaking up on me.

"I said you made five hundred dollars! In one day!" she sang excitedly.

Now I could tell that I had done good. A secret smile spread across my face when all of a sudden, Larry burst into the room and snatched the phone.

"Who the hell is this?" he screamed into the phone.

I couldn't believe this fool! He really had lost what little he had left of his pea brain.

"What are you doing?"

"You up in here whisperin' and smilin' into this phone, I wanna know if this the fool you spent the day with," he yelled.

I looked at the dumb ass like the dumb ass he was. He stood there looking real simple in the face. We could both hear Katina's voice yelling through the phone.

How damn embarrassing. I sat there shaking my head at his antics. His features dropped instantly as he brought the phone back to his ear.

"Katina, here," he said, then shoved the phone back to me and led my son out of the room. No apology, no nothing.

"Damn!" Katina yelled the moment I got back on the phone.

"Yes. That fool of mine is really on one," I said.

"What's his problem?"

"If I knew *that*, it wouldn't be his problem anymore," I said.

"Well, listen, I don't wanna hold you. I wanted to tell you we need to do some stuff on Facebook tomorrow. You'll make even more money and I hope you had a good time," she said.

I hate he did what he did because she no longer had the cool, calm voice she'd had at the beginning of our phone conversation.

"He sure knows how to fuck up a high," I said.

"Let's talk tomorrow," Katina said and abruptly ended the call.

I was fuming. I didn't even bother going out to the living room; I'd get into a heated argument with Larry and I was already good and pissed. I considered getting another tampon, but then remembered I had switched when I got home earlier.

Instead of thinking about Larry, my mind started drifting to thoughts of being Candi. I also thought about how I wanted to make sure Candi was the total opposite of me.

Candi wouldn't take shit from any man! She'd be a sexy vixen and they'd fall all over themselves to be in her presence. Yeah, the more I thought about it, the more I realized exactly what Katina had done for me. She had basically given me what so many women desired, but could never ever have.

Katina had given me something so valuable and now, after the stunt stinky-ass Larry just pulled, I, Candi, realized that I needed to live my new life to the fullest.

# CHAPTER 10

# Quinn

Calvin and I hung out at the gentlemen's club for another hour, watching women parade around on stage for our pleasure. For me it was a great way to forget about Tameecia and my miserable marriage. Most times when coming home from work I'd drive around the block a few times before going into the house or sit in the driveway wishing my life and situation were much different. No matter how I longed for a different life, I felt trapped in the one I had.

"I want you to come by my house either tonight or tomorrow." Quinn's voice was muffled because a stripper buried his face between her breasts. He didn't want to go to the designated area for a lap dance, so he chose to enjoy the pleasure of human contact with a strange woman where he sat.

"Man, finish up your business," I said, getting the attention of a stripper who was dressed as a Greek Goddess. I paid for a lap dance of my own and enjoyed the moment of uncomplicated intimacy, even though it was only brief.

I wasn't able to get to Calvin's house until the following afternoon. I pulled into his driveway and got out of my car. After closing the door on my vehicle, I walked through the bay door of his garage. Calvin was just arriving home from running errands.

He shut the motor off on his Silver Mercedes AMG, a car that retailed at one hundred and eighty grand. I admired his car as he stepped out of it.

"I love this car," I said, smiling with envy.

"So do I. It's my baby," Calvin admitted.

"If you ever get tired of owning it you can feel free to hand the keys over to me," I uttered, wanting him to take me seriously.

"This car is too fast for you. I'd feel bad if I gave it to you and you killed yourself." Calvin had jokes.

"Man, please. I know how to handle myself," I said, slightly offended.

"That's what your mouth says, but I know differently. Follow me," he said with a chuckle. We walked up a spiral staircase that led up to the living quarters above the garage. He turned on the lights. "I call this the mother-in-law suite."

"I wouldn't. I'd call this my private space that no one would be allowed to enter," I said as I admired the décor—chocolate leather furniture, hardwood floors and decorative art mounted on the walls. I followed Calvin down a corridor and into a bedroom that doubled as an office. He walked over to the desk and handed me a package that was there.

"What's this?" I asked, looking at the white box.

"It's a gift for you," Calvin said, slapping my chest with the back of his hand.

"Dude, this is an iPad," I said, feeling the sting of his backhand.

"I have several of them. I use them as prizes for my store managers who reach the sales goals I set for them."

"I can't take this. It's too expensive and I wouldn't be able to pay you back," I humbly admitted as I handed it back to him.

"That's why it's a gift, man." Calvin refused to take it back.

"What am I supposed to do with this?" I asked.

"Build your alternate life with it. Surely you didn't think you'd be able to do it on the same computer that everyone else in the house uses," Calvin said. I hadn't given the idea of truly becoming someone else in cyberspace serious thought. In the back of my mind I thought Calvin was joking. Now I realized he was very serious.

"Come on. I'll help you set it up," he said. I followed him back into the other room and took a seat beside him on the leather sofa.

"Okay. I want you to listen to me carefully. With this device you'll be able to live a double life. This tablet is your portal into that life. I suggest you guard it like it's a government UFO secret. I'll show you how to set a pass code so that if anyone should ever get hold of it they can't access the files on it. With this, you'll be able to access the Internet, send and receive media files and even have video chats. You do have Wi-Fi at home, don't you?"

"No, but I'll get it," I said, feeling as if I were finally in control of something in my life.

"Good. I'm going to download the Facebook and Twitter apps and a few other apps that you'll enjoy," Calvin explained as he began working the device.

Once the apps were downloaded he gave me a crash course on how the iPad worked. We then began working on setting up my Facebook profile.

"So what is the name of your alter ego?" Calvin asked.

"The hell if I know." I leaned back, trying to think of a phony name.

"Let's try another approach. What type of woman do you want to attract?" He glanced over his shoulder at me.

"Anyone other than Tameecia's twin."

"So you want to attract a different caliber of woman?" Calvin asked for clarity.

"I want a woman who desires me just as much as I want her. I want someone who likes to fuck on a regular basis and doesn't bring a lot of drama into the relationship. If she treats me well, then I'll treat her the same," I spoke honestly.

"It sounds to me like you're searching for another wife." Calvin sounded disappointed.

"Does it?" I reevaluated my answer.

"I'm offering you a chance to be a Cyberspace Cowboy. A chance to get on your horse and gallop all over the planet, riding from town to town meeting pretty women. If you play your cards right you'll be able to hook up with a few of them and get you some action on the side. Think along those lines."

"So I need to think like a sailor on shore leave, right?" I suddenly made a connection to what he was saying.

Calvin nodded his head approvingly. "Yeah. Something like that. Now what do you want your name to be?"

I took a moment to think. "How about Julius Apollo Cole? JAC for short."

"I like that," he said. "Now type it in."

He handed me the device and I began creating my alter ego, Julius. In cyberspace, I was single and held a PhD in Cultural Studies. I was well-traveled, loved to read, was interested in women and was physically fit.

"Why in the world did you say you have a PhD in Cultural Studies?" Calvin asked.

"As a used car salesman I deal with all types of people from various backgrounds, so I do feel like I have a PhD in Cultural Studies." Calvin fell off of the edge of the couch from laughing so hard.

"Okay man, whatever. Do your thing," he said as he repositioned himself on the sofa once again.

Threading my fingers together, then cracking my knuckles, I thought of something interesting I could post. So I said, "If you could travel to any city in the world, where would you want to go? Chances are I've been there and could tell you a little bit about it."

"You're probably only going to attract some quiet and nerdy bookworm with a post like that." Calvin seemed unimpressed.

Pointing my fingers at him like they were pistols, I said, "It's the quiet ones that are the freakiest."

Pointing his fingers back at me in the same way, Calvin said, "Oh, you want to see freaky women? Let me show you where the freaks live in cyberspace." Calvin took the iPad, went to another website and bookmarked it for me. He then created an account with my new cyberspace name. He plugged in his credit card information and purchased ten minutes of airtime.

"What are you doing? I always thought it was dangerous to use your credit card on the Internet."

Popping his fingers, he said, "Oh, I'm slipping. I forgot to mention that you'll probably need to set yourself up a playboy fund. This is a debit card linked to my secret bank account that my Mrs. knows nothing about. I keep a thousand dollars in the account and I have all of the statements come to me electronically. That way the wife doesn't have access to the bank statements."

"Smart move!" I made a mental note to do the same. At that moment, a video of a woman dancing around in a room popped up. I stared at the screen. "What the fuck?"

"Yeah, that's my girl right there," Calvin said as he and I both watched this chick tickle her V-Jay Jay with a feather duster. The chick was dancing seductively to music as she moved around the room that was outfitted with cameras.

"Watch this," Calvin said, tapping the iPad screen so that the keyboard popped up.

Calvin typed, "Crawl for me, baby," and then hit enter.

"Hi, Julius baby," I heard the woman's voice come through the iPad. She then got down on all fours and crawled toward a camera. "Here is a kiss for you, Julius." She puckered her lips and blew me a kiss.

"What the hell!" A grin spread across my face as wide as the horizon. "Can she see us?"

"For a little more cash she'll set up a dildo, bend her ass toward the camera and fuck herself, calling out your name while she does it. You can watch her comesquirt all over the place. It's really some wild shit, man. It's like cheating without any of the complications."

"Are you fucking serious?" I was more excited than a teenage boy home alone with his naked girlfriend.

"Hell yeah, I'm serious," he said. "Go ahead. Tell her to put down the feather duster and take you into a private video chat."

I was about to do just that when I saw this other woman come into view.

"Wait. Who is that?" I asked, looking at the woman. She had on a sexy pair of boy shorts and looked nervous as hell.

"Oh, she must be new. An amateur," Calvin griped. "Here, I'll plug in another website for you."

"No, wait. I want to watch her."

"Dude, she's just sitting there painting her fucking toes. What the hell do you want to watch her doing that for?"

"Because I can tell she's nervous. Besides, she looks like a real person and not some weird chick that has banged one too many men or had Dr. Jekyll as her plastic surgeon. She also has a nice ass. I'm a sucker for a woman with a nice big ass and succulent breasts."

"Dude, she's nothing like the woman with the feather duster,"

Calvin complained. I could tell he wanted to move onto the next website.

"Wait a minute!" I noticed that she was warming up. She began rolling her hips and teasing the camera by bending over and showing more of her chocolate ass. "That's what I'm talking about," I said, wanting to see much more of her.

"I tell you what…" Calvin touched the screen and located her name. "Here. Her name is Candi and she has a Facebook page." Calvin tapped the icon and sent a friend request under my name. "There. Now when you get home, you can look her up."

"Cool." I smiled as Calvin typed in the URL of another website.

When I left Calvin's house it was 2:30 a.m. We drank, played cards, reminisced on our youth and talked more shit than politicians. As I drove home I was dreading walking into the house. Tameecia would be there waiting for me with a thousand and one questions because I hadn't called. When I pulled in front of my house, Smokey Love's car was once again parked in my space.

"What the fuck!" I growled as I parked my car on the street and stepped out. I walked up to the door, opened it and expected to find Tameecia sitting on the sofa waiting to curse me out. Instead, the house was quiet and everyone seemed to be asleep. Feeling evil in my heart, I walked down the corridor to LaQeeta's bedroom. I'd planned to wake her and Smokey Love up so that I could put his ass out of my house. Just as I was about to knock on the door, I heard the sound of water splashing. Curious, I followed the sound to the bathroom, where the light was on and the door was sitting wide open.

"What the hell is wrong with you, man!" I snapped off on

Smokey Love, who was taking a misguided piss. He pissed in the toilet bowl and then pissed on the floor and the wall.

"Oh, hey, pimp. What's happening? It's a bitch when your piss comes out as spray instead of a stream." Smokey's eyes were as red as fire and the scent of alcohol was so strong that if I lit a match I was certain he'd burst into flames. He was wearing a purple suit with matching shoes and hat. He looked like a set of drapes from the 1970s.

"You've got to go, man. Get the hell out of my house!" I shouted loud enough to wake the dead.

"Ain't no thang, baby boy. My business here is done anyway," he said, spraying one last stream of urine on the wall beside the toilet.

"Smokey, I'm about to get my gun. When I come back, you'd better be gone," I said as I marched toward my bedroom. When I pushed open my bedroom door, Tameecia was resting on the bed in an upright position, watching television. She had on a hideous black headscarf and a scowl on her face that had the power to make the devil pause.

Tameecia fired angry words at me. "Where the hell have you been?"

I matched her viciousness with my own. "Having myself a good damn time."

"Oh, hold up. Who are you talking to like that?" She tossed back the covers and sprang to her feet. She approached me like a man looking for a reason to get physical.

"I'm going to deal with you in a minute. Right now, I have to deal with Smokey Love." I moved toward the closet where I kept my gun.

Stepping in my path, Tameecia said, "Not until you tell me where you've been. It's three a.m. and the only thing that's open this time of night is a set of legs. This is the second night your ass has been out roaming the streets like a dog who has found a hole in a backyard fence." She pointed her finger at me. "Are you fucking around on me?"

"Move, Tameecia," I warned her.

With daggers in her eyes, she shouted, "Make me!"

"You really don't want to go there," I warned her again.

Looking me up and down as if I were short, she said, "Yes. I. Do." With every word she stepped closer to me.

Placing my hands on her shoulders, I tried to force her out of my way.

"Get your goddamn hands off of me." Tameecia swatted my hands away.

"Look, woman! I'm tired of you bossing me around like I'm some damn kid!" I snapped at her.

"Well, if you were a real man, you'd know how to handle a woman like me!" she barked.

"And if you were a real woman, you'd know when to shut the hell up!"

"What are you saying? The woman you were with is better than me? Is that what you're saying? Who is she, Quinn? Where is she at? I'm ready to beat the bitch down!"

"Please stop fighting." I heard my son Michael's voice. I turned and saw him standing in the doorway.

"Now look at what you've done." Tameecia blamed me for waking him up. She stepped around me and assured Michael that everything was okay. She held onto his hand and walked out of the bedroom. I continued toward the closet where I kept my gun in a box. As I pulled the box down, I heard the sound of Smokey Love's car starting up. I moved over to the bedroom window and saw him backing out of the driveway.

As I put my gun box back, I heard LaQeeta say, "I've got a bone to pick with you, Quinn."

I turned to meet LaQeeta's angry gaze. I exhaled loudly and wished that I really was Julius Apollo Cole—a wealthy man who was well-educated and didn't have any of my issues.

# CHAPTER 11

*Codi*

I loved my new job with Katina. Taylor was back in daycare now that I was making money. We had to pull him out before because we simply couldn't afford the $150 a week, but all of that was a thing of the past now. Larry still didn't know, though. He thought I was home with the baby and occasionally I still took him to Linda's. Slowly, but surely, I was trying to get caught up with some bills. I wasn't pulling the kind of money Katina was pulling, but I was doing okay.

Since Larry went to work before the crack of dawn, once I took the baby to daycare I came back home and had a couple of hours of peace to myself.

This morning I was getting my stuff ready to head out to Katina's when I heard my phone.

"Excuse me, Boss. You have a new text message," the phone announced.

I loved that app. Larry hated it and that probably made me love it even more. When I picked up the phone and realized it was a message from Ree, a smile crept to my face.

Ree was an alias, of course, for this cutie I'd met on Facebook last week. His real name was Austin Reed, and he was the kind of man I'd be with if I wasn't married to Larry's lousy ass. Austin had a real nice body. It looked like he used to be a football player, with thick muscled legs and bulky muscles in his arms, chest, and shoulders.

Austin was the color of milk chocolate and he was stocky, just the way I liked my men. Although we still hadn't met in person yet, I could tell that he didn't smell like shit like Larry did simply by browsing his pictures.

*Aaeeey Sxy. SUP?* his text read.

*U Big Daddy!* I replied.

I loved cyber flirting. It was exactly like Katina said it would be. I was a completely different woman online. When these men reached out to Candi, they showered me with compliments and had nothing but nice and flattering things to say.

Now when I came home and smelled Larry's funk, I simply thought about one of my new Facebook friends, and him and his odor didn't really faze me anymore.

*Can U chat?*

*Getting rdy 4 wrk*, I texted back.

*K. Hit me ltr?*

*U got it Bg Ddy!* I replied.

Most of my things were already together, but I still had to check on the tampons. Since I'd been doing it for a while now, getting in front of the camera was really not that big of a deal to me anymore. I wasn't like Katina, who was really working hard to compete with the porn actresses, but I was loosening up quite a bit.

Even though I was home alone I still went to the front door and tripped the deadbolt. I didn't want Larry busting in on me while I was handling my business.

Once I was sure the place was locked, I rushed back into the bathroom and dug into my secret hiding place. Everything was as I'd left it. I pulled out the plastic container that was sealed shut.

"Okay, I'm gonna need more Vodka soon." I examined the low level of the liquid inside the container. There were three tampons soaking inside.

Using a hand mirror, I spread my legs, inserted and pushed one of the tampons in me as far as it would go. I nearly had this down to a science. When I inserted a tampon, I had a good fifteen minutes to hurry and get to Katina's before my buzz kicked in.

Since my clock had started now that the tampon was snuggled in place, I grabbed my bags, keys, and headed out the door. By the time I made it to Katina's she was wrapping up a set.

I stood off to the side and watched as she gyrated her hips to the music. Of course she was half-naked, but she was sexy as all get out. Katina's hair was fly, her makeup was perfect and her dance moves were tightly choreographed.

"Take off that bra," a voice commanded.

I'll never forget how that freaked me out the first time I heard it. Katina's webcam business was now interactive. For a premium membership, which meant more money, her VIP clients could make requests and she'd do whatever they asked.

I watched as Katina seductively removed the lace bra while using her arm to cover her breasts.

"C'mon, baby. Don't be shy. I wanna see those chocolate nipples," the voice said.

Katina giggled, then snaked her body to the music while using her hands to cover her breasts. Her diamond belly ring sparkled as she moved and the men were whistling and cheering her on. She kept a small monitor that showed four different clients.

Instead of showing her nipples, Katina started massaging her breasts as she continued moving to the music.

Each day Katina ended her set with her theme song, "Super Freak," by the late, great Rick James.

She shut off the cameras and dropped her hands. Her nipples pointed directly at me.

"Hey, girl." She smiled.

"Heeey," I said.

"We got a lunch date in about two hours."

"Oh?"

"Yup. What you got to wear?" she asked.

"I wasn't really prepared for a lunch date," I stammered. There were so many questions swimming around in my head.

"Well, maybe you should borrow something from my closet. We need to come correct. Remember, we're selling a fantasy."

Katina had literally morphed right before my very eyes. She had always been fabulous, but it was like now everything about her had to be over-the-top sexy.

"What are you wearing?" I asked.

"Oh, I have this cute little Gucci shorts suit," she said.

"Shorts suit?" I was confused.

"Yeah. It's shorts and a matching jacket. I'll wear my rhinestone bra and a pair of rhinestone stilettos."

As she spoke, I was getting ready for my set. Today I was planning to clean with my signature boy shorts and baby doll T-shirt.

Once I got dressed and strutted into the room with the cameras, Katina frowned. "You not gonna change it up a bit?"

"Change what up, and why? If it's not broken, I don't plan to fix it."

Frowning, Katina's eyes narrowed as they focused in on me. "Candi, you been drinking?" she asked, like she wasn't sure.

"You know I don't really drink," I slurred.

Her seductively arched eyebrow shot up. "Bitch, I ain't crazy. Now I don't smell liquor, but you high and you know I know you high, so what's up?"

I started stretching. "Well, you know how Larry feels about me drinking, right?"

"Yeah. That's what happens when you got a drunk for a mama," she said.

"Okay, yeah. Linda and her orange liquor. Well, anyway, I basically found a way to get around his little paranoia."

Katina still looked at me like she wasn't sure what I was talking about. "So you smoke weed?"

"Oh, hell no!"

"Okay. Well, what is it? You're slurring every other word, so something is going on. I ain't crazy," she insisted.

"Since Larry freaks out if I smell like liquor, I consume it through the other end." I smiled.

Katina's frown deepened. "What?"

"I soak my tampons in Skyy Vodka, then slip them in."

Katina's expression changed from confusion to bewilderment to stunned surprise.

"You do what?" she yelled.

But it was too late. I was on the clock and that meant our conversation had to end.

By the time I finished my set that consisted of me dusting, vacuuming and painting my toes, all while moving to the music, Katina was waiting.

"I've grabbed every tampon I could find. Now I need you to fix me up," she said.

"I thought we had a date," I said.

"We do, and we're going, but I want a Vodka-soaked tampon in my coochie." Katina pouted. "Why should you be able to have all the fun?"

We both laughed at that.

"Okay, I tell you what. I'll let you have one of mine since they're already soaked. We'll get yours started and that way we can go handle our lunch meeting instead of sitting here waiting for the tampons to fill with liquor."

Katina pulled her car into the parking lot of Pappadeaux.

"Ooohh, seafood," I squealed.

"Yup." Katina swung into a parking spot and turned off the car. "So, look. These guys have money, okay. If you look on your Facebook page, you'll see that both of them have sent you friend requests."

"I haven't logged on in at least three days," I admitted.

Katina sighed like she was dealing with a child. When she spoke, she started slow and soft. "Candi, this is business and we both need the money, so I'm gonna need you to stay on top of your hustle. You've got to be on those pages. I need you friending up these guys."

"Okay, okay. I've just been busy."

She eyed me like I was lying. "Too busy to make money?"

"Nah, never that."

Katina flipped down the visor mirror and checked her teeth. She replenished her lip gloss and puckered her lips a couple of times. Then she turned to me. "Oooh, you're shining. I need you to use these. They'll soon be your best friend."

I took the little blue packet from her and pulled a thin piece of paper from the pack.

"They soak up excess oil from your skin and get rid of the shine," she said.

I flipped my visor mirror down and used the little sheet of paper to dot areas on my face that were shining.

Katina pulled out perfume, sprayed herself, then passed me another bottle. "You never wanna keep company with a man when you smell like outside."

I wondered how she knew all these things that I had never given a second thought to.

When we strolled up into the restaurant in the middle of the afternoon, I was shocked to see such a bustling crowd. I liked the fact that while everyone else was wearing boring business attire, Katina and I stood out in our after-five evening gear. We were classy and turning heads.

She wore her white Gucci shorts and matching jacket with the rhinestone bra, and I wore a cobalt wrap ruffle dress that stopped right above my knees with nude fishnets.

As we approached, the guys jumped from their chairs and I felt so special. I was like, "This is definitely the life."

"Ladies," one of the guys said.

They weren't anything to look at, but they appeared to be polished and expensive.

Katina morphed into this person I hardly recognized. Her voice sounded high and she was giggling excessively. She pointed at me. "This is Candi."

"I'm Norman and this is Rob," the taller of the two said.

I felt like we were at the center of attention, even though the restaurant was full and busy. When men walked by, their eyes lingered at our table. I noticed a few necks craning in our direction and I could tell that Katina was enjoying the spotlight.

Norman commented about Katina's feather duster performance and she threw her head back and laughed so hard and loud I could see her tonsils flaring back and forth. Nothing he had said was anywhere close to being that funny, but Katina was laying it on thick.

The more she laughed and giggled, the more it drew the guys in.

"So, Candi, what do you do?" Norman asked.

"Katina and I work together," I said.

"Oh, really?" Norman's question made me wonder if he was trying to say something.

"I'll have to look you up then," he said.

"Yes, Candi is new, but she's really good," Katina said. When she reached over and grazed my shoulder with her hand, I realized the tampon was working.

She and I were already sitting close. The guys looked at us, looked at each other, then smiled.

"You two ever work together?"

"Yes, every day," I said.

"No, he means, you know, together." Katina winked.

"Oh." I started giggling.

Katina started moving her shoulders like she was about to break into dance, and, with a husky tone, she said, "Why exactly do you want to know?"

"Two sexy ladies like yourselves," Norman said, "I'll bet you guys would be real popular."

Instantly my mind started wondering what the purpose of this lunch was, but our drinks arrived and I didn't think about it again.

I ordered ginger ale, but Katina ordered a margarita. I had already told her the good thing about the tampons was you didn't have to worry about getting sick or suffering a hangover, but still, I didn't go mixing up my clear and dark liquor.

As I nibbled on fried alligator and octopus, Katina slid her chair back, and said, "Fellas, we need to powder our noses."

As if on cue, I got up from my chair and followed her into the ladies' room. Once inside, Katina looked down to scan the stalls for feet. "Look, I love this fucking tampon! Girl, I feel so damn good! I am hooked!"

"Yeah, but you gotta be careful. You're still mixing dark and clear liquor," I said.

"Shiit! I'm feeling real nice right about now," she slurred.

"Okay, but you might wanna slow down a bit."

"Listen, what's up? You wanna make some more cash or what?"

I turned away from our reflections in the mirror and looked at her. "What do you mean?"

"Norman and Rob. We can take them to get a room and make some extra cash."

My heart started banging loudly in my ears. Was she asking me to *hook* with her? What the hell? Katina was out there! I was down for making some extra money, but I wasn't trying to sell my ass!

"Umm," I hesitated. I didn't want to offend my girl, but damn, I wasn't trying to turn any tricks either.

"It's not what you think," Katina said, just as I was about to answer her.

"What do you mean?"

"Well, I can't tell you if you don't want to try it."

"Why not?"

"Because if I tell you and you decide you don't wanna do it, I'd have to kill you." Katina burst out laughing. Either she was crazy or truly drunk. I hadn't decided which one was the case.

"So I'm supposed to answer blindly?"

"Do you trust me?" Katina asked me. By now she was back in the mirror fussing with her hair.

"Of course I do. Don't I work with you?"

"Well, since you trust me, then I can go back out there and tell the guys we can go get a room, right?"

Blank stare.

I swallowed dry and hard.

# CHAPTER 12

# Quinn

I'd just gotten out of the shower after a long day down at the dealership. The bathroom mirror was steamed up, so I took one of the towels and cleared away the moisture so I could see myself. In my opinion, there was absolutely nothing fantastic about me. My skin was an even shade of brown chocolate, my arms were skinny like twigs that had fallen from a tree branch and my belly was round like a Buddha figurine. I didn't consider my gut to be sloppy. I mean, some guys I'd seen on the street had bellies so big they looked as if they'd swallowed the moon. I tried to suck in my gut with the hopes of it instantly disappearing, but I knew from the moment I inhaled that all hope was lost; there was absolutely no change. I exhaled because it was uncomfortable. I watched as my Buddha belly drooled over my waistline.

"Damn," I said aloud as I grabbed my doughy tummy. I squeezed it and wished that there was some pill I could take to make it disappear overnight.

Attempting to ignore my shortcoming, I looked into my own eyes, and said. "My name is Dr. Julius Apollo Cole." I smiled at my reflection. I repeated my fictitious name again, this time adding more bass to my voice. I thought deepening my voice would make me look sexier, but it didn't. I laughed at myself and my silliness.

I finished up in the bathroom and walked down the corridor toward my bedroom. I went inside and shut the door. The house was quiet. I was enjoying one of those very rare occasions when no one was in the house. I locked the bedroom door and headed for the television remote, which was resting on the nightstand near the bed. I got situated on the mattress and turned on the television.

"If you do this program, I promise your body will change." An infomercial was on. Some guy was giving a testimonial about how he'd transformed his body by doing a home fitness program.

"Yeah right." I spoke to the television as if it had the ability to hold a logical conversation with me. Just for kicks, I decided to continue watching the paid program.

"Hi. My name is Josh and I'm thirty-nine years old. I did this program and it changed my life," said another person, who I assumed was a paid actor. That was, until I saw his "before" photo.

"Holy shit," I said as an image of the guy popped up. He looked like the buffet line was the only place he hung out.

"When people who I haven't seen in a while see me, their jaws drop open and they say, 'Oh, my God.' I used to be the fattest guy in the room, but now I'm the fittest. I'm stronger both physically and emotionally. I get more respect now because people don't view me as a chubby pushover. If you're like I was, you're probably sitting at home feeling miserable because you don't have the body or lifestyle that you want. I'm telling you, start here. Buy this program, stick with it, and your results will be awesome."

I didn't understand why the words the fat guy said hit home, but they did. Before I could even talk myself out of it, I wrote down the number on the screen, grabbed my wallet and phoned to order the fitness program. If I was truly going to be Dr. Julius Apollo Cole, I needed and wanted to look like him. I was willing to do anything to escape the wretchedness of my relationship with Tameecia.

Once the infomercial ended, I went over to the closet and retrieved my iPad from the removable wall panel where I kept my gun. I repositioned myself on the bed and pulled up my Facebook account. I was surprised to see that I had a number of friend requests from women. Without giving much thought to who I was agreeing to be friendly with, I approved everyone. Within moments a female inboxed me.

"*Hello*" was all she said. I clicked on her profile to find out more about her. Her name was Helen and she was from Ghana. Her complexion was rich chocolate like my own and her hair was styled straight and plain. Helen had dark black saddle bags directly beneath her eyes. She looked like she hadn't slept in months.

I responded with, "*Hello to you, too.*" I waited for her to reply back, but she didn't.

"What the hell!" I said aloud out of frustration. Why even reach out to me and then not say a word? Irritated, I deleted her from my friend list.

The chat box popped up. "*Hello, handsome.*" It was another stranger. This time, a woman named Zari. I clicked on her profile picture to get some information. Zari was a slim woman with a pleasant smile. She held a master's degree and lived not too far from me. I quickly clicked on a few of her photos and came across one of her in a blue, sleeveless dress with a hemline that stopped well above her knees. I could tell that she was a tall woman by the length and shape of her legs.

"*Hey, beautiful,*" I answered back.

"*What's a handsome doctor like yourself doing being single?*" she asked.

"*You must be reading my relationship status. LOL. I haven't found the right one yet. Why? Are you putting in an application to be my one and only?*" I asked, chuckling at my response.

"*My, don't you have a big ego?*" she typed.

"*I have a lot of big things*," I responded with a cocky answer.

After a long paused, she typed, "*I've heard that one before.*"

"*LOL,*" I said.

"*Where did you get your PhD in Cultural Studies from?*" she asked.

Stating the first college that came to my mind, I said, "*University of Chicago.*"

"*Great school.*" She seemed pleased with my answer.

"*Yes, it is.*" I upheld the lie I'd just told.

"*Well, it was nice talking to you.*" She was about to move on.

"*Wait a minute,*" I typed as fast as my fingers would let me.

"*What?*"

I wasn't ready for her to be done with me. I wanted to talk some more, so I said, "*What about you?*"

"*What about me?*" she asked.

"*What do you do for a living?*" I softly scratched my neck just behind my ear as I awaited a response.

Her answer popped up. "*I'm a high school principal.*"

"*So I'd have to be on my best behavior when I'm around you. That is unless you wanted me to be bad.*"

"*Depends on what you mean by bad.*" she answered back.

Smiling at my iPad screen and happy that she'd taken the bait, I responded, "*Grown ass man, bad.*"

"*Ha, ha. Then if you were in my office, you'd get some grown ass woman discipline.*"

"Hot damn! She's got a little freakiness in her," I said aloud as I clapped my hands and then rubbed my palms together. I began speaking as I typed my response.

"*Maybe you need to make an appointment to see me. I am a doctor, you know,*" I boldly said.

"*You wish. You're not a medical doctor,*" she answered.

"*Why? Are you afraid of meeting new people?*" I asked, wanting to call her out.

"*You're a total stranger. I've known you all of three minutes and already you want to meet me? You're coming off like a stalker.*"

"*Trust me, I'm not a stalker,*" I answered.

"*Trust is earned, honey. Only a fool gives it away freely.*"

"*Okay, I can respect that,*" I said, agreeing with her as I clicked on several more pictures she'd posted. I wanted to be visually stimulated by her body in some way. Looking at her photos also helped me determine if I still wanted to hunt for a steamy encounter with her.

"*What do you really look like?*" she asked.

"*You see my picture, don't you?*" I answered.

"*It's just a head shot. I can't really see you and you have no other pictures posted,*" she pointed out.

"*So you're on my page looking at my photos? Now you sound like a stalker.*" I threw her words back at her.

"*Yeah right!*" I believe I'd offended her.

"*I look nice.*" I wanted to ease any tension.

"*You're probably some colossal guy who has nothing better to do.*" She had good defenses, but I wasn't willing to give up just yet.

Allowing my pride to speak for me, I said, "*No. I'm in decent shape.*"

"*What's decent mean?*" she asked.

"*It means that I look good. What's the problem?*" I asked, getting a little defensive.

"*I don't date or hang out with fat guys.*" She cut straight to the point. I glanced down at my swollen belly and told myself a lie before telling her the same one.

"*No, baby. I'm in great shape.*"

"*That's nice to know,*" she said.

"*Maybe we could have coffee or something one day.*" I put my neck out on the line and hoped she wouldn't chop it off.

She said, "*Maybe once I get to know you better.*"

"*Well, the only way you're going to get to know me is to meet me,*" I pointed out.

"*In time*," she said. I smiled because I realized there was a slim chance we would meet.

For the next four weeks Zari and I chatted online, usually in the evenings. I found her to be interesting and different. I enjoyed listening to her talk about the politics of the educational system. I let her do most of the talking so that I wouldn't sound like I didn't know what I was talking about.

I finally got her to lower her defenses enough to get her cell phone number. The first time I heard her voice, I thought, *Wow, she sounds like Hillary Banks from the* Fresh Prince of Bel-Air. She had a California Valley Girl tone to her voice. From our chat room exchanges, I had discovered that she had been raised in Diablo, California and came from what I considered to be a wealthy family.

"So are you excited about finally meeting me, Dr. Cole?" she asked.

"Yes." I was hoping that, after our dinner date, I'd be able to get her to agree to screw my brains out. Tameecia had once again placed her pussy on lockdown because I'd tried to establish myself as the man of the house. So in my mind, having sex with Zari was fully justified.

"So when I get there, you will have flowers for me, right?"

"Of course!" I wrote a quick note to myself to make sure that I picked up a ten-dollar bouquet of flowers from the guy who sold them at the end of the exit ramp on the freeway.

"I'm excited and nervous about meeting you," she admitted.

"So am I, baby," I whispered; I had taken her call in the house. I was in the basement, standing in a small storage area behind the washer and dryer. It was past 10:00 p.m. and everyone was in the house, so I had to find a place where I could have complete privacy.

"Why are you whispering?" she asked suspiciously.

"I'm not. I'm lying down, that's all," I lied again.

"Would you like me to lay in your super king-size bed next to you?" I got the sense that she wanted to talk dirty to me, and I was more than willing to play along.

"What would you do if you were in the bed with me?" I pressed the phone against my ear so I wouldn't miss a single word.

"Rub on your sexy body, and try to feel what you're working with."

I felt my dick jump the moment her words entered my ear.

"Would you suck on it?" I wanted to hear her tell me how she'd take me into the cave of her mouth and suck the life out of me. She'd told me that before during one of our long chat room sessions.

"I would swallow every drip drop of your love," she answered.

I couldn't help myself. I squeezed my cock, closed my eyes and imagined her down on her knees licking the long vein that ran the length of my *pride*.

"Damn, that sounds so fucking good," I uttered as I became completely lost in the fantasy.

"Maybe tomorrow will be your lucky day."

"Oh shit, really?"

"No!" Her firm answer snapped me out of my euphoria. "We're going to take this slowly, remember?"

"Yes, I remember," I said, recalling several conversations we'd had about her past relationships and how they'd gone sour because they were based on lust and not compatibility.

"Do you mind taking things slowly?"

In the back of my mind I was saying, "Hell yes, I mind!" I couldn't let her know my thoughts, so I said, "Of course not."

"Good. Then I'll see you tomorrow. You get some rest."

"Okay, baby. You, too," I said before we ended our call. I stood there for a moment, smiling to myself. I couldn't believe how right Calvin was. Leading a double life had its privileges and as long as I kept my true identity a secret, nothing could possibly go wrong. I stepped out of the shadow of the closet and startled Tameecia.

"Oh shit!" Tameecia started swinging her fists wildly at me. She landed a shot on my bottom lip. I grabbed her arms and held onto them.

"What the fuck is wrong with you, Tameecia?" I yelled at her.

"What the hell are you doing standing back there in the dark like a fucking burglar" she fired back.

"I was looking for something," I lied.

"In the goddamn dark?" Tameecia didn't like my answer.

"Never mind." I tasted my own blood from the shot to the lip. I moved around her.

"Quinn," Tameecia called me.

"What?" I turned and looked at her. Lately it had gotten to the point where everything she did was irritating. Even the sound of her breathing had become annoying.

"You've been acting weird lately. Are you taking your meds like you're supposed to?"

"You know that I don't have to take those pills anymore. Why would you ask that question?" I glared at her as if she were crazy.

"You may need to schedule a doctor's visit. Seems to me like you're having a relapse or something."

"Thank you for your opinion, Dr. Tameecia," I responded sarcastically as I walked out of the room. "It's a damn shame that you act like I'm the same sickly guy you met years ago," I uttered as I hustled up the stairs two at a time.

# CHAPTER 13

*Codi*

"OHMYGOD, Larry. I'm sorry, but something happened and I'm gonna need you to pick Taylor up from your mother's house," I said into the phone.

When I didn't hear anything on the other end, I wasn't sure if the call had dropped or what was going on.

"Larry? Larry!" I repeated his name, trying to make sure he was still there.

"Uh, yeah, um, you need what?" he asked slowly like he was lethargic.

"I had to rush Katina to the hospital, so I can't get the baby. I need you to call your mom and tell her I won't be able to pick him up," I repeated. This time though, there wasn't as much urgency in my voice.

"What you doin' with her?"

"I had to take her to the hospital! Listen, you have to go get Taylor from your mom's. I need to go, the doctor is coming."

I grinned as I looked up and into Katina's eyes. She was standing guard in front of the bathroom door in case someone came in while I was spinning my tale.

"I thought you was out looking for work or something. What-chu doin' with Katina? And what happened to her, and why *you* gotta take her to the hospital?"

"Larry! I need you to listen!" I said sternly. I knew him, and the questions would go on forever if I didn't take control of this conversation. "I am already at the hospital with her, and I can't leave her. That's why I need you to go get your son from your mom's…"

"Wait, quit fast-talkin' me. Shit! Now, why the hell you gotta be the one stuck with her ass? Now that she at the hospital, you tell them doctors you gotta go get your kid. It's that simple!"

"That's not gonna happen! I'm gonna be here all night if that's what it takes. Now I need to go. I'll call you when I know something," I said and ended the call.

I ended it just in time because Katina's crazy behind started howling. She was laughing so hard I wasn't sure if she was laughing at me or with me, only I wasn't laughing.

"Girl, remind me never to commit any crimes with your ass!" she said.

"What?" I asked.

"You kept stumbling all over yourself, repeating the same shit. It so sounded like you were lying."

"Umm, that's because I *was*!" I yelled.

"Yeah, but damn! You didn't have to be so obvious!"

"Look, are we gonna go do this or what? Who cares what I sounded like when I was trying to get Larry off the damn phone? All that matters is he believed me and now it's time to go handle this business!"

Katina looked at me and smiled wickedly. She then turned back to the mirror and started fussing with her hair again. "Okay, so just follow my lead. I'm gonna tell them we're down, but we want only one room."

I frowned a bit. What, were we about to have, an orgy or something? I needed money like the next broke chick, but I wasn't ready for all of what she was talking about.

"Oh." Katina dug into her bag and pulled out a little rhine-stone-encrusted pillbox. "Here, take one of these. When we get back to the table, I'll announce that we wanna go get a room, but first we need another round for the road. When they get up to go talk at the bar, we need to drop these in their drinks."

What the hell?

Not only was I about to turn tricks, but now I was about to drug them, too? This was all too damn much!

"What's wrong? You look spooked," Katina said.

"Isn't that um, I mean, can't we go to jail for that?" I asked.

Katina looked at me, then sucked her teeth. "You've got to be kidding me!" she deadpanned.

When she realized I wasn't, she sighed and dropped her little goodies back into her purse. "Don't worry about the skittles. I'll handle that part. Shit, that means we'll have to actually *entertain* their asses first!" she mumbled as I followed her out of the bathroom.

Things moved like the speed of light when we got back to the table. Katina wasn't even subtle.

"Everything okay?" Norman asked.

Before he finished his question, Katina damn near leaped over the table and shoved her tongue down his throat. As if the kissing wasn't bad enough, she started moaning and exploring the man's body with her hands.

Rob and I sat there looking as if we were both trying to avoid the massive elephant in the room. When Katina finally came up for air, it was obvious she had stunned Norman. He looked nervous and jittery.

"Wow, what'd you guys do back there?" Rob tried to joke.

"How about we go get a room? That way the four of us could get to know each other better," Katina suggested sweetly.

Rob looked at Norman. Norman looked at me. And I looked at Katina. She got up from her chair.

With three sets of eyes staring up at her, she tossed her hands to her hips and said, "Am I the only one who feels the chemistry at this table?"

I wanted to say, "Um, yes!"

"What do you wanna do?" Norman asked. Only his words sounded even more jittery.

"I'm not the kind of girl who has to ask a man twice to take me to a hotel room and push my back out!" Katina announced in a grand fashion.

I damn near choked on my ice water. Norman looked like he was about to fall while trying to spring to his feet, and Rob looked confused.

"So, you're ready to go then?" he asked Katina as he stumbled upright.

When she started sucking his face again, I rolled my eyes.

"I assume that's a yes," Rob said.

After that kiss, Norman started scanning the room like his life depended on what he was searching for.

"Damn, the service in here is slow as hell!" he said.

"Just leave some cash on the table to settle up our bill," Katina suggested.

Instead of doing that, Norman continued to look around the room. Rob eased up out of his chair and glanced at Norman with wide eyes like he was trying to signal his friend.

When their eyes met, Rob nodded slightly to the left, and a second later, Katina and I were standing alone at the table.

"Just follow my lead," she said. "Don't do shit. Just smile and play along."

As the men approached the table, a waitress came bouncing over. "Anything else for you guys?"

Norman reached into his back pocket and pulled out his wallet. He opened it up, revealing a thick wad of cash. Katina's eyes followed his every move as he plucked out four twenty-dollar bills and gave them to the waitress.

"Keep the change. We're done," he said.

Norman and Rob exchanged knowing glances, and then Norman smiled at me. "Your girl is ready to go. What about you?"

"Yeah. I'm ready, too," I said, hoping I wouldn't have to say too much more.

As I followed Norman and Katina outside, all sorts of thoughts flooded my mind. I thought business was great for Katina. Why in the hell were we turning tricks if she made so much money with the webcam business? None of it made sense to me.

"We'll follow you," Katina said.

In the car there was so much I wanted to say to Katina, but she did all the talking.

"So we'll get to the room, and I'll drop the skittles into their drinks. You just work it. You know, do a little striptease, dance on a chair, and crawl a bit," she said like this was nothing.

"Um, are we really doing this?" I asked with a nervous chuckle.

Katina's head snapped in my direction. "Yeah. Why? What's up? You good?"

"Yeah, I'm cool. It's just that Rob's not really my type," I confessed.

Katina slapped the steering wheel. "Damn, girl. Why didn't you say so? We can switch. No biggie!"

She swung her car into the parking lot behind Norman and he motioned for her to pull up alongside his car. When she did, he lowered his window, and said, "So we getting two rooms or one?"

"Daddy, it's more fun if we're all in the same room." Katina pouted.

"See, told you!" Rob said from the passenger seat.

I was nervous as hell. I had slept with men other than Larry during our marriage so that wasn't the issue, but I had never picked up a stranger off of Facebook and arranged to be paid for sex! The two rendezvous I'd had outside my marriage were both exes. I told myself that those didn't count.

Later, inside the room, Norman pulled out a bottle of Crown Royal and Katina's ass found the dial on the clock radio. The room was far from fancy, but it was clean. There were two beds, but both looked like they'd seen better days. The guys had both lost their pants. Katina and I had our shoes off, but we were still fully dressed.

"We need some Coke," Katina announced after a round of shots went around the room.

"Say, um, Rob, you wanna go to the vending machine? You know, grab a few bottles of Coke?" Norman suggested.

"Oh, yeah, whatever the ladies want." Rob grabbed a towel and wrapped it around his waist. He took some bills from his wallet and left the room.

When Rob walked out, Katina and I started dancing.

"Now that's what the hell I'm talking about," Norman said. He eased into a chair like he wanted to get VIP seating for the show.

Katina and I started gyrating and moving our bodies seductively. Norman seemed to be in heaven. He was cheesing and his eyes were wide like he could hardly contain his excitement.

"Wait, wait, hold that thought," he said, licking his lips. "I need to piss like a race horse. Don't do *nothing* without me," he yelled as he took off for the bathroom.

The second we were alone, Katina rushed over and grabbed her purse. She rummaged through it and pulled out the little pillbox. Looking back and forth between the bathroom door and the hotel room door, she plucked out a couple of pills.

"Shit, I need to crush them up," she said.

My heart was racing. I was more nervous than a hooker trying to work communion on Sunday morning. I went to the front door to try and keep watch out the window. When I looked back over at Katina, she had dropped one of the damn pills! This was too much! She stooped down to pick it up and that's when all hell broke loose.

"What the fuck are y'all doing?"

Norman didn't sound so nervous anymore. As a matter of fact, he sounded pretty pissed off. I wanted to evaporate right where I stood.

Katina was cold busted! With pills in hand and glasses lined up, there was no mistaking what she was trying to do, especially since she already had one pill crumbled on the table.

Rob walked back in the room and stopped. He looked around, frowned, and asked, "What's wrong?"

"That's what the hell I'm trying to figure out!" Norman said. "I come back from taking a leak and it looks to me like these two were about to fix us a real special drink!"

"What? What you saying, Norm?" Rob's frown deepened.

"It's not what it looks like," Katina stammered.

I couldn't help, so I stood silent near the door.

"You know what? Get y'alls shit and get up outta here before I call the police," Norman said. He motioned with his arm like that might help us along faster.

See, that's when we should've eased out the room. No harm, no foul, but that would've been too easy for Katina. And to be honest, I kind of knew it wasn't gonna go down that easily.

"Call the police?" Katina snarled, snaking her neck. "What the hell you gonna tell 'em? But better yet, what you gonna tell your wife?"

I guess she had Norman there because he didn't seem all that big and mighty anymore.

"Let's calm down," Rob said.

"To hell with that. Ain't no telling what these two hos was about to try and do," Norman said.

"Look, let's bounce," I said, trying to reason with Katina. To me, we needed to get out while we were ahead.

"You know what, you're right. Let's find us some real men! We need some who don't mind a few treats to really get the party going!" Katina announced.

Norman and Rob didn't move.

Katina scooped up her purse and shoes. I rushed over and grabbed my shoes and we scrambled out of the room. Once in the hall, we hauled ass and rushed out to the parking lot. We jumped in the car and Katina took off.

"Girl, what the hell was that back there?" My pulse was threatening to burst from my wrists.

When Katina waved two wallets in the air, I couldn't do anything but laugh!

"How did you? OHMYGOD! When did you…?"

I was stunned!

But when we were farther down the road, the joke turned out to be on us.

# CHAPTER 14

# Quinn

I was sitting in one of the used cars on the lot, listening to the radio. A disc jockey had a question of the day and he posed it to his listeners. The question was, "Should well-educated women date men who didn't attend college at all, and as a result make less money?" The question hit home for me because I'd just felt the sting of trying to date someone who was, without question, out of my league.

As I listened to the latest romance-gone-wrong song by Jill Scott that the DJ was playing, I thought about what had taken place a few days ago when I met Zari for the first time.

We'd finally settled on meeting up for dinner. I suggested keeping it casual by meeting up for pizza at this spot in the hood called Italian Fiesta. Although it was in a rough neighborhood, their pizza was the bomb. It was something about their butter-flaked crust that made my taste buds water.

"I know you didn't just suggest taking me to a gang-infested neighborhood for our first date." Zari sounded as if the thought completely offended her.

I should've known better than to suggest such a place, but I honestly couldn't think of a really nice restaurant I could afford to take her to. The most expensive restaurant Tameecia and I had ever gone to was Red Lobster, and hell, we considered that to be eating high on the hog.

Laughing as if I were joking, I said, "Where is your sense of humor? I'm sure you want to go someplace downtown."

"Well, I was actually thinking of a place in the suburbs, but I like your suggestion of downtown better. We could go to the Brazilian steakhouse called Fogo de Chão."

"Fogo who?" I blurted out because I'd never heard of the place.

"How could you never have heard of the Fogo de Chão? It's received great reviews on websites and in newspapers all around the city and even the country for that matter." She sang the praises of the eatery.

Not wanting to sound completely unknowledgeable, I answered, "Maybe I do recall hearing something about the place." After I said it I made a mental note to treat myself to someplace other than Red Lobster.

"Hello, my name is Vonda, and I'm from Tallahassee, Florida. I'd like to answer your question about women dating men who aren't educated." I turned up the volume to listen to Vonda's response.

"Tell us what you think," said the DJ.

"I'm not dating anyone who doesn't have a place for me to sit, eat, or sleep. I'm also not going to hook up with someone who will be jealous of what I can do with the money that I make."

"So you wouldn't date a man who made less money than you?" the DJ asked, for clarification.

"No, I wouldn't," answered Vonda. The DJ began to segue to another song and once again encouraged people to call in with their opinions. I turned the volume down again and thought some more about my date with Zari.

For our first meeting I knew that a suit and tie would give off the best impression and hold up my image of being an educated man. I put on the best suit that I had which, admittedly, was fitting me a bit snug around my belly and thighs. I had to really suck in my gut in order to fasten my slacks and zip them up. Although the slacks were tight on my thighs, once I put on my jacket, I figured Zari wouldn't notice. I grabbed my black shoes, which needed a new sole and heel, and needed to be polished, but I didn't have time to do it without running the risk of being late. I was thankful that Tameecia wasn't home so I wouldn't have to answer a ton of questions about where I was going.

I got into my car and headed toward a nearby cash station. I stood in front of the ATM and tried to decide how much money to get.

"Damn. I should've looked up their menu prices before I left the house," I spoke aloud to myself. "A meal for two people shouldn't be more than sixty bucks," I told myself and then withdrew that amount.

"Yeah, this is Larry from Houston. I want to respond to your question about women dating men who make less money." I was once again snapped out of my mental trance by the voice of another caller and turned up the volume.

"Good, let's get a man's perspective on this." The DJ encouraged Larry to speak his mind.

"Okay, it's like this here," Larry said.

"First of all," the DJ interrupted Larry before he got started. "Tell the listeners what you do for a living, Larry."

"I'm a working man. I work for the City of Houston as a sanitation worker," Larry proudly said.

"So you're a garbage man?" the DJ asked just to be sure.

"Yes, I am!" Larry's voice was strong and confident.

"Okay, Larry. Tell us what you think. Should a college-educated woman date a man like yourself?"

"Okay, here's the thing. I'm a hard-workin' man who handles

my business. The reason all of these single, stuck-up, college-educated women don't have a man is 'cause they don't know what a good man look like. I ain't got no degree, but I got good common sense and that goes a long way with or without a degree. I know people who think they all that just 'cause they have a piece of paper in a frame. It's a damn shame so many college-educated women have they identity hung up on a wall."

"Wow. There you have it, folks. A working man's opinion about college-educated women. Thanks for your call, Larry."

"You got it, man. Oh, can I say one more thing?" Larry asked.

"Sure, go ahead," said the DJ as music began playing once again.

"These women need to understand they role. When a hard workin' man come home, he don't wanna hear a bunch of drama. When he walk in the door, have his food ready, a cold beer waitin' and the TV remote nearby. On Sundays, when the game is on and his boys are over, she need to make a little dish for them and leave them alone. If women would understand that, this here world would be a better place."

"Thanks for your opinion, Larry. We've got to go," said the DJ.

I turned the volume back down and laughed at Larry. Some of his points were valid, but his last comment seemed like a personal issue he was having in his current relationship. I popped my fingers and sang along with the next song.

"You dropped a bomb on me, baby!" I sang the lyrics to the classic Gap Band song.

I sighed as I reminisced about my date with Zari and the bomb she'd dropped on me.

I arrived at the restaurant fifteen minutes late because traffic was horrible. I also refused to pay $30 for valet parking and drove to a self-park parking lot six blocks away. I walked some and ran the rest of the distance back to Fogo de Chão. When I finally got there I was sweating because it was unbearably hot outside.

My plan was to head to the bathroom, freshen up, and then come out and find Zari. My plan didn't work because as soon as I walked in Zari spotted me from her table. She was sitting near the front door. When our eyes met, I didn't dare duck into the bathroom first, especially since I was already late. I exhaled as I felt droplets of sweat trickling down my back and forehead.

"Hi," I said as I approached the table.

"Dr. Cole?" she asked as if she didn't believe I was standing before her.

"Yes." I smiled. I was waiting for her to stand up so I could hug her, but she didn't. She glared at me as if something was wrong.

"It's very hot outside," I said, realizing that my sweaty body didn't look very attractive. "I'll be right back." I excused myself and made a quick dash toward the bathroom. Once I cleaned myself up I returned to the table.

Zari was everything she said she was. She was beautiful, fit, and looked like she came from wealth. I gleefully sat opposite her and smiled. My eyes landed on her succulent breasts and I instantly visualized myself circling the tip of my tongue around her erect nipples. If I had my every wish we would've skipped dinner, headed for a motel, and spent the next several hours fucking. We could get to know each other later.

"You really are single, aren't you?" she asked. Appearing as if I were truly single was very important to me. I'd almost blown everything because, as I was running to the restaurant, I realized I had my wedding band on. I had pulled it off while hustling across an intersection like Superman about to leap into the air and placed it in my pocket.

"Yes. Why would you think otherwise?" I said, trying to seduce her by adding more bass to my voice.

"That suit you have on..." She looked at me oddly.

"Yes. It's nice, right?" I popped my collar; I just knew I'd dropped a few inches during the run from the parking lot. I could tell because my suit wasn't fitting so snugly around my thighs. The color had faded around the pockets from being ironed too hard. You couldn't really tell unless you looked really hard.

"You have on a burnt orange suit."

"Yes. I shop at designer stores all of the time. I have a closet full of suits like this. Feel the material. This is the good stuff," I proudly boasted. Most of my suits came from Sears, but the one I had on came from a place called Mr. G's Suits and Fashions. It was a place in the hood that sold unique fashions for men. They sold the type of stuff you wouldn't see everyone wearing.

"Really?" she asked as she leaned back in her seat.

"Yes." I paused briefly. "You look fantastic. What do you think about me?" I asked, wanting her to return the compliment.

"I never imagined you looking the way you do," she admitted.

"That's a good thing, right? I look better than you imagined?" My confidence was soaring.

"I have to go to the ladies' room. Would you excuse me for a moment?" she said, rising to her feet.

"Did you order yet?" I asked.

"Yes. Go ahead and place your order," she said as she smiled at me before heading toward the bathroom, which was situated behind me. I turned around in my seat, so I could get a glance at her ass. It was round and I could almost feel my hands caressing it.

"Can I get you something to drink, sir?" The waitress got my attention.

"Yeah. Let me have some Skyy Vodka and orange juice," I said.

"Do you need more time to look over the menu?" she asked with a pleasant tone of voice and smile.

"Yes," I answered.

The waitress stepped away as I picked up the menu and began going over my options.

Zari seemed to be taking an awfully long time. I turned around in my seat and glanced toward the direction of the bathroom to see if she was returning. I didn't see her so I turned back around. As I was repositioning myself I glanced across the restaurant and looked out of the window on the other side of the room. I adjusted my focus to make sure my eyes weren't lying to me.

"Oh, hell no!" I said as I noticed Zari hailing a taxicab. As soon as one pulled to the curb she got in and took off. I couldn't believe that she'd literally run out of the restaurant and left me sitting there looking as if a pigeon had taken a crap on my shoulder.

"Yeah, this is Sugar from Little Rock, Arkansas." A woman with a high-pitched voice made me focus back on the radio.

"Hello, Sugar. Tell us your opinion. Should college-educated women date men who have never attended college?" asked the DJ.

"Okay. First of all, I'd like to respond to Larry, who called earlier. If he wants his woman to do all of that for him, then he needs to make sure he's treating her right. My ex-husband thought that I was his mama and expected me to do everything for him, including give him a bath."

"What?" asked the DJ.

"You heard me. He wanted me to run his bath water, get down on my knees and wash his body while he just sat there. He told me that he was a hardworking man and as his wife it was my duty to bathe him."

"So you don't like catering to your man's every need?" asked the DJ.

"To a certain extent I will, but not to the point that I feel like a slave."

"Okay. Now what's your answer to today's question?"

"This answer is from my perspective. After I left my hardworking ex-husband, I went back to school and got my master's degree. I'm doing better as a single woman than I ever did when we were together, living with two incomes. So for me, I would want a man who is as educated or more educated than I am so that our incomes can complement one another."

"What if the man has no formal college education, but is an entrepreneur who is financially well-off?" asked the DJ.

"Then I'm okay with that," answered Sugar.

"So for you it's about the money?" asked the DJ.

"This may sound like I'm shallow, but yes. Money does matter." With that last comment the DJ played a song called "For the Love of Money" by a group called the O'Jays.

I sat in the car and sang along as I thought about ways to get more money, so I would actually look like Dr. Julius Apollo Cole. I was at the point of doing anything to be someone other than who I was. I reached for my cell phone and called Calvin.

I'd just had a crazy thought and wanted to run it past his ears.

# CHAPTER 15

*Codi*

I needed a break from Katina for at least a minute. Yeah, I liked the money I was making, but the drama was taking its toll. Larry was on the warpath and my ass was tired! Katina didn't do anything but eat, sleep, and think of ways to separate men from their money. While I loved money as much as the next chick, I wanted the cash without the drama.

Besides, the last thing I needed was to lose my marriage behind some of her drama. Larry wasn't the best thing in the world, nothing close even, but his shitty ass was mine and after I had to sneak into the house like some delinquent teenager a few weeks ago, I decided to pump the brakes on Katina and her antics for a minute. My bank account had been hurting ever since, but still I needed to chill out for a little bit.

Even though I was staying clear of Katina, it seemed like I exchanged one bad habit for another. In the three weeks I'd been away from her I was becoming more addicted to social networking sites.

Once I got the baby off to daycare, instead of coming home and looking for work, I got on the computer and sometimes I wouldn't get up for hours. Facebook was my favorite, but I'd been doing them all, including Twitter and some of the other less popular ones.

I had already been chatting it up with several guys. One in

particular really got me going. His name was Marvin and he seemed like the perfect man. At this point, I was always thinking about him. In my mind, he was a better lover than Larry, he smelled nicer, had a better job that didn't require him to get his hands dirty and he always knew exactly what to say, unlike Larry!

Earlier tonight when Larry came in saying he was going out with the fellas, I wanted to jump for joy. I kept looking at the clock, wondering when in the hell he was leaving, but it seemed like the more I looked, the more he stalked around the house, moaning and groaning about little insignificant things.

"Okay, you taking the car?" I asked when it looked like he was finally dressed and ready to go.

"Yeah, I told the guys I'd drive. We going to a bachelor party," he said. "I dunno why they decided to do this shit on a Friday night though."

One look at Larry and it was obvious he was on something totally different. He was so out of touch it was sad, but whatever. I just wanted him out of the house, so I could hop online and chat with Marvin. I eyed Larry up and down, but didn't say a word.

He was wearing a pair of stonewashed jeans with some church shoes and white gym socks. He had the nerve to put on a V-neck sweater with a polo shirt underneath. He looked a hot mess and I couldn't tell if he had even showered. I kept thinking that those would have to be some desperate strippers to be grinding all over him, but whatever. That was their problem, not mine.

"Aeey, what you doing tonight?" he asked like he suddenly remembered I would be home alone. Lately he'd been walking around with his little bony chest sticking out because he thought he had laid down the law and stopped me from seeing Katina.

"Nothing. Looking up some positions I wanna apply for," I lied.

"Hmm. You bet not be hangin' with your girl!"

I looked at him and rolled my eyes. I wasn't in the mood.

"Yeah. After that shit y'all pulled a few weeks ago, I hope you know fo' sho she's off-limits!"

Ignoring him was very hard, but I had to. If I didn't he would never leave.

"...come sneakin' up in here right before the sun! You musta lost your mind! Ain't no respectable married woman got any business out in the streets after ten at night! Umph! You betta be glad your girl nearly choked in that restaurant and them doctors found that thing on her throat and had to do that emergency surgery. What'd you call it?" he asked, frowning like he was struggling to remember what was found on Katina's throat. Larry was so pathetic.

"A polyp," I said unenthusiastically.

"Yeah," he said, checking his profile in the mirror, then smiling like he was checking his teeth for trapped food.

I wanted to tell his ignorant tail where a polyp would really be found, but figured I'd let him think he had done something to keep me away from Katina for a little while.

The truth was when Katina realized the two wallets she had skillfully lifted from our dates contained a whopping thirty-six dollars between them, that fool wanted to turn back around.

"Are you crazy?" I screamed at her. "What are we gonna go back there and do? Curse them out for being broke, but frontin'?"

"No! I'm pissed. How the hell were they gonna pay us if we'd fucked them?"

Was she for real?

"We weren't going to. *Remember*?" I couldn't believe she was upset because they didn't have any money in the wallets she'd *stolen*!

"But we saw a thick wad of cash when Norman opened it to pay the waitress," Katina shrieked. She was firecracker hot!

"It *was* a wad, but who knows whether it was a bunch of one dollar bills. I mean, think about it. He paid for the drinks, then paid for the room. For all we know he might've had a few twenties and a bunch of ones.

"Girl, I need cash and I need it like nobody's business. Shit! What to do? What to do?"

That scared me; I didn't understand why she was so desperate for money.

"Katina, I thought the business was doing real good," I said softly.

"It is, but until you get up to speed it's only doing *good*. I mean, um, we need it to do great and we need it like yesterday," she said.

"...I'm serious! I ain't playing," Larry warned. His ranting pulled me back to the moment.

I hadn't heard a word he said. I wanted him to hurry up and leave. I had some friends waiting for me online and him and his *BS* were holding me up.

When he finally left I didn't know if I should laugh or cry. My son was asleep, my husband was gone, and I had a date with a bunch of handsome, rich men who didn't care what I looked like or who I ran around with. They just wanted their Candi and I wanted to give it to 'em!

Nearly two hours later I pulled back from my computer screen and laughed. I tossed a handful of popcorn in my mouth, squinted my eyes, then moved in closer and decided Marvin's picture looked nice.

He was handsome, model handsome, and I liked that. After taking in his glamour shot picture I smiled and my fingers started dancing on the keyboard.

*So, whassup?* I typed, then waited for him to respond.

*U Ma, like what U C?*

*No doubt!*

I had come to love cyber flirting.

*Is that right?*

I didn't care too much for the chat rooms because everyone knew that was where the freaks and weirdos hung out. Usually, I exchanged emails here and there, but I didn't like the fact that I had to wait close to forever for a reply. Facebook had changed all of that and I loved it!

*Daddy, it's all good from where I'm sitting.*

At first I wasn't sure about Marvin. He didn't have a profile picture, there were very few personal details about him on his page and I couldn't tell anything by browsing through his friends list. But a few days after I had accepted his friend request he sent me a private message and we'd been chatting ever since.

*Tru Tru.*

When I commented about him not having any pictures on his page, he asked how badly I wanted to see him. I had to think about that for a second. Katina's warning sounded off in my head, but I ignored it. What did Katina's butt know anyway? She was doing all the wrong things online. While I wanted to make some money, too, I also enjoyed being Candi and being desired by an entirely fresh new crop of men.

Technology had moved dating from the clubs to the Internet and I didn't have a problem with that at all. As far as I was concerned this was the new singles bar and I didn't have to worry about getting dressed, made up, leaving the house, or even getting caught.

*So we gon' hook up or what?*

I realized that lately I'd been spending quite a bit of time on Facebook, but Candi's life was far more exciting. Even though she only existed in cyberspace, she was still living *the* life!

*Yeah, that sounds hot.* I quickly typed back.

*You cuming to me or am I cuming to you?*

I started laughing again. I liked Marvin. He was witty, clever, and really fast on his feet, and in his picture he looked really good. He was buffed in all the right places and had a very nice smile.

*When you talking about meeting and where?*

Even though I didn't know him, I didn't want him to think I didn't trust him, so I figured playing it that way would be best. He didn't respond right away.

By the time my phone rang minutes later, I was still waiting for him to respond. It was Katina on the phone.

"Hey, girl. What's up?" I said, keeping an eye on the computer screen.

"Hey, guuurrrl," Katina sang. "What's going on with you tonight?"

"Nothing, guuurrrl! I'm right here. The baby's asleep, Larry's gone, and I'm playing a little," I said, then giggled as my eyes fixed in on the text message.

"Who you playin' with?"

"I'm chatting with this dude on Facebook," I explained.

"Umph. So listen. What's up? When you coming back to work?" Katina asked, cutting to the chase.

"Not sure. Maybe in a couple of weeks or so," I said. "Why?"

"'Cause I'm wondering if I should try to bring in someone else. I really need money and I can't do it all alone," she said.

I didn't want Katina to bring in another girl, but I also didn't want to be having this conversation right now. I was more focused on Marvin and our conversation online.

"Besides, there's this guy out of Chicago. He's one of my best customers and he was asking for you," she said.

That gave me pause.

I wondered if Katina was just saying that to get me back sooner than I wanted to come. Since when was one of *her* clients asking specifically for me?

"What does he want with me?" I asked.

"Said something about his boy really digging you," she said.

As I read Marvin's text, I listened to Katina.

*Thought u liked the pix*, the message read. Then he said, *Let's meet at Pappadeaux on 610*

So he's in Houston, too!

"...you know me. I'm already packing my bags and thinking about us shopping on the Magnificent Mile," she said.

"Katina, you always got champagne dreams and shit, then we wind up sippin' on Mad Dog," I said.

"No, girl. Not this time. This dude got serious money. I'm trying to tell you, girl!"

"Yeah, like the two dudes the other night, right?"

"Oh, you ain't still trippin' off of that! Girl, that's been what, two months ago now? That's water under the bridge. So what's up? I ain't been to the Windy City in a long while, and when we get there we could stock up on some Garrett's Popcorn," she said. Katina sounded really excited like a little kid. Me, on the other hand, I wasn't about to go getting my hopes up.

And the disaster with the last two chumps was a mere three weeks ago, which was not quite water under the bridge as far as I was concerned.

"I may come back next week," I said, hoping that would shut her up and get her off the phone.

"So I can tell ol' boy to tell his friend you'll be back next week?"

"Yeah, Katina. I need some money anyway."

"See now that's what I'm talking about!" Katina was hyped. "Girl, let's make this money!"

But I still wasn't completely buying her Chicago story. As we hung up I told myself that, if nothing else, I could use the cash.

When Marvin sent a series of question marks, I realized I hadn't responded to his request about Pappadeaux.

*When?* I typed back.

*Saturday night*

*What time*

*Six-thirty*

*K. C U then.* I quickly typed before I changed my mind.

I figured it was time to get off Facebook.

I was thrilled, excited, and scared all at the same time. After all, I had less than twenty-four hours to pull my hair, outfit, and myself together.

Oh, how I loved the social networking sites.

# CHAPTER 16

## Quinn

I t had been one month since my date with Zari. At first I was really feeling shitty about the way she'd played me, but as it turned out she had actually done me a favor. She'd let me know that I needed to step up my game if I ever had any hopes of living my double life as Dr. Cole. I had to learn how to be cool, charming, and most of all, have the necessary tools to seduce any woman I damn well pleased. For tips on that, I had to go see Calvin, and have him teach me what he'd learned from my father, the King Mack Daddy.

It had been a while since I'd seen Calvin, so I knew he'd be shocked to hear from me the moment I called him.

"Hey, Calvin. It's me, Quinn," I said as I turned on the hands-free device in my car.

"My God! Pigs must be flying. Let me go and look out of the window because I can't believe you've decided to catch up with a brother."

"Ha, ha," I said.

"It's good to hear from you." Calvin sounded genuinely glad I'd called.

"What are you doing right now? I'm in your neck of the woods and I want to drop by and see you."

"Nothing. Hanging out on my favorite site, talking to this chick named Katina that I want to fuck."

"That's the chick we were watching a few weeks ago, right? The one with the sex website? The one who has the amateur friend?"

"Yup. That's the one," he confirmed.

"Ask her how her girlfriend is doing. I'd love to do her," I said, laughing.

"I'm trying to get her to come to Chicago. Maybe I can get her and her girlfriend to come," Calvin said.

"That would be cool, but isn't that kind of dangerous? You know, playing in your own backyard?" I asked.

"Yes, it is, but that's one of the things that makes fucking around so exciting. It's the danger and risk of it all that's an aphrodisiac." He laughed.

"I guess," I answered, wondering if he was thinking with a clear mind.

"How close are you?"

"I'll be there in about ten minutes."

"Cool. I'll see you then."

I pulled into Calvin's driveway, got out of my car and rang his doorbell. I heard his dogs, Huckleberry Hound and Astro, barking. When he answered the door both of his dogs began sniffing me while wagging their tails.

"Hey, fellas. Leave him alone. Go on now." The dogs obediently walked away.

Calvin was wearing workout clothes and looked like he'd lost a little weight since the last time I saw him.

"You working out now?" I asked, noticing the difference.

"Yeah, dude. A few weeks ago I went in for my annual checkup and the doctor told me that I needed to shed a few pounds. He tried to put me on high blood pressure pills and I told him to go fuck himself. That shit will make your dick go soft."

"Yeah, I've heard that," I felt slightly envious that he'd started working out and had gotten noticeable results. "What kind of workouts are you doing?"

"Weights and cardio, the same stuff I did when I played in the league. I know how to get the weight off. I'd just gotten lazy and comfortable." I followed Calvin down to the family room that was situated in the basement.

I plopped down on the leather sofa and placed my feet on a nearby ottoman.

"So what's up?" he asked, taking a seat on the leather La-Z-Boy recliner.

"I need to know everything that my father taught you about women and seduction."

Laughing out loud, Calvin said, "What brought this on?" I was quiet for a moment as I thought about where I should start. Then I laid it all out to him. I told him about Zari, our hook up, and how things had gone wrong. I told him about my desire to sleep with other women and how I wanted my cake and ice cream, too, at least for a little while.

"Wow. You mean to tell me in all the years you've been with Tameecia, you never once tipped out on her?"

"No. I've been loyal to her," I answered truthfully.

"Damn! That's fucked up. I mean, it's cool if you have the right woman who is a lady in the streets and a freak in the bed and respects you, but shit, man. If I was married to Tameecia and she treated me the way she treats you, I would've run around on her a thousand times by now and dared her to say something. Then, when I got tired of fucking around on her, I'd leave her."

"I don't have that type of thug in me," I admitted.

"Yes, you do. You just don't know how to tap into it. If you ever do get gangster on Tameecia, it would fuck her head up," he said, chuckling.

"Maybe and maybe not, but answer this for me. You have a wife who is a lady in the streets and a freak in the bed and you still fuck around. Why do you do the things you do?" I was hoping he'd give me an honest answer.

Shrugging his shoulders, Calvin said, "I like fucking a variety of women, just like your dad did."

"So you a ho?" I teased him.

"No. Promiscuous women are hos. Promiscuous men are called playas. That's another one of your father's lessons."

"Speaking of him, please tell me what he taught you. I need to know everything."

Calvin rubbed the stubble on his chin. "Honestly, man, you need money to truly become who you want to be. Pussy is not cheap and women control the price of it."

"I have money."

"I'm not talking about money from your job. I'm talking about Richard Gere money like in the movie, *Pretty Woman*. You need to be able to blow two or three thousand dollars without blinking an eye."

"Did you blow that kind of money on women?"

"Hell yeah, especially when I was in the league. I was flying women to exotic islands. I've blown a shit load of money on pussy," he admitted.

"Okay, so I'll have to manage my expectations with the cash I've got. I get that," I humbly admitted.

Calvin repositioned himself in his seat. "I don't believe I'm going to do this for you."

"Do what?"

"Grant you your wish. I feel sort of bad that you weren't very healthy when you were in your twenties and missed out on chasing skirts. That's a rite of passage all men need to experience."

"I couldn't help that," I said defensively.

"I know. Look, I'm going to give you a gift to help you out."

"What are you talking about, man?" I was confused.

"I'm going to set up a playboy fund for you and hook you up with my tailor."

"I don't want your money, Calvin." My pride wouldn't allow me to take what he was offering.

"Look, fool. Don't look a gift horse in the mouth. Do you want the full-blown fantasy or not? Once the fund I set up for you runs out, that's it. You'll have to deal with your life the way it is, but you should at least experience some of what you've missed out on."

"Dude, I…"

"Yeah, save it man." Calvin tossed up his hand, cutting my comments short. "Now, about your dad. In order for you to seduce a woman you have to first be appealing to her and, like me, you need to lose weight."

"I bought some workout DVDs that I haven't really used yet. I could start using them. The program guarantees results if I stick with it."

"Then that's what I suggest you do first," he said.

"Then what?" I asked.

Calvin got up and walked toward the bar on the opposite side of the room. He grabbed a small key and asked me to follow him. We went out to the coach house above the garage. He opened a safe that was hidden inside a wall. He pulled out a box and handed it to me.

"What's this?"

"Material for you," he said.

I set the box down on the desk and opened it up. Inside were a ton of DVDs. I picked one up and read the title out loud. "*How to Blow Her Mind*." I chuckled.

I picked up another one. "*The Knack of Seduction*," I said.

"That's a really good one," Calvin said.

I picked up another one that read, "*Common Fantasies Most Women Have.*"

"Wow! Where in the hell did you get this stuff?"

"Some of it belonged to your father and the other stuff I picked up over the years. There's a lot of material there. It's pretty self-explanatory."

"*Sex and the City?*" I picked up a DVD collection of the first two seasons.

"Oh yeah. Pay attention to all of the women and learn them. They give you all types of information on fashion and how women think. There are DVDs on sexual positions, toys, Kama Sutra and how to give massages. There is even an erotic DVD in there called, *Sock It to Me.*"

"No shit," I said, feeling as if he'd just given me the holy grail of sexual knowledge.

"I want my shit back when you're done," he said, relocking his safe.

"No problem," I answered as I put the lid back on the box.

"Come on. I'll walk you to your car," Calvin said as we headed toward the driveway.

I wasted no time transforming myself. With the extra funds Calvin had generously provided, I purchased a set of weights to build muscle with. I set up a makeshift gym in my garage and started following the workout DVDs. The shit I was doing was basically a get-in-shape-quick boot camp. By the end of the second week, I'd lost five pounds.

Feeling encouraged, I doubled my efforts by working out twice a day—once in the morning and then again in the evening. By the end of the fourth week, I'd lost ten pounds and had noticeable muscular definition on my arms.

Tameecia, as usual, thought I was crazy and doing too much. She told me so one morning during my workout. She came out to the garage and stood in the doorway. She glared at me as I did pushups until I was exhausted.

"Fool, you're going to kill your damn self." She tried to interrupt my flow with her negativity.

"Is that what you think?" I stood up and wiped sweat from my brow. For the first time in my life, I felt invigorated and strong. My chest had become broader, my biceps had gotten bigger and my stomach had gone down considerably. I no longer felt bloated and miserable and the back pain I'd been experiencing for most of my life was gone because I'd strengthened my core muscles.

"You're doing too much. You're going to have a relapse and hurt yourself. I don't feel like you being sick again. I got this new job and won't have the time to take care of you when you hurt yourself."

"You let me worry about my health," I said as I picked up a pair of 35-pound dumbbells to do arm curls with.

"Just stop, Quinn!" Tameecia gave me a command as if I was a dog. I immediately turned my attention to her and shot flaming daggers at her with my eyes.

"There's no way that I'm going to stop just because you said so!" I snapped. For the very first time, I saw Tameecia flinch. She looked at me like I was someone who'd just betrayed her.

I got a twisted sense of pleasure from it. It made me feel powerful.

Without saying another word, Tameecia left me alone.

# CHAPTER 17

*Codi*

After the weekend I had, I was actually glad to get back to Katina's on Monday. I walked in just as she was wrapping up her set.

I was stunned to see that Katina had installed a pole and she was working it like a pro. When she slid from the top to the bottom, upside down, and kicked out her leg to land with the other leg still wrapped around the pole, I wanted to make it rain.

"Damn, girl!" One thing about Katina was when she set her mind to do something, she did it to the hilt.

"I'm glad you came back," she said as we sat talking after she finished.

"Man, you've changed a lot," I said, looking around.

"Yeah, gotta keep up. It's getting crowded in this biz, so now I've gotta work three times harder than before," she said.

"Why's that?"

Katina looked at me. "There's this chick, DeeLish, and she's got a team with her and they are wicked. It's like they'll do anything for a buck, so that means I've gotta work harder. Otherwise, I won't keep any clients."

"Hmm," was my only response.

"So what happened with dude you were chatting up the other day?" Katina asked.

I didn't want to come right out and ask her about her client from

Chicago. I needed her to bring it up, so I wouldn't seem as desperate as I really was.

"Oh, girl, wait 'til I tell you what happened!" I said.

Katina scooted closer on the sofa. She was eager for me to start dishing.

"So we agreed to meet up at Pappadeaux Saturday evening. Girl, just talking about it takes me back there and oooh!"

I looked around the restaurant and felt like I'd just stepped into a serious club. I immediately felt uncomfortable, but I was like, "Let me calm down." Lord knows after all I had to do to get out of the house, I needed Marvin to be everything I had fantasized about.

I'd worn the jeans, a red wrap sweater and red suede pumps so Marvin would be able to pick me out of a crowd. Sometimes people didn't look like their online pictures and I was cool with that.

The bar was packed, there was very little standing room, and the music was so loud this place could easily be dubbed as a poppin' nightclub.

I kept looking around, trying to see if any of the guys were paying extra attention to me or looking in my direction. I was also trying to see if anyone looked familiar.

"This seat taken?"

I whipped my head around and didn't see anyone.

"This chair. Is anyone sitting here?" he asked again.

This time I realized a midget was talking to me. My heart took a nosedive when suddenly two and two came into focus.

"Um, no. No one is sitting here." I managed to find my words.

I watched in horror as the midget climbed up on the barstool and adjusted himself close to the bar. My head was spinning as thoughts of the old bait and switch played out right before my eyes.

The little midget started snapping his fingers toward the bartender.

I was fuming. I couldn't believe I had fallen for this shit. What was I gonna do with a freakin' midget! Just as I was about to say something real nasty to him, another voice stopped me.

"You Candi?"

I froze at the sound for two reasons. First, I'm only Candi online. Second, the voice did not belong to a man. I turned my head slowly, and said, "Yeah, who wants to know?"

The woman standing in front of me sounded like a female, but she was sporting a fade haircut and had tattoos all around her neck and arms. She wore a pair of baggy jeans and several white T-shirts.

"It's me, Marvin," she said.

I nearly upchucked right there.

"Um, you're who?" Now all of a sudden the midget didn't look bad after all.

"Well, I'm Marvina, but everybody calls me Marvin," she said.

I frowned. "I um, I thought you were a man."

Marvina smiled nervously. "Baby, I'm better than any man you've ever had."

I looked at her and couldn't believe she was serious. She looked like a dude, but she was *not* a man!

I eased off the stool and grabbed my clutch from the bar. Between her and the midget, I was fit to be tied.

"I'm outta here," I said. As I took off she was right behind me.

"So whassup, ma?"

I was so mad. I had snuck out of the house and left Larry and the baby to come and hook up with a female who was having a gender crisis? I was pissed.

"Marvina, I don't go that way," I said and rushed toward the car. Larry would be pissed. I told him the baby needed milk and diapers. That was nearly two hours ago.

The thought that I nearly hooked up with another woman had me on the edge. How could she be on Facebook pretending to be a damn man?

"Guuurrrl, no!" Katina squealed. Her eyes were wide and she looked like she was anxiously waiting for more of the story.

"*He* was a *she*!"

"What did you tell Larry when you got back home?"

I sighed. "More drama there, too, girl." I rolled my eyes. "I told him I'd been driving around because the first three stores I went to were out of both diapers and milk."

"He bought that shit?"

"Larry is simple, girl. Then when he looked at me, and was like, 'You weren't wearing that when you left.' I told him I didn't expect him to pay attention to me, but this was proof that he never did because he didn't even notice what I was wearing when I left the damn house!"

"You changed?" she asked.

"Yes, girl. When I thought I was meeting Marvin and not Marvina, I sure did. I walked out of the house in sweats and a T-shirt, but my real clothes were in my hobo," I said. "The minute I turned the corner I changed in the backseat of the car, then I got on the freeway and rushed off to meet who I thought was the perfect man!"

"Yeah, that's the problem with Facebook and the rest of those sites, even with online dating," Katina said.

"What's that?"

"You never know what you're getting."

"Ain't that the truth!"

Katina looked at the clock. "Oh snap! I need to get ready. This is about the time my Chicago sugar daddy likes to peek at me."

She sprang up and flipped the switch to activate the camera.

As the music started Katina twisted her hips and started moving to the beat. The way her hips swayed back and forth and twisted in a circular motion, she was working it. The more she danced, circled the pole and dropped it like it was hot, I just knew her clients were happy.

The numbers were spiking, too. All of a sudden Katina reached over and snatched me off the couch. Reluctantly, I got up and started moving to the music with her.

When we started taking off our clothes the numbers spiked even more. Katina was really serious about this voyeur business. In addition to the ticker she had that counted the number of callers at any given hour, she had music and monitors on automatic control and her set up was pretty nice. I realized she was right. There was much money to be made, and I needed it.

The next day my phone rang early and I wondered who it could be. Before seeing the caller ID, I assumed it was a bill collector. Who else called at eight in the damn morning?

It was Katina.

"Hello?" I sounded groggy.

"Girl! Didn't I tell you dude from Chicago was feeling us? See you thought I was bullshitting you, huh?"

"What happened?" I felt my pulse begin to race from excitement.

"Girl, he left me a message. I got his number and he wants us to call him."

"Who is he?" I asked. Katina was talking so fast, her words were all jumbled.

"We finally hit the jackpot," she said. "This is the one!"

"Katina, who is this man?" I asked again.

"Girl, are you sittin' down?" Katina asked.

She could be so over-the-top. I wanted to know what she knew about this man she was getting all worked up about. So far our track record wasn't looking good.

"I'm sitting," I said.

"Girl, he used to be in the NB fuckin' A!" Katina announced. She sounded like she wanted to cry tears of joy. "His name is Calvin Hamilton. They used to call him Can do Cal. I mean, he was big time! A starter, girl!"

"What? Is he single?" I asked.

"I don't know yet, but when he left me that message I got his name. Girl, I Googled him and couldn't believe when I saw all this stuff about him on the Web! Dude got bank!" Katina said with such conviction she had me trembling with excitement.

"So what are we gonna do?"

"I'll tell you exactly what we're gonna do. We're gonna reach out to him and his friend, tell their asses we are not afraid to travel, and then we're gonna go to the Windy City and fuck them both so damn good they'll be willin' to pay to play."

If I knew Katina like I thought I did, I knew she was as serious as cardiac arrest.

"Oh, and Calvin said you need to accept Julius' friend request on Facebook," she said.

"Who the hell is he?" I asked.

"Have you been listenin' to me talk? I told you about his buddy. Remember I told you they were watchin' us and he and his friend were checkin' us out? Girl, this is it! This is pay dirt!" Katina yelled.

"Can you at least wait 'til you talk to the man?" I asked.

"No need. I feel it. I realize that I've stumbled onto something real special here. I'm tellin' you, I smell money with this one," Katina said.

I didn't want to remind her about the last time she thought she smelled money. I didn't want to seem like I was hating. She was excited, but after Marvin turned out to be Marvina and some of the other stuff on Facebook, I wasn't so quick to get all worked up.

"Is Larry gone yet?" she asked.

"Yeah, why?"

"'Cause I wanna call his ass. I wanna call with you on the phone. His message did say for *us* to call him."

"What are you gonna say to him?" It's not that I wanted to know. I just couldn't fathom that we were about to call some random man who saw us on her site. What would we say?

"Girl, puuhleease. He's a man! Just hold on, listen and learn," she said.

Before I could protest, she clicked over and the next time I heard her voice, another line was ringing in my ear.

A few seconds later a man's voice answered.

"Hello?"

"Hi. May I speak with Calvin Hamilton, please?" Katina said in a husky and breathless voice. I rolled my eyes at her and her antics.

"Um, this is Calvin Hamilton. Who's calling please?"

"Hey, Daddy. I should've known this was you. The minute I heard your voice I felt my wetness coming down."

For a second there was a pause and I thought Katina had gone too far.

But suddenly the man said, "Damn, girl! I knew you were as sexy as you look on that site!"

"Yes, Daddy. I'm sexy, and so's my girl, Candi," she said.

"Candi?" he asked.

"Yes, I'm extra sweet, so naturally, I'm the only Candi your mama wouldn't mind you eating," I said.

"Oooh! You ladies sound like a whole lot of fun," he said.

"We're even more fun in person," Katina offered up.

"I'll bet you are," he said.

"So, Daddy, where do you live?"

"In Chicago. You ladies been to Chicago?"

"Not lately," Katina said quickly.

"Well, we'll have to see what we can do about that. You two are in Houston, right."

"Yes," I said.

For the remainder of the conversation, I only dropped in a few times. Katina did most of the flirting and Calvin seemed to be eating it all up. I had to admit, the girl was good. When she started talking about swallowing and back door action, I had to mute my phone.

By the time Katina was done with him, I knew Calvin would soon be buying tickets regardless of whether he knew it or not.

"I sure hope you're excited about seeing us," Katina said.

"Hey, listen. I need to take this call that's coming in, but I want to talk to you ladies later. Let me check with Dr. Cole and we can check our schedules and get you two up here to the Windy City," he said.

"Oh, okay. Well, go work your jelly, Daddy," Katina said. "We'll talk later, but until then, be sure to check out my site in about an hour."

When he got off the phone, Katina was screaming at the top of her lungs.

"Guuurrrrl, did you hear him say his friend is a doctor?"

"I know! I know!" I squealed. I really was excited now.

"Did I hook you or what?"

"Oh, you hooked me!" I said.

"Cool, so why don't you get dressed and get over here so we can handle this business, and, of course, talk more about our trip to Chicago."

I may not have admitted it then, but I really was very excited about the possibilities with Mr. Chicago and his friend, the *doctor*.

# CHAPTER 18

# Quinn

"How do pants feel in waist?" asked my silver-haired Korean seamstress who had a thick accent and spoke in broken English. She was on her knees behind me, placing pins at the bottom of my slacks.

"I can't believe I've lost so much weight. I've gone from a forty-two-inch waistline down to a thirty-six-inch waist," I said, as if she really cared about my transformation.

"You look very nice. Handsome. Girls be all over you in new expensive suits you about to buy."

I snickered loudly. I loved the idea of being irresistible to women. I'd never experienced that before, but that was all about to change, thanks to Calvin. I didn't know how I'd ever repay him for the gift he'd given me. Even if it would be short-lived, I was going to enjoy every minute of it for as long as it lasted.

"Someone must like you very much. They spend lot of money on Armani suits for you," said the Korean woman as she rose to her feet, stepped around in front of me and asked me to extend my arms out to form the letter "T."

"The suits are a gift from a family member," I explained.

"What you do? Give kidney?" She was clearly being nosy.

"No," I answered. "It's just a gift."

"Seven Armani suits. Very expensive gift," she said, continuing to pry.

"I know," I answered as she finished up her measurements. As promised, Calvin hooked me up with his tailor who made all of his suits. Since he stood 6'7", it wasn't easy for him to go to Sears and buy off of the rack. All of his clothes were custom-made. Calvin was feeling extra generous and told me that he'd cover the cost of the new suits for my new look. That way I wouldn't have to spend the money he'd previously given me to live out my fantasy on new threads. He'd selflessly given me twenty thousand dollars to play with. To me it was a boatload of cash, but to him it was nothing, especially since each of his restaurants made thirty-five thousand a week on average. I used seven thousand dollars of the money he'd given me to buy a red and black Chevy Camaro that had come into the dealership.

The owner, Big Sam, wanted ten thousand dollars for the used car. After I had it inspected for any potential mechanical problems, I made Big Sam an offer his greedy ass wouldn't refuse. That left me with thirteen thousand dollars in cold hard cash to blow on my once-in-a-lifetime adventure.

"Suits will be ready in three days," said the seamstress as I walked back into the changing room to put my street clothes back on.

I stepped out into the bright sunlight and smiled at my new ride, which was glistening. The black rubber on the tires looked as if it was wet and the tinted windows made my baby look smoking hot. I'd even given my wheels a sexy name. I called her Silky.

I walked over to Silky, opened the door and ducked inside. The black leather seats seemed to wrap around my back and I felt as if Silky was hugging me. I fired her up. I loved the growl of the motor. I put on my sunglasses, plugged in my iPod and selected one of my favorite songs, "Atomic Dog," by George Clinton. I leaned to the right, tossed my left hand on the steering wheel, checked my side mirror before pulling out into traffic and zoomed off toward the expressway, barking like a dog along with the music.

"Why must I feel like that? Why must I chase the cat? Nothing but dog in me," I sang aloud as I turned onto the highway and let Silky run wild.

I'd been studying the videos that Calvin had given me. I'd learned a lot, but I really loved the DVD on how to be a charismatic man. There were tips like: Women love compliments, but only if they're sincere. The instructor on the DVD said to avoid compliments like, "Your eyes are so pretty." Instead, men needed to compliment on a comment she may have made like, "That was a really smart point" or "You're really funny." It also helped to have a funny story that got laughs every time it was told. And I needed to work on listening and timing my responses during the course of a conversation. There was nothing more awkward than being interrupted when you were trying to make a point, or when you cut someone off to interject your thoughts.

I had to admit, I was truly enjoying my new fantasy life. It was the ultimate escape from my reality. In my alternate world, I had no nagging wife and no free-loading sister-in-law who'd recently learned that she'd lost her lawsuit and wasn't going to get a damn dime. I also had no children. I was a ladies' man, and being physically fit gave me a newfound confidence I'd never known before in my life.

Another one of the DVDs that Calvin had given me talked about the science of sex appeal and the importance of having a sexy walk. The DVD explained how women who believed they were being watched by men tended to walk more sexily by swaying their hips more. Men who believed they were being watched had a tendency to swagger their shoulders and puff out their arms to visibly increase their size. A man with swagger made a woman swoon. Denzel Washington had it, my father had it, and President Obama definitely had it. I was, without question, sharpening my swagger.

My radar detector began bleeping. I glanced down at my speed and noticed I was doing 90 mph. I tapped the brakes to slow down so that I wouldn't get a ticket from some state trooper. At that moment my phone began to ring. I saw that Tameecia was calling me.

"Shit," I hissed as I answered the phone. I just knew she was about to start nagging me.

"Where the hell are you?" she blasted me.

"In my damn skin!" I snapped off. I wasn't about to let her push me around. The old Quinn would've, but not the new and improved version. I'd upgraded and she needed to recognize that.

"When are you going to come clean about how you got the money for that car?" she asked. Tameecia wasn't happy at all about my purchase. She couldn't stand it when I did things without her input or permission.

"I know you're not trying to clock my money." I almost dared her to admit it.

"Quinn, if you have extra money you need to tell me. The kids need new clothes, the refrigerator is about to go out and you know we need to call a plumber about that leak under the sink in the bathroom." Tameecia clearly wanted me to care about her concerns, but I had an answer for all her complaints.

"Tameecia, I've called the repairman about the refrigerator already. I will fix the leak under the sink and I'll take care of getting the boys a few outfits. In fact, I'm on my way home now. When I get there, I'll take them to the mall," I said.

Tameecia was silent. I could tell she was thinking.

"So how did you get extra money? Did you sell a bunch of cars at the lot?"

"Stop adding me up, Tameecia!" I blasted her for trying to get into my private affairs.

"Excuse me?" I could hear anger in her voice.

"You heard me the first time. I didn't stutter." I waited to hear her response. Tameecia remained uncharacteristically quiet. I assumed she was thinking. She was probably trying to figure out how to deal with the new me. I liked that because I was now unpredictable and it kept her on her toes.

Once my new suits arrived I had my son take some photos of me and I updated my profile picture on Facebook. It didn't take long for friend requests to start pouring in from women all around the country. I got all types of messages in my inbox. Allison from California wrote, *Damn, baby! You look sexy in that suit. Look me up if you're ever in Cali.* Dawn from Philadelphia wrote, *Can I see a picture of your dick?* Linda from Chicago inboxed me a photo of her tits along with her phone number and a note that said, *Call me if you want some of this.* I was becoming addicted to social media. I loved all of the attention and online flirting and Linda and her tits would definitely be hearing from me in the future.

On Saturday morning I got up early to give Silky a bath. I hated for any type of dirt to get on her. As I was hosing her down my cell phone rang.

"Yo," I answered.

"Where are you at right now?" Calvin asked.

"I'm at home."

"I need you to meet me somewhere real quick. We need to talk."

"Sure. Is everything okay?" I thought something had gone wrong.

"Oh, everything is perfect, man. I need to talk to you about something. It's best that we talk about this matter in person." He sounded secretive.

"Where do you want me to meet you at?"

"Why not meet up at Home Depot on Lincoln Highway? I have to pick up some cleaning supplies for one of my stores," he suggested.

"Cool. Going there was actually on my list of things to do today. I'll see you there in about forty-five minutes."

"Great. Oh, and come alone. Don't bring the kids with you."

"No problem."

When I arrived at Home Depot, Calvin was sitting in his car. I pulled into the parking space next to him and stepped out of Silky as if I'd just pulled up to some red carpet.

"What's going on, playa?" I asked.

"Hold up! When did you get the Camaro?" I could see a little envy in his eyes and that made me feel good.

"I've only had it a few days. It came into the dealership and I was able to get it at a steal," I explained.

"So is that what you used the playboy money for?" Calvin asked.

"Some of it," I admitted as he opened the door of my car and took a look inside.

"Nice," he said, nodding his head approvingly. "I hope you still have enough money left to wine and dine several women because pussy costs money. You can't forget that."

"Of course I know," I said as he shut the car door.

"Then listen to this. Do you remember when I was showing you the website with the two chicks dancing around?"

"Of course I do," I said, recalling the girl named Candi.

Calvin started laughing before he could get more of his words out. "Dude, I told them that I'd fly them to Chicago for a weekend."

"You did what?" I didn't want to believe my ears.

Continuing to laugh, he said, "I gave out my number and I got a phone call from Katina. I told her that I was an ex-NBA player and that I'd love to hook up with her for something a little more intimate."

"And she agreed?" I asked.

"Hell yeah. She was damn near willing to drive to the airport while I was talking to her," Calvin said, smiling.

"What are you going to do when she gets here?"

"No, you mean what are *we* going to do when they get here?" Calvin corrected me.

"They?" I was perplexed.

"Yes. They. I told her to bring her girlfriend, Candi, for you."

"Bullshit!" I said, not wanting to believe him.

"Now you know me, Quinn. I don't bullshit when it comes to getting me some new pussy."

"Damn. When are they going to get here?" I asked, trying to figure out what excuse I'd use to get out of the house.

"That's the thing. I was going to fly them in this month, but I've got to fly out to Los Angeles to participate in a reunion party with my old teammates and look into opening a new restaurant out there. I'll be gone for at least three weeks."

"Okay, that's cool. It'll give me enough time to figure out how I'm going stay out all night."

"Just say you're staying at my place," Quinn offered.

"That works for me. So what are we going to do with the ladies when they arrive?"

"Feed them and then fuck them. Maybe they'll even get freaky and do each other while we watch." Calvin laughed.

"Now that would be some wild shit," I said, liking the idea.

"Sounds like we're going to have a private party," Calvin said. "I'm putting them up in a room at the Ritz-Carlton Hotel downtown."

"Nice." I thought about how elegant the luxury hotel looked. I'd seen several news stories on the hotel because guests of the *Oprah* show stayed there.

"So bring your 'A' game and plenty of condoms."

"You got it," I said, giving him a fist bump as we made our way inside.

# CHAPTER 19

*Codi*

After I had shook my ass in front of a camera damn near all day, Larry came walking in the house with an extra-large chip on his damn shoulder.

What was he doing home early?

"I'm tireda chicken! Every damn day fried chicken, baked chicken, chicken soup, leftover chicken. Damn, girl! Ain't yo' mama teach you how to fix anything other than chicken?"

This was what I heard shortly after the front door opened then closed. I was trying my best to ignore his simple behind, but he wasn't making it easy. I was on the phone with my mom and trying to finish the chicken and pasta dish I had made for dinner.

"That Larry I hear in the background?" my mother asked.

"Yeah, that's him," I said.

"What's he fussing about? Y'all doing okay?" she asked.

"Yeah, we're good. He over there fussing about work. Who knows, Ma," I said.

We were having a nice conversation about this TV show we enjoy watching. Maybe it was wrong to lie to my mom, but telling her that Larry was complaining about my lack of skills in the kitchen would only lead to a lecture from her, and that I did not need. So I kept it simple.

"Lemme say hi to my son-in-law," she said.

"Oh, he just went into the bathroom, but I'll tell him to call you when he gets out the shower," I lied again. Before she could say something else, I said, "Okay, well, let me get dinner ready. I'll talk to you later." I ended the call abruptly because I really didn't need those two talking while he was bitching and moaning.

When I ended the call I turned my cell phone off and slipped it into a drawer. As I turned around, Larry walked into the kitchen and the look on his face told me he wasn't done complaining.

"I'ma have to hold out on this here good stuff if you don't act right in the kitchen," he had the nerve to say. Larry's sense of humor was lame, but he was clueless.

When he slapped me on my butt I really had to struggle not to go upside his head. I wanted to ask, "What good stuff?" Not only did Larry stink in everyday life, but he also stunk in bed!

"Don't tell me. We havin' chicken again, huh?" He chuckled.

I rolled my eyes at him and turned off the oven when the timer rang.

When I turned to reach for a potholder I bumped right into him.

"Get out my way!" I screamed.

He grabbed me around the waist and tried to kiss my neck.

"Larry, quit!" I screamed, swatting in his direction. "You playing and I'm trying to get food on the table."

"How 'bout I bend you *over* the table," he said as his hot, sour breath assaulted my personal space.

This was Larry's idea of foreplay. To say I was not the least impressed or aroused was an understatement. He could at least try to clean up before he tried to get some, but no, that would be asking too much.

"Where the baby at?" he asked.

"I didn't pick him up yet. I told you he can stay there until six-thirty, and it's only five-forty-five."

What did I say that for?

"Girl, come get some of this good stuff," Larry said.

I wondered what had gotten into him. If I knew he was going to pop up early, I would've found something to keep myself busy until time to pick up Taylor from daycare.

"I dunno why you like to play hard to get. You only hurtin' yourself!" he insisted. He pulled me closer to his midsection where I could feel his hardness.

"Yeah, you know you want me. Quit playin'," he whispered and slobbered my neck with more kisses.

Larry backed me into the corner between the stove and the pantry and there was no turning back. I didn't want to admit it, but my panties were wet. I hated when my body betrayed me.

Being the borderline male chauvinist he was, Larry reached up under my skirt and fingered me before I could squeeze past him.

"Oh, look how wet it is, and you tryin' to act like you don't want it!"

He was so disgusting and so not romantic that he made me sick.

"Quit, Larry!" I feigned anger.

When he moved to unbuckle his pants I was able to get past him, but I didn't move fast enough. Larry caught me near the table and grabbed me at my waist from behind.

"Quit! Let me go," I yelled.

"Oh yeah. See, I told you you wanted it on the table."

He was huffing like we had already done something.

Larry hiked my skirt up, pushed my panties to the side and slipped into me. He had me leaning over onto the table as he humped me from behind.

"Ugh yeah. This what you wanted. Yeah, girl," he groaned as he moved his hips.

Soon it started feeling good and I began to wiggle my hips in response to his thrusts.

"Oh yes," I cried. He was hitting my spot.

"Yeah! I'm comin'!" he suddenly announced.

I stopped moving.

"You what?" I bolted upright.

But Larry quickly shoved me back down. "Hold still," he begged.

I was pissed.

Larry kept humping away.

"Yeah, that's right. Whose pussy is this?" he huffed, moving his hips even faster.

*It's up for grabs if you come before I get mine!* I thought to myself.

"Who's your dadd... Uurrgghh!" he whimpered.

I couldn't believe him!

Right when I tried to move back into an upright position, he squealed. Then I felt his warm juices running down my leg.

"Ahhh, that was the shit!" he had the nerve to say as he slapped me on the ass and moved away with his limp dick hanging. I turned and looked at him. Satisfaction was all over his face. I was still hot and horny while he reached down to pull up his pants.

"Damn, I'm hungry. Food gonna be ready when I get out the shower?" he asked.

"Larry, you not done," I said with my panties soaking wet now.

He looked at me like I was speaking gibberish, yawned, scratched his belly, then said, "Aw, girl, you can't expect a man to hit a home-run every time he goes up to bat. I'ma hook you up later." He winked like that was an acceptable answer, then turned and left.

I was so mad at him I wished I had someone else to fuck right there in front of him! I glanced at the clock and saw that it was five minutes to six and that pissed me off even more.

Days later at Katina's, we wrapped up our fourth session of the day when she turned to me, and said, "Wanna hang tonight?"

It was Friday. Taylor was staying with Linda and Larry and his Neanderthal friends were going out. So technically I was free, but I was leery about spending my free time with Katina. I was still a little put out with her over that whole Chicago trip. First, she was all hyped, saying dude was flying us in. Then when I started asking about a date, she said dude was out of town. It seemed odd to me, but he could've up and gone out of town after making plans to fly us up. Or Katina could've taken the money for our tickets and done God knows what with it.

The last time we were working for him and his friend, we got on Skype later and it was all gravy. Julius, the doctor, had even started posting on my Facebook page. I tried not to bother him too much because he was a doctor and all. And Katina and I agreed we needed to handle these two just right. What were the chances of her snagging a big baller who had been in the NBA and me pulling a bona-fide doctor? I decided to ride it out because you don't luck up on that kind of pedigree too often.

"Where you talking about going?" I asked.

"Not sure, but I figured we could find something to get into," she said. "Why? You got plans?"

I didn't have plans, but one of my Facebook friends invited me to this party and I wasn't gonna go at first, but now that Katina was looking for something to do I was considering it.

"Not really, but this dude on Facebook did invite me to this party out in the Woodlands."

Katina's face was twisted. "Damn, the Woodlands. That's kind of way out there."

"Yeah, but he's been promoting the hell out of it on Facebook. I don't know much about him, but there's free food, liquor, and live music in a mansion."

Katina's eyes lit up.

"Whoa! The Woodlands, mansion, live music, and free liquor?

Girl, you trippin'! Hell yeah, we need to roll, and you know what else? We need to take a stack of postcards about the site."

Was she serious? I waited for her to realize what she was saying, but she was serious. I didn't need anybody in Houston knowing about her website.

"Think about it. We need more clients. I got bills and shit, so this party sounds like just the type of circle I need to be rubbing elbows in. Here, let's get on your Facebook page and see what's up."

After perusing my Facebook page and analyzing Pier, the guy hosting the party, and the invitation he sent, as well as other Facebook friends he invited, Katina was sold.

"Yeah, this all looks good from where I'm sitting," she said. "How well do you know dude?"

I frowned. "I don't really. I mean, I comment on some of his posts and he comments on mine, but I don't *know* him, know him."

"Well, based on his pictures, it looks like he's some kind of promoter or something. We should call him before we drive all the way out to the Woodlands, though."

"I only know him from Facebook. I don't have his number."

"Girl!" Katina pulled the laptop away from me. After a few keystrokes she grabbed her cell phone and started to dial. "You know people's numbers are on Facebook!"

Really, I didn't know that.

"Hey, I'm looking for Pier," she said. After a few seconds of silence she started giggling. "Yeah, this is Candi. My girl and I were thinking about rolling out to your party, but I'm trying to figure out if it'll be our type of crowd."

I stared on as Katina listened. She started nodding.

"Wwwhhhaaat? Umph, okay then! Yeah, that's what's up!" said Katina excitedly.

Two hours later Katina and I were taking shots in her parked car outside the mansion's gate in the Woodlands. Pier's place had more than curb appeal. It looked like an ad for the rich and famous.

"Girl, I can smell the paper from all the way out here." Katina giggled as she tossed another shot back. She frowned and smacked her lips. "Ooohweeee! Yeah, my right and left hand are itching," she sang.

I swallowed the liquor and cringed as its hot trail blazed down my throat. Katina touched up her lip gloss and I looked toward the house again.

"Yeah, Pier was talking about just have an open mind and shit. He just needed to show my ass a picture of this damn house and I'da been willing to open more than just my mind!"

"What do you mean he said have an open mind?" I asked. But Katina was already getting out of the car.

We walked into a marble foyer and blue lighting illuminated overhead. I heard music playing off in the distance and it seemed to mix with laughter and chatter. The woman who greeted us at the door was friendly enough, even though she kind of eyed us up and down.

"They're in the kitchen," she said, pointing us in a direction over her shoulder.

I followed Katina into a grand red-hued kitchen. All of the major appliances blended in with the cherrywood cabinetry. Women were hovering over snacks and drinks on a massive marble slab that served as an island and the men milled among them.

A few heads turned when we walked in, but for the most part the crowd was socializing, sipping, and snacking in their own world. The women seemed to know each other.

The men looked like they were on something totally different. They were dressed in silk boxers, boxer briefs and pajama bottoms.

I couldn't remember the last time I had seen so many six-packs, bulging biceps, and ribbed stomachs.

One of my eyebrows went up when I looked toward the pantry and saw a half-naked woman with her head flung back and her ecstasy-induced expression nearly frozen as this fine chocolate specimen held her by the waist and sucked on her neck like he was feeding.

I tugged on Katina's arm, but her attention was focused on the action near the French doors that led to the backyard.

A couple stood there hugged up and kissing. The woman's hands traveled up the man's washboard stomach, lingered at his chest, and then her slender fingers squeezed his nipple. After the kiss they stood staring into each other's eyes. He licked his pretty lips, she licked hers, and then their faces connected like steel pulling toward a magnet.

When Katina leaned back, I whispered, "What the hell? Umm, what's going on up in here?"

"Girl, please. These people got money," she said, dismissing my question and concern.

I was starting to wonder if we had stepped into an orgy. Katina didn't seem to mind and she was always in search of dollar signs. When she took off down the hall I wondered where the hell she was going. As I was about to take off after her, a vision of perfection stopped me in my tracks.

"What's your name, Lovely?"

"Uh, Cod-um, I mean Candi," I said. Suddenly, I wasn't all that worried about what we had stumbled onto.

He had to have been the most beautiful man I'd ever laid eyes on. He was tall and built like a stallion. I saw muscles everywhere my eyes traveled on his magnificent body. His skin was the color of rich dark chocolate. He stood blocking my path wearing nothing but a pair of snow white boxer briefs and I wanted what was bulging in them.

He took my hand and placed it on the left side of his chest.

"You must be new," he said. His teeth were blindingly white and his smile threatened to weaken both my vision and my heart. I was in heaven. All I could think about was what it would feel like to kiss his lips.

He moved in closer.

I swallowed hard.

He even smelled good.

Just as he touched my waist, a crashing noise spoiled the scene and anything that could've happened next. I turned around in horror when the words I never thought I'd hear rang out.

"Everyone, stop right where you are. This is a raid! We're with the FBI and the house is surrounded!"

# CHAPTER 20

## Quinn

"What in the hell do you mean, you're tired?" I asked as Tameecia tumbled off of me like a lethargic tree tumbling to the ground in the forest.

"Damn! We've been at it for almost three hours," she said, squeezing her thighs closed and curling up.

"Oh, hell no," I said, jumping up to stand on the side of the bed.

"Get on your knees and put your ass in the air. It's time to do it doggie style again," I ordered.

"Quinn, you've fucked me raw. Are you taking pills or something? Because your dick is hitting spots it's never hit before. I feel like you're busting me wide open."

"So what? You're just going to leave me standing here with a hard, wet dick?"

"Just let me rest a minute," she said as she repositioned her body on the bed. "Come lay next to me," she uttered as she repositioned her head on a pillow.

Frustrated, I said, "I'll be back," and walked into the bathroom. I flipped on the light switch and caught a glimpse of myself in the mirror. I could see the silhouette of my six-pack. I still had a little stubborn belly fat, but not much. My shoulders and arms were bulging and when I glanced down at my dick I had to grab onto it and squeeze it because it felt so hard and strong. I loved the way my dick looked when it was wet with pussy juice. The way my chocolate skin glistened, the way the veins ran through it and the weight of it defined my masculinity. I inhaled deeply and then exhaled. It was a scientific fact that as fat accumulated on the lower abdomen, the size of a man's dick changed. In some cases, abdominal fat all but buried the dick. Tameecia thought I'd been taking pills to increase my dick size. Ha, what a laugh. The reason I felt bigger to her was because I'd lost weight. I knew one thing, she needed to step up her game or get left behind.

After admiring my new body, I went back into the bedroom for another round. When I got there Tameecia was snoring loud enough to wake the dead.

"Oh give me a fucking break," I griped. I marched over to the bed and shook her shoulder. "Tameecia, wake up," I whispered.

"Leave me alone," she said. Her words sounded more like gibberish than English. I realized at that moment that she wouldn't awake for hours.

"What the hell?" I complained as I walked over to the closet and removed my iPad. I logged on to the website to see if Candi was there. I figured I'd invite her to do a private session and I'd masturbate while she did her thing. Unfortunately, she wasn't available. I was about to click around and go to a random porn site and jerk off when I got an instant message from someone on Facebook.

It was Renee, a woman who'd inboxed me a photo of her breasts.

"*What are you doing up this late?*" she asked.

"*Looking for some trouble,*" I typed back to her.

"*Trouble is my first, middle and last name,*" she said.

I laughed and typed. "*How much trouble do you want to get into?*" I asked because I really wanted to take Dr. Julius Apollo Cole out to play.

"*The kind of trouble that will have my legs open,*" she answered.

"*So do you want to fuck me?*" I cut straight to the point. I didn't know the woman from Jack Shit, but I didn't need to in order to bust a nut and keep moving.

"*You know you can't handle what I've got,*" she said jokingly.

"*Ha! You may not be able to deal with what I've got swinging between my thighs,*" I answered.

"*Oh, your shit swings?*" I could tell she was excited.

Feeling bold, I aimed my iPad at my erect and glistening dick, took a picture of it, and then forwarded it in my next message which read, "*Does this answer your question?*"

"*Oh damn! I can put my mouth all over that,*" she said.

"*Yes, you can,*" I answered.

"*With all that dick, why are you single?*"

"*Because I haven't found a woman who can handle a load like mine,*" I said, feeling cocky.

"*I can handle it,*" she answered.

"*Can you handle it tonight?*" I asked. There was a long pause. "*I guess not,*" I said and was about to disconnect.

"*Yes,*" she finally answered. Now I was the one who paused.

"*Hello. Are you still there?*" she typed.

"*Yes,*" I said as I tried to see a photo of her, but all she had on her Facebook page were pictures of animals and none of herself.

"*Where do you want to meet?*" she asked.

"*What do you look like?*" I asked.

"*I look nice,*" she said.

"*How do I know you're not some guy pretending to be a woman? You don't have any photos on your page.*"

"*Trust me. Now are you going to give me what's swinging between your thighs or do you want to talk all night?*" At that moment I thought about the old saying, "Be careful what you ask for because you just might get it." I glanced over at Tameecia, who was still snor-

ing, and gave myself permission to let Dr. Cole and Silky go out
and play.

"*Yeah, baby. Let's meet at the Baymont Inn on One Hundred Forty-
Seventh Street. Do you know where that is?*" I asked.

"*Yes. I'll be there. I hope you don't play me for a fool,*" she said.

"*I won't. I'll see you there in about forty-five minutes,*" I said.

"*Okay. Here is my number. Call me when you arrive.*" I plugged
her number into my phone, then got up, took a shower and was
out of the house in no time flat.

When I arrived at the hotel I sat in the car, which was positioned in a location that allowed me to see everyone who walked
in and out of the lobby. I was waiting to see if and when Renee
would show up. After waiting for another five minutes, I saw a
woman walk into the lobby. From my viewpoint, I couldn't tell
what she looked like because I was too far away. However, she
did step back outside and seemed to be searching for someone. I
called Renee's number and when I saw the woman before me dig
into her purse to answer, I knew she'd arrived.

"Hello. Where are you?" she asked.

"I'm here," I said, getting out of the car.

"I can't wait to see all of you." Her voice sounded very husky,
which was something I hadn't expected. I couldn't tell if she was
just trying to sound sexy or if she had allergies.

"I'm walking toward you, baby," I said.

"Oh, there you are. I see you walking across the parking lot,"
she said just before she hung up.

As I approached I could tell that she was a tall woman. She had
very long legs. "Oh yeah," I said aloud to myself. As her features
came into view my eyes widened with horror and my heart nearly
stopped.

"Oh, you are so handsome," Renee said, spreading her arms to
give me a hug.

I didn't allow her to touch me; I was still trying to process what my eyes were showing me. Renee had a very husky voice like a man. She had very large breasts, but her facial features were undeniably masculine. Like a woman who looked too much like her father. She had strong cheekbones and a hideous-looking black wig, and when she smiled, she showed more of her red gums than her teeth.

"Oh, don't be afraid now, baby. I won't hurt you. Not unless you want me to." Renee stepped closer to me and I took a step back.

"You're a hermaphrodite, aren't you?" I asked, noticing what appeared to be a cock print in the skirt she was wearing.

"We need love, too, baby. I'll rock your world." Renee grinned at me.

"Oh, fuck no!" I said, taking an even larger step backward.

"How can you not like something you've never tried?" Renee had the nerve to get defensive. Suddenly, with the way the light was casting shadows on her skin, she began to look like Lurch, the grim-looking butler from *The Addams Family*.

"I know I like regular pussy. I don't want anyone who's working with the same equipment as me," I said, turning my back.

"Can you at least let me suck you off? I'll give you a blow job that will make your eyes roll into your skull," she shouted out behind me. I hurried over to Silky, got in and burned rubber getting the hell away.

The following afternoon I was fixing the leak under the bathroom sink when Tameecia interrupted me.

"What's going on with you?" she asked.

"What are you talking about?" I asked, crawling from beneath the sink.

"Who have you been fucking?" Tameecia asked flat out.

"What in the hell are you talking about?" I glared at her as if she were nuts.

"You've been fucking around on me, Quinn. Some bitch out in the streets had to have taught you some new tricks because you've never been able to hit it like you did last night."

"What?" I was highly offended.

"I'm calling a spade a spade. Last night was totally different. It seemed like you...I don't... You just have me wanting to cook you breakfast and shit, and that's not like me." I wasn't sure if she was complimenting or insulting me.

"I do know what I'm doing," I said, taking the viewpoint that she was actually insulting me.

"I'm sore, Quinn, and I feel as if I've been with King Kong. You put it down last night and I'm trying to figure out if you've been holding back or creeping around on me with that new chick magnet of a car you have."

I rose to my feet, stood before Tameecia and met her gaze. "Maybe you need to figure out who the other woman is and thank her. Because one thing is for sure, she would have finished me off and would not have left me with a hard dick," I said as I walked around her. I knew that I would ruffle her feathers with a comment like that.

"What! I know damn well you don't have another woman! I'll beat a bitch down." Tameecia's ghetto side had reared its ugly head.

"Go on." I laughed at her. "She's sitting out in the driveway. Her name is Silky and she gets my rocks off every time she hugs me."

"I'm serious, Quinn. Something or someone has happened to you. You just don't suddenly learn the moves you put on me overnight. I swear if I find out that you've been creeping around on me, nucca, there will be hell to pay."

"Tameecia, grow the hell up," I said and walked away from her.

Four weeks had passed and Calvin was finally back in town. He'd set everything up and had the Houston ladies flown to Chicago. We arrived at Midway Airport in his Cadillac Escalade and parked.

"Let's go do this," he said as we both stepped out, looking sharp. I was wearing my black Armani suit, my Movado time-piece and a new pair of Italian leather shoes. Calvin was wearing a smoking brown suit designed by actor Blair Underwood. He had on some watch that he'd purchased during a trip to France and a pair of designer sunglasses. We had the cock of the walk as we swaggered through the airport. I noticed women turning their heads. Women were checking us out and adding up our expensive clothes. When I got on an escalator a woman standing in front of me turned, met my gaze and smiled at me.

"You look nice," she complimented.

"Thank you, baby." I swept my tongue across my lips. When she stepped off the escalator, she rocked her hips a little as she watched Calvin and me.

"You made her panties wet," Calvin said.

"Is that what that little twitch was all about?" I asked.

"Damn right it was," he said with absolute certainty. Calvin removed his cell phone from its holster. "I just got a text message. They've landed."

"I certainly hope these women are the ones we saw dancing around and not two chicks who look like Renee," I said appre-hensively.

Calvin started laughing loudly. "I still can't believe that shit happened to you."

"Fuck you, man," I said jokingly.

"Stick with me and learn from a master. We're going to make this a trip these ladies won't soon forget," Calvin said confidently as we stood and waited for them near baggage claim.

# CHAPTER 21

# Codi

"I wasn't worried," Katina had the nerve to say.

"Oh really?" I asked.

We'd been talking about the raid in the Woodlands. I had no idea we had walked into some prostitution ring. Thank God the Feds had been watching the house for months and could verify that we really were not regulars.

We were waiting for people to shuffle off the plane. I was so hyped about being in the Windy City that I could hardly contain my excitement.

I decided I'd worry about Larry and home in a couple of days. For now the only thing on my agenda was having a damn good time.

"So what's up? We fuckin' this weekend or not?" I asked Katina.

"What men do you know gon' spring for plane tickets and not expect any ass in return?" Katina asked.

I couldn't stop laughing when we walked down to baggage claim at Midway and two men immediately caught my eye.

The one in the bad-ass suit was holding a sign that read: *Katina & Candi*. Katina elbowed me and started giggling. That girl didn't know subtle to save her life.

As we got closer I was so happy to see that Dr. Cole looked like a real important doctor! After all I'd been through on Facebook and that mess we barely avoided in the Woodlands I was more than a little bit skeptical, but I was finally pleasantly surprised.

"That you, Daddy?" Katina purred, then ran and jumped into Calvin's arms. You'd swear the two were long-lost lovers reuniting after a lengthy separation.

"Yeah, baby. It's me, it's me." He smiled.

I approached slowly, not knowing how to act with the good doctor. I smiled easily and stepped closer to him. When our eyes met it was like an instant connection. A smile curled at the corners of his lips and we fell into a comfortable and quiet embrace.

"It's so good to finally meet you in person," I whispered in his ear. He smelled good, too.

"Candi, you look good. Real good," he said. When we broke our hug he even spun me around, then said, "Yup, it's all there, baby, real and in the flesh. I been dreaming about this moment for more than a minute now."

The four of us started cracking up. He sounded so serious and sincere.

When we walked out to Calvin's tricked-out Escalade I prayed Katina wouldn't say anything stupid. She was speechless because she didn't utter a single word. She was cheesing so hard I could see the decaying molars in the back of her mouth.

Outside, Dr. Cole opened the front door for Katina, then opened the back door for me. When I slid into the soft, butter leather seat, I wanted to fuck right then and there.

When Dr. Cole slid in next to me, I felt really special.

"You ladies hungry or you wanna check into your rooms first?" Calvin asked.

Katina leaned over, and said, "Daddy, we not goin' to your place?" She pouted.

"Oh, ah, my kids are there with the nanny, and um, you know

I'm not into taking new people over to the house. You understand, don't you?"

"Um, yeah, I guess so. It's just that I thought we'd, you know…" Katina said, then glanced toward us in the backseat.

"It's all good," Dr. Cole said.

He was so easygoing, quiet and laid-back. I liked everything about him. In the backseat I had to *will* myself not to stare at him. I was so happy to be in his presence. When he reached over and held my hand I was regulating my breathing, but I was screaming on the inside.

We pulled up on North Michigan Avenue and the butterflies really started going crazy in the pit of my belly.

"I hope the Ritz-Carlton is good for you ladies," Calvin said. He was so sweet.

"Yup. Works just fine, Daddy," Katina squealed.

When we walked into the lobby I was so impressed.

"Why don't you ladies go over to the bar and I'll get you checked in," Calvin said.

Katina grinned at me and it was like I could read her mind. We had finally hit the big time for real. I was excited, too, but I wanted to strangle her when, the moment the men turned to leave, she grabbed my arm, and loudly said, "Cha-ching!"

I was mortified, but relieved, when I turned to check and noticed they were already at the desk.

"Girl, we need to fuck them real, real good tonight," she said. "I don't wanna mess this up!"

"Calm down," I said to Katina.

She looked up and around and reminded me of a small kid standing in wonder. A couple walked by us, talking about dinner.

"We should have a steak at the Michael Jordan Steakhouse tonight," the man said.

Katina broke into a fit of laughter.

"Gurrrl, did you hear that? Michael Jordan has a steakhouse down the street from here. Oooh, I wonder if he ever goes there to eat." I could see the dollar signs ringing in that child's eyes.

Just as we were about to hop onto one of the high seats at the bar, the guys showed up.

"We can have a drink here or we can go up to the suite," Calvin said smoothly.

Suite?

I swear my panties were so damn wet I nearly felt ashamed.

When my cell phone rang I wanted desperately to ignore it, but the truth was, I had already ignored Larry's calls and I needed to answer eventually.

"Um, can I meet you all up there? I really need to take this call," I said.

Katina looked at me with a threatening glare. The truth was we hadn't discussed how we were gonna handle this, but I knew for sure I didn't want to mess this up in any way.

"I'll step outside real quick," I said.

Calvin gave me a keycard. "You'll need your key to access the suites on the higher floors."

"Okay." I took the keycard, then eased out and caught Larry's call right before voicemail picked up.

"Aeey," he screamed into the phone. "What's this my mama saying about you havin' to go somewhere with Katina?"

"Oh yeah. Her dad died, so I had to ride up to Dallas with her," I lied.

"Oh snap! Really? I didn't even know she knew her old man."

"What? Katina? Girl, don't cry. Um, Larry, I'm gonna call you later okay. She needs me. We stopped for gas."

"Oh okay. Um, yeah. Tell her to err...hang in there."

I ended the call and rushed back into the hotel. It was the nicest I'd ever stayed in and I was so hyped.

Katina shot me a text to see where I was. I quickly answered that I was on my way.

I hopped on the elevator and got off on the floor leading to our suite. When I opened that door two things stunned me, but I wasn't sure which the most.

First, the music was blaring and drinks were flowing. Then as if that wasn't enough, Katina was up shaking her behind.

"Candi, girl, let's show these guys what's really what," she said just before she dropped it like it was hot.

I was floored.

I wanted to snatch her up and ask what the hell she was thinking. We may not have worked out a plan, but I thought we agreed we didn't want to mess this up with these guys. These were not your typical roughnecks who got off on that sort of stuff. The only time I saw doctors was when I went to the emergency room and I damn sure never thought I'd be able to snag one!

I was trying to gauge Dr. Cole's temperature. I couldn't tell if he was into Katina's booty shake or if he was just trying not to be rude.

When Calvin stood up and got behind Katina I felt a little better. Except then I got scared she'd try to screw him right there in front of us.

"I thought we were going out to eat," I said nervously.

"Oh yeah. We'd better do that so we can come back and get comfortable," Katina said. It was so obvious that she was ready to get busy. They were just about dry humping each other by then.

I wanted to remind her that we still had an entire day and a half with these guys and we needed to slow our roll if we wanted to make this last, but I couldn't tell Katina anything. I braced myself because it was gonna be a long weekend.

Later that evening, after we ate at a restaurant located on the seventieth floor, I was too through. We had such an incredible view of Lake Michigan and the surrounding areas. The night sky twinkled so much that everything looked magical.

Dr. Cole and I were hugged up across from Katina and Calvin. I was so excited that I wanted this to be my life every day. To be safe, I turned off my phone so Larry wouldn't keep calling.

We had dinner and drinks afterward. Everything was perfect.

That night, when Julius was between my thighs, I knew for sure I was in love. He was such a strong and intense lover that I wanted to stay in bed until it was time to fly out.

There wasn't none of that quick five-or ten-minute action with him. He was an awesome lover and he whispered sweet things in my ears, which turned me on even more.

"This is the best pussy ever!" he cooed.

"Squeeze me tightly!" I insisted.

"Oh shit! You got the bomb-ass pussy!" he said, and then released his essence.


Days later, back in Houston, I couldn't stop thinking about Dr. Cole. The way he dressed, his fancy car, and his body. Everything about him gave me goose bumps. I especially liked how witty he was on Facebook. Like now, we were Skyping before my next session started.

"What you do is so daring," he said.

Daring? Who said that? If Larry found out about my gig with Katina he'd flip out, but Dr. Cole was different. Everything about him was different. He wasn't about to go screaming and yelling and acting all ghetto like he ain't had no damn home training.

Sometimes now when Larry worked my nerves, I'd fantasize

about being with Dr. Cole. I bet my life would've been so much better with him versus Larry. My mother would trip at first, but when she learned that her daughter had landed a *doctor*? Umph, I bet she'd get to liking Dr. Cole real fast.

"Thank you, Daddy." I chuckled. I loved me some Julius, the good doctor.

"Codi? You ready yet?" Katina's voice asked.

I rolled my eyes.

"Hey, Big Daddy, I gotta run. Will you see me on the other side?" I asked.

He looked so cute on my monitor.

"Yeah, babe. You know I'll be tuning in. Why don't you blow me a kiss or something, okay? I'll make sure you're paid well for the cyber kiss."

"Okay, but I'd love to give you that kiss in person. When are we gonna talk about you guys coming down to Houston? Me and Katina would show y'all a real good time."

"It's gonna happen a lot sooner than you think, baby girl," Julius said.

I didn't wanna go work. I wanted to sit there the whole day and video chat with him. If I knew I could pull a man like Julius, there was no way in hell I would've wasted my time with Larry in the first doggone place.

Katina came walking in with her titties bouncing all over the place.

"Girl, whatchu doin' back here?"

"I was on Skype with Dr. Cole," I said.

"Umph, girl that man got your nose wide open," Katina said.

"Yeah. Larry better be glad we got Taylor because I'd kick his ass to the curb in a heartbeat. Imagine how much better my life would be."

"Look, why don't you imagine all the money we could make if you get your ass in front of that camera?" Katina quipped.

I know she wasn't hating on me and Julius.

"You need to put on some clothes," I told her.

"And you need to take some off!" she snapped back.

I had on my trademark fitted T-shirt and a pair of boy shorts. I had also added a miniskirt that was pleated and a pair of thigh-high socks with tiny bows on the sides. When I stepped into my stacked platform shoes I tried to get into the zone. No way was I about to let Katina get to me.

After us nearly being arrested a few weeks ago, I told myself I wouldn't be so quick to follow her behind. Katina was all about the money, no doubt, but sometimes, no, most times, when she got to drinking her judgment went completely out the window.

The only reason I was still with her was because of the trip to Chicago and how it finally panned out. I was so ready to wash my hands of her after the Feds let us go with a warning because we were the only two people in the mansion wearing street clothes.

But I had to admit, the trip to Chicago reminded me that if it wasn't for her I never would've met Dr. Cole.

Something told me that Dr. Cole had a bunch of surprises in store for me and I wanted to be front and center on the receiving end of them all!

# CHAPTER 22

# Quinn

I felt sad when Candi had to end our Skype call to go to work. Although I watched her show off her body to god only knows who, I could tell by the way she was looking into the camera that she was thinking about me. It was in her eyes. I just knew she was thinking of me. Once her show ended I turned off my iPad and relaxed on the bed. I was thankful that Tameecia, LaQeeta and the kids were out of the house. I had solitude and I couldn't help but reflect on the time I had with Candi when she was here in Chicago.

On the second day of their visit, I decided to show Candi more of the city. Calvin and Katina were content with staying in the suite, drinking and fucking all day, which was cool, but I really liked Candi and wanted to offer her more than casual sex. I wanted to romance her so she'd never forget me.

"Have you ever been to Navy Pier?" I asked her as we walked out of the lobby of the hotel.

"No, I can't say that I have," she said, looping her arm within mine. I had the bellman hail a cab for us. I gave him a nice tip as I ducked into the backseat with Candi.

"Navy Pier," I told the cab driver. Candi snuggled up next to me and rested her head against my shoulder. With that move I felt as if I were being asked to take care of a delicate flower. In my heart I felt as if she were actually waiting for a man like me to come into her life. The cab driver dropped us off at Navy Pier, which was bustling with tourists. I took Candi by the hand and led her inside.

"O.M.G.! Look at this place. We don't have anything like this back in Houston." She glanced around at the multitude of shops.

"What? You guys don't have a tourist trap?" I asked jokingly.

"Of course we do, but this is just really, really nice," she said as I led her through the mall.

"Where are we going?" she asked.

"Relax. You'll like it," I said as I made my way to the giant Ferris wheel, which was a signature ride at Navy Pier. For a brief moment I felt strange. I was actually on a real date with someone. In all of the years I'd been with Tameecia I don't think we ever truly dated each other. We just sort of started fucking and then the kids came along and the next thing I knew, I married her.

I was taking Candi, a woman who was for the most part a complete stranger, to a place I'd never even consider bringing Tameecia. Mainly because I knew we'd end up arguing. Candi, on the other hand, was very easygoing. She wasn't loud, she wasn't annoying and she didn't treat me as if I were some sickly guy who needed to be rescued. Instead, I felt like a man with her. A romantic man who was proudly showing his woman a good time.

"Oh, my God! That thing is huge," Candi said, glancing up at the Ferris wheel.

"You're not afraid of heights, are you?" I asked, genuinely concerned.

"No," she answered to my relief.

"The view from up there is going to be wonderful," I said, even though I'd never been on the ride. It was a shame. I'd lived in the city all of my life and never once had I taken the time to enjoy it the way I did with Candi. I paid for two tickets and we sat down on a bench seat and strapped ourselves in. Before long we were hoisted high in the sky where we could see the entire city from all viewpoints—the lake, the skyline, and even the cruise ships docked at the pier.

"This is so beautiful," Candi said, glancing around in all directions. My heart swelled with pride. I knew she'd be returning home a better woman. As Candi turned back around to face me, I stopped her from focusing on the beauty of the city to look at me.

"Hey, you," I said.

"Hey, Daddy," she answered. I took her cheeks into my hands and leaned toward her for a kiss. When our lips met, I enjoyed the softness and fullness of her lips. The taste of her lips was like an aphrodisiac. I was instantly aroused. It was as if the very flavor of her went to my brain.

"Damn! What are you doing to me?" she asked, pulling away.

"I could ask you the same question," I said.

"You don't understand. I'm not used to this. I mean, I'm not used to being treated like this."

"Am I doing something wrong?" I asked.

"No, you're doing everything right. Where I come from…I mean, I'm just not used to romance in my life."

"Well, maybe that's a void I can fill for you," I said, helping myself to another kiss. Candi cradled the back of my head. The pace of her breathing shifted and before long, she surrendered her neck to me. I placed soft kisses on her chocolate skin while my hand softly stroked her thigh. She parted her legs for me and I knew that she would've enjoyed my fingers exploring the soft moist folds that led to the gate of her paradise. I pulled my lips away from her skin and whispered in her ear.

"I want to taste you so badly." My words hit her just right. She reacted by placing her hand on my dick, which was straining against the fabric of my slacks.

Speaking purposely in my ear, she said, "I'd love to put you in my mouth right now. I can't believe how hot I am. I'm so wet, I feel my juices trickling down my thigh."

"Take off those pants and I'll lick your juices off of your skin," I said unashamedly.

"Okay, folks, the ride is over," said the ride operator. I hadn't even realized that we'd come back down.

"Whew," Candi said as she rose to her feet and stepped off of the ride. After we got off the Ferris wheel, I took her over to where the boats were docked and paid for us to go on a one-hour cruise around the lake. I held her hand the entire time and even stole a few more passionate kisses. After the cruise I took her to Carmen's, a nice place I'd looked up that was on Rush Street. The food was fabulous and afterward we were both stuffed. Instead of taking a cab back to the hotel, I suggested that we walk. We held hands, talked and laughed the entire time. Once we got back to the suite we found Calvin and Katina naked on the sofa with wine bottles littering the floor.

"That's my girl." Candi laughed, but also had a look of disappointment in her eyes. I wasn't sure if she approved of her girlfriend or not. Either way, I didn't really care at that particular moment because she said, "I'm going to take you into the bedroom and ride you."

Not wanting to waste any more time, I followed Candi into the bedroom.

After Candi and I took a shower together, she dried my back for me. Then she squatted down and began drying my legs.

"You have a sexy dick," she said as she lifted it up and ran the tip of her tongue along the long vein on the underside. When I felt the warmth of the cave of her mouth pull me inside, I couldn't help but toss my head back and enjoy the moment.

"You like that, baby?" she asked, looking for my approval.

"Oh, hell yeah. Suck it harder," I said, glancing down at her. She was working me over and I felt my knees buckling.

"Ooo. Damn, girl," I said, threading my fingers through her hair. I loved her nakedness—her chocolate skin, neatly trimmed black pubic hair and succulent breasts that I couldn't wait to place in my mouth.

"Come on, baby. Let's take this party to the bed," I said. Candi walked in front of me, swiveling her hips as she moved along. Her ass was perfectly round, chocolate and begging to be spanked. I couldn't wait to get her into the doggie-style position and stroke her until her body trembled. Candi rested on her back and met my gaze.

"Come here," she said, smiling at me.

I positioned myself over her body. She looked up at me and I looked down at her, and that's when it happened. I could almost hear her eyes talking to me, pleading with me to not judge her. She reached down and took hold of my *pride*. She spread her legs a little wider and guided me inside her. Her back arched, she gasped, and her eyes widened. She completely surrendered to me. I was inside of her, feeling her juices explode all over me. I could feel her pussy squeezing my dick and holding onto it as if it never wanted to let go. She screamed as my strokes became deeper, longer and more powerful.

I listened to her body and paid attention to every detail of the moment and before I could stop myself, I said, "You're making me fall for you."

There was loud pounding at my bedroom door that snapped me back into my reality.

"Quinn, what the hell are you doing in there?" Tameecia was banging hard on the door. "Open the goddamn door!" she barked at me.

"Hang on a goddamn minute," I said, pissed off that she'd fucked up the mental movie that was playing in my mind.

"Why do you have the door locked anyway? You afraid to be in here by yourself or something?" she asked.

I opened the door and gave her the stank eye.

"Why are you looking at me like that?" she asked.

"Like what?" I asked with a tone of utter disgust. Ever since I'd connected with Candi, everything about Tameecia annoyed me. It was the little things that got in my craw. The sound of her voice, the way she chewed her food and even her dumb facial expressions were now the subject of my mental criticism and ridicule.

"Did you miss me while I was gone?" she asked.

"No," I answered truthfully. My answer stunned her.

"Yes, you did." She insisted that I was lying. I laughed and walked out of the room to go see how my boys were doing.

A few days later, I caught up with Calvin in the back office at one of his restaurants. I needed to talk to him. I needed his opinion. I couldn't stop thinking about Candi. I wanted to be near her. I needed to see her again.

"Man, don't tell me your ass is sprung," Calvin said.

"I don't know what it is about her, man. I can't stop thinking about her. We've been talking, Skyping and sending text messages, and it's still not enough for me. I need to see her again."

"Quinn, listen to what you're saying, dude. This thing you're doing is about sowing your wild oats. It's about being with multiple women and living the life of a playboy. It's not about finding someone to fall in love with. Especially since you're already married with kids! I kicked Katina a few extra bucks for showing me a good time."

"You paid her?" I was completely surprised.

"I gave her a few dollars to show my appreciation, that's all," he said.

"Cool. I understand. Listen, man. I'm not saying that I'm in love with her. I'm just saying that I need to see her again," I said with a more persuasive tone.

"And then what, Quinn?" he asked as he got up to close his office door.

"I want to spend some more time with her, that's all," I explained.

"You don't know her like that, man. You don't know a damn thing about her, except for the fact that she's a good fuck. Think about the group Bell Biv DeVoe. You never trust a big butt and a smile." He tried to talk some sense into me, but my head was as thick as a brick.

"You just don't understand. We made a connection. There is something about her that I've got to have." I was speaking with pure honesty.

"You can't have her, Quinn. You're married with two children. If Tameecia ever finds out, she's not only going to whip your ass, but place your butt in the poor house as well."

"I don't give a fuck about Tameecia!"

"Hold on, man. I'm not the one." Calvin didn't like the tone of my voice.

"I'm sorry. I didn't mean to yell at you. I just need to see her again to find out if what I felt was real."

"So what are you going to do? She's in Houston and you're in Chicago," Calvin reminded me.

"I'm going to fly to Houston to see her," I said. I'd already arrived at that decision during my drive over to see him.

"When?" he asked, surprised.

"Tomorrow. I'm going to call in sick, go to the airport, buy a plane ticket and surprise her." Calvin's mouth opened as wide as the sky when I told him of my plan.

"What are you going to tell Tameecia?" he asked.

"I'm going to tell her I'm with you. You're my alibi," I said with a smile. Calvin took a deep breath and then exhaled.

"Why don't you just come with me? You can hook up with Katina again. I know you'd love to tap that ass again," I said, feeling as if I'd said enough to convince him.

"Not this time," he said. "I've got too much going on. Do you know where you're going to stay in Houston?"

"With Candi, at her place," I said.

"How in the fuck are you just going to fly there and not know where the hell you're going?"

"I'll just call her and she'll give me the address." .

"No. If you really want to surprise the shit out of her, you need to be able to walk up to her front door."

"Well, I'll get her address. I'll tell her that I want to send her some flowers or something."

"Or I could help you do something really crazy."

"What?" I wanted to know what he had in mind.

"I needed an address when I made the airline reservation for Katina. Katina tried to get me to send her cash, but I wasn't about to do that. She could've taken my money and never come. So I charged their plane tickets to my secret credit card. I believe she and Candi live together because she told me to use the same address for her as well."

"So you have her address?" I asked excitedly.

"Yeah, I have it," he said as he began typing information into his computer. A few seconds later he wrote the address down on a piece of paper.

I read the address aloud. "Seven Fifty Jackson Hill Street, Houston, Texas."

"That's where they live," he said.

"Thanks, man." I respectfully gave him a fist bump.

"Quinn, be careful when you go. Always expect the unexpected. Remember, these are women we met online. Everything that glitters isn't gold," he warned.

"Dude, I got this. There is so much more to Candi. I feel it. I want to know everything about her. I want to get to know her and I want her to know me," I said conclusively.

"Do you mean Dr. Cole? Or Quinn? Because Quinn is not who she met. She met Dr. Cole. Don't forget that," he reminded me.

Popping my fingers, I exhaled and was about to say something, but no words would come to me. My mind went blank. I thought I'd have a logical answer, but I didn't. All I had was a burning desire to see her at all costs.

# CHAPTER 23

## Codi

I may have been married, but I had a bona-fide *sidepiece* and I couldn't be happier. Now, the shit Larry did, didn't seem to bother me as much anymore. When I saw his dirty clothes piled in the middle of our bedroom floor I simply stepped over them.

If he came home and I hadn't cooked anything, I'd drop a few hotdogs in boiling water and call it a day. When he and his lame friends came over, I went to the store for a couple of hours, which meant I was really a few blocks away parked and Skyping with Dr. Cole, or I ignored them while secretly Skyping and texting with my sidepiece.

Because of Julius I was able to face my husband with a smile on my face every day no matter what he threw my way.

"Aeey, you look like you getting a lil thick around the middle," Larry said to me this morning.

*Who says shit like that to their wife?* I thought to myself.

Normally, a comment like that would have ruined my day. I would have been pissed at him and would've started questioning whether I really was slacking off, but the minute the words tumbled from his mouth, I looked at him, and said, "Really?"

His eyebrow shot up.

"Yeah really! You need to watch that shit. I don't want no fat broad," he defended.

Julius had never complained about a single inch of my body. Actually, it was like he couldn't get enough.

Before Larry could finish complaining I walked out of the room and thought about the next time I'd get to see Julius. That was all I thought about. All I wanted was Julius.

At home, we were nearly caught up on most of the bills. I still had some other things I needed to take care of, but for the most part, the money I made with Katina was helping.

On Facebook, I was doing just enough to keep the guys tuning in to our site, but mostly I was only concerned about Julius. The daydreaming had kicked into high gear, too. I sat around writing my first name with Dr. Cole's last name just to see how it would look in print. I felt like a schoolgirl with her first major crush.

"You doing another shift or you rushing to Skype with your boyfriend?" Katina had been acting a little salty with me lately and I wasn't sure why.

Maybe it was because Dr. Cole and I were always on the phone, texting, Skyping, and loving all over each other, but she rarely spoke about Calvin.

I didn't understand why she couldn't be happy for me. I had finally found the one! Well, the *other* one.

"I'm gonna work. Taylor is at Linda's today because he was sick, so I'm not rushing off to pick him up," I said.

Katina fixed her face to smile. Making money was the only true way to make her happy.

We did two additional sessions and afterward I was tired. Instead of going straight home, I decided to hang out and Skype with Julius.

"Hmmm," I was confused. When I couldn't get him on Skype I tried texting him. When that didn't work I called.

"What's the matter? Can't find lover boy?" Katina asked.

I didn't know whether to answer or ignore her. This was most unusual. Julius was always available when I reached out. Because I was married, I didn't reach out late at night or too early in the morning, but he never asked any questions, which was another thing I loved about him.

"You wanna go to happy hour?" Katina asked.

"I don't know," I said.

"Why not? I need a drink," Katina whined. "I still have a couple of hours, but we should go have a drink and unwind."

My mind was racing with thoughts of where Julius could be and what he was doing. The more I thought about it, I hadn't heard from him since earlier. This was strange.

"Let me do this last session. After that we can go to Saltgrass Steakhouse for a drink. If we're lucky we'll find some old retirees willing to blow their Social Security checks," Katina said.

She was too much. I laughed, but decided that if I waited through her session, it would give me a chance to wait around for Julius to call me back.

While Katina did her thing I called and left a message on Larry's voicemail.

"Hey, it's me. Since the baby is at your mom's, I'm gonna go to happy hour with Katina. You know she's still sad over her dad, so I'll see you at home later."

After I ended my message I turned off my cell phone. When I didn't want to be bothered by Larry I'd turn off my cell and deal with the consequences later.

When the bass started thumping from Katina's dance song I started thinking of all the possible reasons Julius wasn't responding.

The ringing doorbell broke my train of thought and I jumped up to catch the door before it distracted Katina.

When I pulled the door open my knees buckled a bit. I stood speechless.

"You gonna just stand there or you gonna give your man some love?"

"Julius!" I squealed. I jumped into his arms and plastered his face and neck with kisses. I couldn't believe he was here in Houston!

Shit! He. Was. Here. In. Houston!

"Surprise, baby," he said.

I turned and looked over my shoulder.

"Sssshh!" I placed a finger over my pursed lips. Katina was working. I quietly ushered Julius into the back bedroom.

"Baby, I'll be back in a sec, okay? Stay here because Katina is still working."

I closed the bedroom door and pressed my back against it in hopes of catching my breath. What the hell was I going to do? Julius had hopped on an airplane and come to surprise me.

"Oh shit! Oh shit!" I repeated to myself silently.

After finding a piece of paper and a pen, I wrote a quick note for Katina.

*Help! Julius popped up to surprise me. He's got to stay here! I'm gonna call Larry later, but for now I just wanted to let you know what was going on. I'm about to make love to my man, so if your bedroom's rocking, please don't come knocking!*

I added a smiley face at the bottom of the note, then I stepped to the edge of the room Katina used for taping and stuck the letter on a wall where I knew she'd see it. She looked at me as she spread her legs in front of the camera.

I eased back down the hall and entered the bedroom. I was so happy to see Julius that I wanted to cry tears of joy. He was stretched out on the bed.

"You surprised?" he asked.

"Yes, Daddy. You got me. Now what you gonna do with me?" I asked teasingly.

I gave him a wicked smile, then I started to do a slow and sexy striptease. The music from Katina's session was playing softly, but we could still hear it. It worked perfectly to help set the mood for me while I was entertaining him.

Julius was on his back. He laced his fingers behind his head and watched my every move. When I was naked I dropped down on all fours and started to crawl over to him.

"You are so damn sexy! I can't stop thinking about your fine ass!" he said.

At the bed, I helped him undress until he wore nothing but his boxers and his socks.

I stuck my hand into the opening of his boxers and took out his dick that had sprung to life. I started planting light kisses on its head. I looked up to see him squeal in sheer delight.

"Talk about a mouth," *kiss*, "full," *kiss*, *kiss*, "of joy," *kiss*, *kiss*. "Emmm hmm," I hummed as I tried to deep throat him.

Julius looked like he was struggling to hang on. I had him up against the ropes and he was going down fast.

I got up and looked at him.

"Stand," I commanded.

Julius stumbled up from the bed.

"Damn, Candi," he said breathlessly.

I took him again, no hands, and suckled him like he was my favorite flavor. He started wobbling back toward a small couch near the window, but the more he inched backward, the more I hobbled on my knees.

For every two steps he took, I followed, with my lips still holding on to his stiff dick. I had a grip on him like a powerful suction cup. When he finally made it to the couch he collapsed back onto his ass and I pounced on him. I sucked and sucked, then slopped and sucked some more. I was trying my best to suck every ounce of juice from his dick.

"Aaah, girl, you good. Real good," he cried out.

I felt his body jerk.

I wanted to be more than good. I wanted to put a hex on him. He grabbed the back of my head, holding me in place while I sucked harder. Just when his warm fluids began to erupt, I pulled back and watched with pleasure as he exploded.

"Goddamn! Your head game is serious," Julius declared.

I pulled him up by his arms and guided him back over to the bed. We lay in each other's arms, but about thirty minutes later he was kissing on my breasts and my stomach. Julius situated himself between my thighs.

He raised my legs and cradled them in the crook of his elbows. Without warning, he rammed into me, then held himself very still.

Julius stared into my eyes like he was searching my soul. At that very moment I had never ever felt closer to *any* man.

"I been waiting so long for you," he said as he reached down and sucked a spot on my neck.

I wiggled, trying to stop him from leaving a mark. "Hold on, Daddy. I ain't going nowhere. This is yours!"

"It's mine?" Julius asked in a sexy husky voice.

"It's yours, Daddy!"

He moved his hips with a rhythm that was driving me crazy.

"Tell me it's mine."

"It's yours, Daddy! It's yours!"

"I want you to ride."

I wanted to do what he wanted, but it felt so good I didn't want him to stop. He didn't want to stop either because despite all the talking he did, he kept moving his hips.

"Okay, Daddy. I'm gonna ride."

We switched positions. On top of him, I swung one leg over, then looked down. I felt full. I wiggled my hips and tried to suck more of him inside me.

"C'mon, girl, that's it. You almost there," he cheered.

I wiggled some more, another two inches. I released a breath, prepped myself and wiggled my hips a bit more.

A few minutes after getting into a good slow rhythm, I had to fight *that* feeling. But my body wouldn't listen. I started to feel the tingling sensation in the tips of my toes.

"Oh shit!" I cried.

"I'm about to come, baby! I'm not ready yet!" I yelled.

"Girl, your body's saying something else. Give in to it. We got all night. Do your thang. Do your thang with this sweet tight pussy of yours," he said, egging me on.

After I came, Julius turned me over and rode me doggie-style. He howled when he came and I grinned hard. We were so compatible it was crazy. In the afterglow of incredible sex we lay in each other's arms and soon he was snoring.

When I felt like he was in a good sleep, I hopped up from the bed and ran outside. Katina was on Facebook when I tapped her on the shoulder.

She jumped. "Girl! What the fuc…"

"OHMYGOD, Katina! He just popped up. I need your help! Seriously. You know I can't stay here all night. I don't know what to do."

Katina looked at me like I had three eyeballs. "What are you talking about?"

"I figure I can stay 'til about midnight or one, but after that I need to put his ass to sleep so Larry won't be trippin'. I'll be back in the morning, but you know damn well I can't stay here tonight."

I couldn't believe Katina was acting like she didn't understand, but soon she got up and went to get her purse. When she came back she gave me the pills. I looked at them, then looked at her.

"Well, you need him asleep, right?"

"Yeah, but," I stammered.

"But my ass!"

I accepted the pills like a fiend buying crack. By the time I got back in bed, Julius was stirring. He reached for me, threw his arm around my midsection and pulled me close. I enjoyed spooning with him. I loved being with him. I only wanted everything to go right with us.

"Baby, you hungry?" I asked.

"Mmmm. I could eat something," he muttered.

I giggled. "I mean food, silly."

"Oh, food, yeah, food. Okay, baby. I could eat something."

"Let's go grab a bite, then come back here and enjoy some drinks. Besides, I wanna do you all night long, so you're gonna need your energy!"

"Shit, I like the way that sounds."

When he got up to go to the bathroom, I prayed over the pills and hoped Katina's plan would work. I didn't know what else to do, but there was no way I could lose Dr. Julius Apollo Cole.

# CHAPTER 24

## Quinn

We went to the Breakfast Klub. I ordered the grilled sirloin and Candi ordered the Creole mustard salmon. I'd stepped away to go to the bathroom once the waiter had taken our order. When I returned there was a glass of wine on the table for me.

"I hope you like wine, Daddy," Candi said.

"As long as you ordered it, I like it," I answered, feeling really great about her. I started visualizing myself with her on a more permanent basis. Sure, I could've continued chasing skirts and spending money, but Candi was something special. In the short amount of time I'd known her, I'd connected with her in a way that I'd never thought possible. Maybe it was because she was a new lover to me, but then again, maybe not.

I smiled at her, then winked as I picked up my glass of wine and took a healthy sip of it. After swallowing the wine, I looked at the glass oddly.

"What's wrong, Daddy? Everything okay?" Candi asked.

"Yeah, baby. The wine just tasted a little funny."

She leaned toward me. "It's probably because you still have the taste of my sweet pussy on your lips."

I smiled, then laughed. After drinking the entire glass of wine I felt a massive headache forming and my vision started getting blurry.

"Oh no," I said, feeling as if something was horribly wrong. My right arm and cheek went numb.

"What's wrong, baby?" I felt Candi touch my left hand.

"We should go back to your place. We could bring the food we ordered back with us. I suddenly don't feel so good," I said, trying to figure out why my head was hurting so badly.

"You're probably just exhausted from the flight and all the lovemaking we've been doing," Candi said.

"Maybe you're right. Maybe I just need some rest," I agreed.

"Why don't you go get in the car? I'll take care of things here," she suggested.

"Okay," I agreed and made my way out to the car. I could barely keep my eyes open. My vision had worsened and I felt as if I couldn't even stand up. Candi would have to drive the rental car, so I got in on the passenger's side. As soon as I sat down, I felt as if the world was spinning. I looked through the windshield and saw Candi coming out of the restaurant. From what I could gather, she was fussing at a couple of women, one of whom was wearing orange. I rolled down the window to try and listen to what was happening.

"Taylor is feeling better. Been picked up earlier. Darlisa and I had dinner. Where have you been?" I only heard slices of what the woman in orange was saying.

"Linda, I really don't have time for this right now." Candi's voice was panicky.

"Why are you getting in that car? And who is that? He looks sick," the woman in orange asked. I willed myself to stay awake a little longer.

"It's Katina's brother. He's upset about the death of his father." I wasn't sure if I'd heard Candi right because her voice sounded very lethargic, as if she were trying to speak and yawn at the same time.

"I'm telling!" The woman in orange seemed angry. I thought there was about to be a fight. I was about to get out of the car to see what was going on, but I passed out.

When I awoke I felt sicker than a junkie trying to shake the effects of some bad dope. My head was pounding and my arm was still numb. I tried to sit up, but felt too weak. My stomach was sour and cramped up at the same time. I hadn't felt this bad since being sick in my twenties. My body ached all over and I was having difficulty breathing.

"Candi?" I didn't get a response. I tried to clear my mind. I tried to remain calm, but I feared that I was having a relapse.

"Candi?" I still got no answer. I glanced around the room, taking in the décor. The walls were a light shade of blue with a cathedral-styled ceiling. The drapes matched the wall color and there was a chaise lounge on the opposite wall.

"What's going on?" I glanced over in the direction of the voice and saw Katina.

"I. I. I." I couldn't fucking form words. What the hell!

"Are you okay?" A look of horror formed on Katina's face.

"I'm not sure," I answered as best as I could.

"Hang on. Let me call Codi," she said.

"Codi?" I asked because I didn't know who the fuck Codi was. Katina held up her hand to silence me. She walked to the opposite corner of the room and began whispering.

"How many pills did you give him?" I heard her whisper.

"Are you sure? Because Dr. Cole is looking real fucked up right now." Katina turned and looked at me. She placed a fake smile on her face and then turned her back on me once again and whispered. I don't know if she thought I couldn't hear, but I could.

My problem was I was having difficulty speaking. Plus, for some reason, in that short amount of time, I began sweating.

"He's looking pale, girl! I'm telling you, Dr. Cole is looking really creepy. You need to get over here and deal with this!" I could hear the urgency in Katina's voice.

"I'm fine," is what I believe I mustered up the strength to say, but when Katina turned and looked at me again, my words must've sounded like gibberish to her.

"Oh, my God, Codi. He can't form words!" Her whispering became louder.

"I don't know. His words sound like nonsense." Katina paused and I could hear Candi's voice saying something to her.

"What do you mean, you can't get away?" She paused again and listened.

"What the fuck was Linda doing at the restaurant last night?" She paused again as Candi spoke. I felt as if someone were hitting my head with a sledgehammer. I tried to speak again, but my words now sounded like rubbish to me. Suddenly, everything felt surreal. It was as if I was watching myself in a movie and there was nothing I could do.

"What do you mean call an ambulance? And tell them what? That you…" She turned and glanced at me again, but held on to her words. "I'm not going down for this," she continued. I heard Candi shouting into the phone at Katina.

"I didn't sign up for this shit! You need to talk to him," Katina said. She turned and marched over to me.

"Here, it's Candi," she said and extended the phone to me. I raised my right hand to take the phone, but it was still numb. As best as I could, I held it to my ear.

"Hey, Daddy, what's wrong?" Candi tried to sound upbeat.

"Something is wrong. I don't know what's happened to me."

"Oh, my God. You sound like you're having a stroke. I don't understand a word you're saying. Give the phone back to Katina!" I looked into Katina's eyes and handed her the phone.

"Stroke! Oh, hell no. I don't care what you have to do. You need to get your ass over here, pronto!"

When Katina hurried out of the room, I heard her say, "Fuck, Larry! You've got bigger problems." At that moment my cell phone rang. With my left hand I reached for the nightstand where it was sitting. It was Tameecia. I answered.

"Why the fuck haven't you called me? You didn't leave me any information about where you'd be staying in Houston for your important sales conference, which I know is a total damn lie! Yeah, that's right. I know you've lied to me, Quinn. I went by your job today and Big Sam said that he didn't send your ass to a sales conference in fucking Houston! So where are you at, Quinn? Huh? Tell me! That's okay. You don't have to tell me where you are. I've got your iPad. The boys helped me figure out your password and I'm about to Skype this Candi bitch you been talking to."

"Call Calvin. He knows where I am. I need to go to the hospital."

"What the hell did you just say? Why do you sound like that? Why do you sound like a crack head? What the fuck is going on with you?"

I hung up the phone. Then I pulled up the text screen and typed a message to Calvin.

*Had relapse. Arm numb. Lost speech. In big trouble. Need to get to hospital. Girls will not help. Send ambulance to Katina's address b4 it's too late.*

# CHAPTER 25

# Codi

I arrived at Katina's house just as the ambulance was pulling off. Katina's simple behind was out on the lawn bawling like a baby while a police officer tried to calm her down.

"What the hell is going on?"

"What the hell is going on!" my son repeated from the backseat.

I sighed real hard and pulled over next to the curb. Everything in me screamed, "Keep driving! Keep driving!" but I couldn't.

Once I parked, I got out and removed Taylor from his child seat. As I approached, I tried my best to look like a concerned friend instead of a guilty party.

"Ma'am, we need you to calm down. We need to know what happened here," I heard the officer say to Katina.

"I didn't do it! I didn't do it," that dummy kept sobbing.

I wanted to bitch-slap her. Was she trying to get us sent to jail or what?

"Officer?" I said softly.

The moment Katina's eyes focused in on me, she started screaming. "I told you to get over here! I told you something went wrong! I told you!"

The officer turned his attention to me. His red, puffy cheeks and beady blue eyes looked like he wasn't in the mood to play. "Do you know this woman?"

"Um, yes, sir. I do. That's my best friend, Katina." I swallowed hard. I also glanced around at the neighbors who were still out-side. Some were pointing and gawking, but I told myself to focus on the task at hand—staying out of jail!

"We were trying to question her about the gentleman who was just rushed to the hospital," he said, "but it doesn't seem as if she knows much about him, even though he was staying at her house."

"I believe I can help. The gentleman, Dr. Cole, suffered an allergic reaction to some medication," I said with a straight face.

The officer looked at Katina, then back at me. I saw the frown on his face, but I was about to ride this lie until the wheels fell off.

"A what?" he asked.

"Yes. Dr. Cole suffered an allergic reaction. He's a guest of mine and the reason Katina here is so frazzled is because she didn't know he was coming to visit."

"How could she not know a man who is staying in her house?"

I chuckled. "See, what had happened was, Katina was at work when Dr. Cole got here. I didn't tell her about him coming because I knew she'd try to get more rent money out of me and well, I figure he's only here for two nights, so I was planning..."

"Whoa! Hold up a sec. So you live here?" The officer looked really confused now. "Hold on a sec. You come over here," he said to Katina.

She stumbled next to me and I prayed she wouldn't say any-thing else stupid.

"This is your roommate?" he asked.

"Um, yeah, when she pays her share of the rent," Katina managed.

"So you snuck a man in the apartment without her knowing and what happened?"

"I had to go get some milk for the baby." I moved my hip just so, in case he hadn't noticed Taylor bouncing on it. "And, well, I left some medicine on the nightstand and I believe Dr. Cole accidently drank it."

"So the medicine is yours?" he asked.

Just then he held up a finger to quiet me. He dipped his head over to the radio on his shoulder and listened.

When I heard the words One-Eight-Seven and a street that was two blocks over, I started to breathe a sigh of relief.

"Sir," I began.

He looked at Katina and me, then said, "Uh, I gotta go. We'll send someone back later if we need any more information."

Suddenly, he raced back to his cruiser, talking into his radio.

I turned to Katina and looked at her pathetic behind.

"You almost got us arrested! Again!" I took off toward her front door.

"I told you he got sick," she screamed at my back. "You gave him too much! What were you trying to do, kill the man?"

Just as we made it to the door, a horn started blaring from the street. I looked up to see Linda's orange Buick and Larry behind the wheel. I rolled my eyes.

"Oh God! Not more drama!" I screamed.

Katina looked at me. "What the hell?"

"This is what I was trying to tell you over the phone. Linda saw me with Dr. Cole. That's why I couldn't get over here. This fool is trippin'!"

"So what you gonna…"

"Where that fool at?" Larry yelled. "Where he at?"

"Larry, I don't know what you talking about. Don't be coming over here clowning," I warned.

Taylor started crying. That bitch, Linda, had the nerve to snatch my baby.

"I just knew something wasn't right," she said, shaking her head and making her orange earrings dance. I ignored her.

"My mama say she saw your jezebel ass!" Larry screamed. "She saw you with some other man!"

"Larry, you are trippin'," I said.

Katina looked like she was at a tennis match. Her head bounced back and forth between Larry and me.

"I told you. Katina's dad just died. That was her brother in the car with me! I don't know why you gon' let your mama get all up in our business," I said.

He looked a little confused.

"He trippin' off Julius?" Katina asked. She even looked offended.

"You got a brother?" Larry asked her cautiously.

"Yeah, and like she said, when my dad died, he had to come here because my dad left some stuff for him."

"I hear what they're saying, but son, it didn't look right to me. The man looked drunk and it looked to me like they were on a date!" Linda said. "Darlisa even said so herself. None of it looked right!" she insisted.

"Linda!" I screamed at her.

"You bet' not be doing no runnin' around on me," Larry warned. "I don't play that shit!"

"Larry, go on home. I'll be there soon."

He looked at Katina real hard. I was scared he was about to swing on her or something.

"Her brother, huh?" he asked.

"Larry, when would I have time for another man? Think about it. Between you and Taylor and me looking for work, when would I have time for another man?" By now my hands were on my hips. "You know how your mama be trippin'. Why would you let her get all up in your head? Am I not next to you every night? Wouldn't you know if I was with another man?"

I could tell I was wearing him down. Now his chest wasn't all puffy like it was when he ran up on us.

"Baby, I'd keep my eye on this one here. Brother, my ass!" Linda mumbled.

Larry finally turned to leave. Before he walked away, he looked over my shoulder, and said, "I ain't for none of this kind of bullshit, Codi!"

"I know, baby, I know. Let me just talk to Katina for a little while and I'll be home."

"And I'ma want some ass, too," he tossed in.

"Okay, Larry. Just go home," I said. "Here, lemme give you the baby's car seat."

Larry and I walked behind Linda, who was now playing with the baby.

"When you get home I'ma tear that ass up. I ain't playin'. You think I'm dumb or something, but I don't want Katina's brother gettin' no damn ideas! You hear me?"

"Larry, Katina's brother is gay!" I said.

"Whhhhaaaat?" He turned around and glanced in Katina's direction like that might explain something. "Ain't that some shit!" he exclaimed.

"Listen, so there. You ain't gotta worry about him wanting me. Your mama was way off base when she told you whatever she told you," I said.

I rushed, grabbed the car seat, and all but shoved it into Larry's arms.

"I don't know if I like the idea of you hangin' around no gays," Larry said, like he had an afterthought.

I just wanted him and his nosy-ass mama gone.

I watched as they pulled off, then when I was sure they were gone, I ran inside. Katina was waiting. "What are you gonna do? How you gonna fix this shit?"

"The first thing I need is for you to calm the hell down!" I screamed.

"Look, I ain't about to go to jail over those pills. I didn't tell you to try and kill his ass. I told you to give him one!" she yelled.

"You didn't say give him one. You gave me the pills. How was I supposed to know he only needed one?"

"How many did you give him?"

"Two," I said.

Katina was pacing. She looked nervous and scared.

"Listen. All we gotta do is get over to Memorial Hermann and see about him. When he sees me I'll explain what happened."

Katina stopped walking and looked at me like I had just insulted her dead daddy.

"You think I'm about to go to the damn hospital? Girl, you don' lost your mind for real! His buddy keeps calling, I ain't answering his calls, and I damn sure ain't about to go up to no doggone hospital. To say what? To do what? Thank God someone got shot and that cop had to hightail it up outta here. We'd be on our way downtown right now," she admonished.

"Why you putting all these extras on it, Katina? All we have to do is play this cool. If we don't show up at the hospital, that's when someone is gonna get suspicious." I tried to reason with her, but she wasn't hearing it.

Katina plopped down on the sofa, then looked at me.

She pointed as she spoke. "You can take your ass down there, talking about mixing up medicine if you want to, but you on your own! Ain't no way in hell I'm getting all up in that one."

"So you just gonna leave me hanging?" I asked.

"You damn straight, I am! And you know what else? I'm gonna need you to call Calvin back and tell his ass to lose my number!"

Now I knew for sure Katina must've fallen and bumped her head. There was no way in the world this could be the same woman I knew.

"So you don't want Calvin anymore? You giving up his money, too?"

That gave her pause.

"I just can't deal with this. What am I supposed to say to him? I mean seriously. His boy comes down here, but he didn't even bother to come and try to surprise me, so what he calling me for?"

Oh! Now I realized the problem. Katina was hating because Calvin wasn't all over her the way Julius was with me. I couldn't believe this shit. So as far as she was concerned, I was on my own because Calvin hadn't been checking on her.

"So you're gonna let me go up there by myself?" I wanted to be clear.

"What am I gonna do up there? I don't know him!" she yelled.

"Katina, I don't really know him either, but I'm gonna at least go up there and see about him. We can't just leave him in the hospital by himself!"


Reluctantly, Katina came to Memorial Hermann hospital with me and the entire ride there I had to hear about all that could've gone wrong.

I rolled my eyes as she bitched and whined, but I was glad to have her with me because I didn't want to deal with this mess alone.

When I pulled up in the parking lot I turned to her, and said, "Give me your cell."

No questions asked, Katina dug into her purse and pulled it out.

"Look how many times this fool has called. After I flew up there and rocked his world he ain't said as much as "Hi cat, dog," but the minute his boy is here, he calling every hour on the hour!" She sucked her teeth and rolled her eyes. "Take it!"

After inspecting her missed calls, which were all from Calvin, I swallowed the lump in my throat and called him back.

The phone barely rang before he answered, sounding anxious.

"Um, Calvin? Hi, this is Candi," I said.

"Where's my cousin?"

"Your cousin?"

"Yeah, where the hell is Quinn? What did you guys do to him? I swear, if he's hurt in any way whatsoever, I will not only have you two hos tossed in jail, I'll sue you both for every red dime you have!"

"Dude, calm down!" I yelled back.

"Why are y'all yelling at each other?" Katina had the nerve to ask.

"Who you calling a ho?" I screamed.

"Oh, no he didn't! Who he calling a ho!" Katina yelled like a really bad recording. "What he saying? Put him on speaker," she said, clawing for her phone back.

"Listen, I don't have time for no games. I'm about to call the police again and tell them some foul shit so that they raid your apartment!" Calvin threatened.

"Let's all calm down. The name-calling, screaming and yelling ain't gonna do anybody any good," I said.

"How the hell y'all not gonna take Quinn to the hospital when you knew something was wrong?" Calvin asked.

"Who the hell is Quinn?" Katina asked, looking at me confused.

"Yeah, he did say Quinn. Who is Quinn?"

"Ah, I mean Julius," Calvin corrected himself.

"He wasn't sick," I quickly added.

"That's not what the text message he sent me said. Who do you think sent the ambulance and the cops to Katina's house?"

Katina and I were stunned.

"We would've taken him to the hospital. I didn't know he was sick," I screamed.

"I don't even think yo' ass was even there, so you can save that shit!" Calvin said. "Let there be something wrong with my cousin and the two of you will regret the day you ever met me!"

Before either of us could say something else, he ended the call.

"See, this shit is all messed up," Katina said. "We should leave. If you go in there, it's gonna open up a can of worms. Think about it. You already smoothed things over with Larry and his mama. Why go in there?"

I felt what she was saying, but something in me said I couldn't turn my back on Julius like that. When would I ever have a chance at another doctor ever again?

"You stay here. If I don't text you in twenty minutes or come back out, then you'll know something is wrong. But for now I need to go see about him. I just have to."

As I got out of the car and walked toward the hospital's entrance, my phone vibrated. I looked down to see a text message from Katina.

*Don't do it girl, come back! Let's run!*

I ignored her text and walked inside when the automatic double doors opened.

# CHAPTER 26

## Quinn

"What is your name?" I heard someone ask me. I opened my eyes and I felt as if I were looking through a prism. Everything looked like an illusion. Then I began seeing sparks followed by zigzag lines. I had a monstrous headache that made me want to put a gun to my head and squeeze the trigger just to stop it. I blinked rapidly, trying to bring my vision into focus.

"What is your name?" I was asked again.

"Quinn Hamilton," I said, but I still couldn't articulate my words.

"Can you hear me clearly? If so, nod your head once," the voice said. I nodded my head once as instructed.

"Okay. I'm going to touch your body and if I touch you some-place that's in pain, I want you to nod your head again, okay?" The voice waited for me to acknowledge that I understood. I felt someone touch my head and I nodded.

"Your head hurts?" the voice asked. I nodded again.

"Did you fall or hit your head?" the voice asked. I moved my head from left to right, answering no.

"Do you have a headache?" the voice asked. I nodded yes.

"Is it a small headache?" the voice asked. Using the motion of my head, I answered no.

"You have a big headache?" the voice asked. I nodded yes. I now realized from the sounds around me that I was in the hospital, probably the emergency room, and the doctor there was trying to figure out what was wrong with me.

"Are you on any medication for migraines?" the doctor asked. I answered no.

"Have you taken any pills or drugs?" he asked. I answered no once again.

"How about your vision? Can you see?" he asked. I answered no.

"I'm going to have a neurologist come and look at you. Okay, just relax," he said. A few minutes later I heard another voice come and ask me a question.

"Have you ever had a severe migraine headache like this before?" the voice asked. I answered no.

"Open your eyes for me," the voice said. I was almost afraid to because I didn't feel like seeing sparks and zigzag lines again. However, this time when I opened them up, I could see the silhouette of the doctor hovering above me. My vision seemed to be getting better.

"Everything is blurry," I said.

"Blurry vision. Is that what you said?" asked the doctor.

I nodded my head and said, "Yes."

"Okay, your speech is starting to come back. Did you experience any numbness of your face or extremities?"

"Yes. My right arm went numb," I answered.

"How does your right arm feel now? Can you feel me touching it?"

Strangely enough, I did feel his touch and my numbness had disappeared. "Yes, I can feel you touching me."

"How long has it been since his arrival?" I heard the second doctor ask the emergency room doctor.

"It's been about fifty minutes," the emergency room doctor said.

"Okay. I believe I know what has happened to you. The neurological symptoms you were experiencing earlier are reversing themselves. I'm going to check back with you in about fifteen minutes to see how you're progressing. Just relax, okay?"

"Okay," I said. This time I heard my voice and it was sounding more normal. I closed my eyes and rested.

I was awakened by someone shaking my shoulder.

"It's me again." I recognized the voice of the second doctor. When I opened my eyes I could see him clearly.

"Can you see now?" he asked.

"Yes," I answered with a normal voice. My head was still pounding, but not as badly as it was before.

"You sound better, too," he said.

"What the hell happened to me?" I asked. I didn't know what to think.

"I believe what you were suffering from was something called a complex migraine headache. It's a severe headache that can cause vision problems, numbness, and in some cases like yours, loss of speech. This type of headache closely resembles a stroke."

"A stroke!" I didn't want to believe what I was being told. I glanced down at the doctor's name badge. It specified that he was with the Neurology Department.

"You did not have a stroke. You only had a very bad headache."

"Dr. Banks, how did I get it? I've never felt anything like that in my life. Shit, my head is still hurting."

"I'm going to give you something for that. A variety of things can trigger it. Changes in your diet, changes in the weather, stress, and pretty much anything else. Sometimes people just wake up with them."

"Damn! Do I need to get a CAT scan or something to make sure everything is okay?" I asked, feeling as if I were a prisoner in my own body.

"You'll be fine for now. Talk to your regular physician regarding a follow-up CAT scan. I'm going to write you a prescription and release you," said Dr. Banks. I watched as he went over to the nurses' station. He said something to one of the nurses and then pointed back at me. I sat upright and opened and closed my hands to make sure that everything was back to normal.

An hour later I walked down a long corridor toward the waiting room. I was told that there was an exit there. I couldn't wait to step outside, so I could get a cell phone signal and call Candi back to ask her some questions. Just as I was about to step outside, I heard Candi talking very loudly to a hospital employee who was trying to help her.

"His name is Dr. Julius Apollo Cole and he was brought in here over an hour ago. How long does it take for his name to show up in your damn system?"

"Miss, if he hasn't been, admitted then his name will not show up. I've left word for the Head E.R. nurse to call me as soon as she can. When she does I'll ask her about his status along with everyone else you see in here who is waiting to hear something. Until then, please take a seat."

"I don't have the time to be sitting around here all damn day, waiting to hear something. I need to know if he's alive!" Candi's voice was edgy and hostile.

"Hey, babe. I'm over here," I called out to her. Candi spun around and rushed over to me. Before I could even say hello, she wrapped her arms around me and held on to me tightly.

"I'm so glad you're okay." She continued to smother me with her love.

"I'm okay," I tried to assure her.

I could hear her sniffling. "I thought I'd lost you."

"You haven't," I said as I pulled her away from me. I looked into her eyes and I could see both tears of terror and relief. "Where did you go?"

"Shhh. Let's just get you back to Katina's place."

"You mean Katina's and your place," I corrected her.

"Yes," she hesitated. "Come on. Katina's outside waiting for us." I followed Candi out to the car. When Katina saw me, she glared at me as if she were looking at a ghost.

"I told you it wasn't that bad," Candi snarled at Katina as we got into the backseat of her sedan.

"What the fuck!" Katina blurted out. "How in the hell are you even walking?"

"Katina, just take us to the damn house. Time. If you know what I mean!" Candi gave Katina a very hard glare. She also seemed unusually irritated with her girlfriend.

"Shit, can he talk now?" Katina asked.

"I'm fine," I answered her.

"See, he's fine. Just get us back home." Candi spoke through clenched teeth.

"I have a question to ask you," I said as Katina pulled off.

"Oh shit," I heard Katina whisper.

"Baby, now is not the time for a thousand and one questions." Candi snuggled up close to me. She began massaging my neck.

"Damn, baby. You're very tight. All that lovemaking we did didn't relax you?" Candi asked as I surrendered to her touch.

"I'm still trying to figure out what the hell happened. I was feeling fine up until dinner. There must've been something in the wine. I swear I feel as if I've been slipped a mickey."

Katina suddenly started coughing violently. Candi glared at Katina as if she'd murder her if she continued her odd behavior. Katina suddenly stopped coughing.

"That's ridiculous. You were extremely tired and that was your body's way of letting you know to take it easy."

Candi was insisting that my episode was nothing more than an anomaly. She began stroking my *pride* through my slacks, and it immediately got hard. She then leaned closer and spoke purposely in my ear.

"See, Daddy. You're fine. You're hard and ready for some more Candi, aren't you?" she asked as she placed moist kisses on my neck.

"Damn, girl. What are you doing to me?" I whispered as I spread my legs wider. I noticed the sun was going down as Katina turned onto the highway. Feeling bold, I lifted up Candi's shirt, unhooked her bra and began sucking on her breasts.

"Oh, damn," she cooed as she cupped the back of my head. "Suck it harder, baby." I enjoyed the taste of her. I enjoyed the way her body responded to me. I enjoyed being with her. I unfastened her jeans and slipped my fingers inside of her panties. My fingers combed through her pubic hair and found her moist folds. She repositioned herself so that I could penetrate her with my long, middle finger. The pad of my finger searched for and found the rippled flesh that was on the inside of her pubic bone. I massaged it softly.

"Oh damn. Oh shit, baby. You know my spot," she cooed as my tongue danced around her erect nipple. I glanced at Katina briefly and noticed she'd adjusted her rearview mirror, so she could enjoy our unbridled passion.

"Oh, God! I'm about to come!" Candi shouted out. She clamped her thighs closed and trembled.

"You have me acting so recklessly. I don't understand why I behave the way I do when I'm with you," I whispered in her ear.

A few moments later we pulled up in front of their apartment. The streetlights had just come on as Candi fixed her clothes. I stepped out of the car and waited for her. Once she was out I held her hand and followed Katina toward the door of the building. I palmed Candi's ass because I couldn't wait to go inside and make love to her.

"Codi! Why the fuck does that faggot have his hand palming your ass?" Candi shoved me away from her so hard that I tumbled to the ground.

"Larry! What are you doing here?" Candi sounded nearly hysterical.

"I told you I wanted some ass from you tonight. When you didn't bring your motherfuckin' ass home like you were supposed to, something told me to come back over here to see what the fuck was up! Now explain to me why that punk bitch over there was palmin' your ass!"

# CHAPTER 27

*Codi*

I froze at the sound of Larry's voice. I didn't mean to push Julius off me like that, but Larry was about to act a plum fool and I didn't know how much more drama I could handle.

It didn't take long for me to come to my senses. I rushed to Larry and ushered him toward the car.

"Sssshhh," I said as we moved toward the car. I could see Julius on the ground, shaking his head like he was a bit dazed. When Katina rushed to his side, I figured she had finally found a clue because the shit was bound to hit the fan.

"Baby," I said to Larry, "I didn't tell you, he ain't out yet!"

Larry's nostrils flared. He looked at me, but also kept looking over at Julius and Katina.

"What the hell you talkin' 'bout, Codi? All I know is I walk up and see some punk feelin' on my wife's ass! What kinda shit is that?"

"Baby, yes. You saw him touching my butt, but it wasn't what you thought."

He looked at me sideways.

"I'm serious. We were talking about him being gay and how he was still in the closet, so I told him that he wasn't doing a good job because, I mean, look at him." I glanced in their direction and Katina was helping Julius up off the ground.

Luckily for me, he stumbled a bit and it made him look like exactly what I was describing.

"What's a closet got to do with this and what I just saw with my own two eyes?" Larry asked.

I sighed real hard. "Are you gonna listen to me or not? I'm trying to explain to you what was going on. I know what it looked like, but I'm telling you, Julius and I were talking. He's not ready to come out the closet just yet, but I was telling him that everything about him screams gay! So I said to him, act like a straight man. Show me what you think straight men do."

Larry looked like he was considering believing me. "And that's when he grabbed your ass?"

"Yes, babe. That must've been right when you walked up. Trust me, I was stunned when he grabbed me, too, but it wasn't a grab like say, what you do. No, he was trying to show me that he could be straight."

"What kind of shit is that?" Larry said, looking back toward the front door where Katina and Julius were. Thank God they'd gone inside. "So he don't like a woman's ass?" Larry asked, like the thought itself was blasphemy.

"Baby, he told me he don't do fish!"

"Fish?" Larry asked.

"Yeah, that's what the gays call pussy, baby." I shook my head. "They don't want fish. They want meat!"

Larry's eyes grew wide, then his face twisted. "Now that's some nasty shit right there. It ain't natural," he insisted.

"I know, but I'm sorry you had to see that. I don't want you thinking I'd ever let another man touch me like that. Believe me when I tell you, Julius is harmless. He don't want what I got. Actually, I'd be more worried about him trying to get with you."

Larry jumped back. "Don't even play like that, Codi. That shit ain't funny!"

"So listen. I'm about to take him and Katina to the airport, then I'll be home so I can handle my business."

"Well, you tell that fool I'ma let him slide this time, but where I'm from, you don't go grabbin' on no married woman's ass. That's a straight violation and a guaranteed ass whuppin'. Trust, Codi, no jury would ever convict!" Larry said with his chest all poked out.

"You know when you talk like that it turns me on," I said.

Larry's eyebrows jumped up on his face, a smile curled at the corners of his lips and he pulled me close. "You like that?"

"You know I do," I purred.

"See that's what I'm talking about. I wanna get all up in your womb. You know how I do."

"Let me handle this. I'll be home later and you can do whatever you like, however you like."

"You bullshittin' me?" he asked.

"No, I'm not. Seeing you and how you was about to go smooth off on poor Julius, oooh, Larry, I gotta tell you. It just made me…" I licked my lips.

Larry's eyes were glued to my lips and they grew wide.

"What you talkin' 'bout, girl?" he asked, smiling hard.

I reached down and grabbed his crotch. He was already hard.

"You feel that?" Larry thrust his hips. "Huh? You feel that? All that's for you, girl! Hurry home."

I kissed him and stood by as he got into the car.

"Don't make me come back over here," he yelled as he pulled away. "And tell that punk what I said."

Once he was gone I rushed inside. Julius was laid out on the couch with a pack of frozen peas across his forehead. I eased up next to him on the sofa.

"Daddy, you okay?"

"Nah, I ain't okay," he snapped. I rubbed my hand up his chest and snuggled next to him. "Candi, who was dude out there?"

"It's a long story." I planted soft kisses on his cheek.

When he shoved me back I was stunned. I couldn't lose him.

I started pouting and I folded my arms across my chest.

His cell phone rang and he dug into his pocket for it.

"Yeah?" he answered. "Nah, I'm good. My head was all messed up, but I'm good. Where you at?" Julius said into the phone. "The airport? Nah, man. I'm good. I'm good. Actually, I'll be back in a few hours. I changed my flight a few minutes ago. I'm heading home tonight instead of tomorrow."

I felt somewhat relieved by that because that meant I wouldn't have to figure out how to stay out real late or all night after the drama that played out earlier.

"She right here," he said. Then he looked at me. I couldn't gauge his temperature, so I figured I'd let him finish his conversation, then I'd try to mend things. I couldn't let him get on that plane feeling the way he was about us.

"You feeling okay?" I asked the minute he hung up the phone.

I didn't like the way he was looking at me and I needed to do something to fix things. Otherwise, I could just about kiss him good-bye and that was not an option.

I started picking at my cuticles, then I looked up at him, and said, "Okay, I'm ready to come clean and tell you everything."

"I knew this shit wasn't adding up," he said. "I'm not crazy!"

"Okay, okay. I'll tell you everything, but I don't want to talk here." I started choking back tears. I had to make this good. "Let's go talk in the back. You need to get your stuff ready to go anyway, right?"

"Yeah," he said.

He followed me into the back bedroom. Once inside alone, I turned away from him and willed myself to cry. I squeezed my eyes shut tightly and counted to ten in my head. When I opened them they had watered enough. I spun around and started talking.

"I'm sorry, Julius. I'm sorry about everything. I never meant for it to come out this way. The truth is I was so afraid of losing you. I thought if you knew the truth you'd walk out of my life for good, and I couldn't bear the thought of that."

"Hold on, hold on. What are you talking about? What's that got to do with me getting sick and that crazy man showing up over here like that?"

"Have you ever heard of Spanish Fly?" I asked bashfully.

"Uh, yeah. What about it?"

"Well, I was so worried about us being together again that I wanted to show you an incredible time. So I went and bought some Spanish Fly. Only I couldn't find any, so I got something off the Internet that's supposed to be just as good. I ordered it as soon as I got back from Chicago. I intended to use it during our next encounter, but I didn't think I'd see you so soon."

"Wait. You drugged me?"

"Well, I didn't really *drug* drug you. I must've added too much to your drink, but I put it in both our drinks. You must've had an allergic reaction to it or something. But the thing is, if you're healthy, it's not supposed to do anything to you."

Julius looked like it was now his turn in the hot seat.

"I'm healthy!" he screamed.

"Ookay," I said.

"But what about dude who bum-rushed me? I hit my head on a brick out there. Otherwise, I would've torn his ass up!"

"See that's the part I didn't want to tell you about. That's my ex. The problem is he's very abusive and it seems like the restraining order does no good."

"Restraining order?"

"Yeah, it's gotten worse. He is having trouble letting go. He still thinks we're an item, but trust me, we're not. Whenever he shows up I try hard not to make matters worse. You see, what

I've learned is if I can just calm him down enough to get him away from the scene, it all works out. If I fight him and start yelling and getting all loud, the situation escalates into something ugly. Sometimes he misses the good times we used to have and he thinks we're still together," I said sadly.

"He hit you?" Julius asked. Finally, his voice softened up and he seemed sympathetic.

"It was horrible." The tears suddenly gushed out and that was all she wrote. Julius took me into his arms and held me close.

"Baby, you could've told me all of that." He pulled back and looked at me. "And you tried to get us some Spanish Fly?" He laughed. "That's the sweetest thing anyone's ever done for me."

I closed my eyes and said a silent prayer.

"Now I wish I hadn't changed my flight."

"Oh, you really did that?"

"Yeah, Calvin was flipping out. He was on his way here and I didn't need the drama, so I changed the flight."

"Well, how much time do we have?" I asked. I felt good because my doctor was mine!

He gave me a wicked smile and I knew it was on!

Once he put on the condom I spread my legs wide and I felt him as he entered me. Immediately, I sucked him in deeper.

"Shiit, Candi. Your fine ass got some good pussy," he cried out.

"Fuck it like you mean that then," I said.

And he did. We fucked on the bed, then moved to the chair. And if that wasn't enough, he lifted me up from the chair, then held my ass in his hands and slammed my back up against the wall.

"How you like it? How does it feel?"

"Oh, Daddy, I love it. You hitting my spot, Julius. You hitting my spot," I purred.

"Gooo-ood. Thha-t's whaaa-t I'm here to do. Hit your sppp-ot!"

"Yeeesssss! That's it. Right there. That's it, Julius, right there," I screamed.

"Where? Right there?"

"Yes, baaa-by. Ohhh yessssss!"

Julius bent his knees, grabbed my hips tighter and dug deeper into me.

Sweating and panting now, I couldn't believe I was about to come again. Julius and I had been fucking for nearly two hours!

"You say that you want it...you say that you need it...Is it gooood to you?"

"Oh, fuck yes! Yes! Yes! Yeeesss! Please don't stop! Don't you dare stop! You hitting my spot, Julius!"

We were nearly startled into stopping when we heard banging on the wall, but that only encouraged Julius to take me to the bed. Before he had the chance to lay me on my back good, I flipped him over and mounted him.

I stretched my back to his knees, then rotated my hips in a slow and seductive grind. With his dick still inside me, going strong, I slowed my rotation and moved my hips in circular motions.

All Julius could do was throw his head back and release a menacing grunt from the pit of his belly. I used the muscles in my pussy to clutch his hard dick. With a tight grip on his member, I eased up with my hands, cupping my breasts.

Julius opened his eyes and caught a glimpse of me squeezing my nipples and he started moving his hips faster to match my pace. I leaned forward and allowed my breasts to hang into his face.

"Suck 'em," I begged.

He grabbed my breasts, squeezed them together and slopped each nipple before taking one between his teeth. This drove me insane. I grabbed his chest with my nails and dug into his flesh.

"Please don't stop. I'm almost there," I huffed.

"I'm with you, girl. I'm with you. You like this, huh?"

"Oh yes! Yeesss!" I cried. "Right there! I'm, I'm, I'm commming!" I screamed.

"It's about fuckin' time!" Katina yelled through the walls.

But Julius and me, we were both in the zone. He exploded the second he felt my juices overflowing. We collapsed next to each other, struggling to breathe.

"Damn, girl. That's some bomb-ass pussy you got there," Julius said.

"And you knew exactly what to do with it," I purred.

Now when I looked at the clock, I was sad. I knew him leaving would make things easier for me with Larry, but the thought of not being with him had real tears seeping from my eyes.

# CHAPTER 28

# *Quinn*

The last thing I wanted to do was leave Houston. I wanted to stay there and protect Candi from her abusive ex. I swear if I ever got wind that he put his hands on her and harmed her in any way, I'd catch a case because I'd put a bullet in his ass.

After Candi and I exhausted each other during our lovemaking, we both wanted that moment, the feeling and the glow of our intimacy, to last just a little longer. After I'd exploded inside of her, Candi collapsed on me. I loved the weight of her body on mine. I began threading my fingers through her hair as I listened to her labored breathing begin to subside. I closed my eyes for what I thought would be a quick moment.

"Candi!" I heard Katina call her name. Opening my eyes, I glanced over at Katina who was standing in the doorway. I smiled at her.

"Will you wake her ass up?" Katina insisted.

"Baby," I whispered in Candi's ear. She didn't move, so I began caressing her perfectly shaped ass. "Baby, wake up," I whispered again.

"You may want to speed that process up, Dr. Cole, because you might end up missing your flight." That got my attention.

"Oh shit!" I said, glancing at a clock that was on a nearby night-stand. I'd been asleep for over an hour and my flight would leave in about fifty minutes.

"Baby, get up. I've overslept!" I said to Candi.

"Seriously?" Candi was lethargic.

"Come on, baby. I've got to go," I insisted.

Inhaling my scent deeply, she said, "Just hold me for a few more seconds."

"Candi. T.I.M.E., if you know what I mean." The way Katina said it snapped Candi out of her euphoria instantly.

"How much time has gone by?" Candi asked nervously.

"Enough for Yrral to be within ten minutes."

"Shit!" Candi immediately sprung to her feet.

"What's a Yrral?" I asked curiously.

"Yrral is uhm..." Candi was frantically putting on her clothes.

"What I mean is you all have about ten minutes to pack up and get out of here if you're going to make it to the airport."

"Listen, baby," Candi sat on the edge of the bed. "Now is not the time to talk. You need to get a move on."

"You're right," I agreed as I rose to my feet. I glanced at Katina who was still standing in the doorway. She unashamedly glanced at what I was working with. I even saw her sweep her tongue across her lips at the sight of my glistening manhood.

"One thing is for sure, Candi. I understand why you were screaming."

"Will you go start the car, so we can get the hell out of here?" Candi asked as she stood up and slipped her feet into her shoes. Although I wanted to take a shower, I knew that there wasn't much time. I put on a fresh pair of underwear, slipped into my jeans and slung everything I'd come with into my luggage.

"Come on, come on, come on. Let's go, baby!" Candi combed her fingers through her hair, which had clearly been sweated out from our intense lovemaking.

"You don't have time to worry about your hair now, girl. You definitely look like you've been fucking. You need to get the hell out of here before Larry..I mean Yrral…"

"I got it, Katina!" Candi barked as she and I ran out of the apartment, hustled over her to sedan and got in. Candi sped off down the block and zipped around a corner before she turned on her headlights.

She glanced over at me in the passenger seat, and said, "I'd buckle up if I were you, baby."

"Oh, you're about to do some shit, right?" I asked, even though I already knew the answer to my question.

"Oh, I'm going to get you to the airport on time," she assured me. Candi zoomed through a red light without so much as slowing down or looking to see if traffic was coming.

"Don't get us killed, girl!" I complained.

"No one is ever at that intersection. That's the dumbest place for a stoplight." She defended her traffic violation as she cut to the right and hopped on the interstate. Candi then floored it. The motor whined loudly as the car picked up speed. Candi switched lanes without signaling and flashed other motorists with her high beam headlights if they cut in front of her or moved too slowly.

"Damn, baby. Where did you learn how to drive like this?" I asked as I felt adrenaline rush through me.

"My daddy," she said sweetly as she veered into the shoulder lane to zip around an eighteen-wheeler. I glanced over at her speed and noticed she was doing 110 mph.

"Shit!" I said, double-checking to make sure my seatbelt was really clicked in.

"I got this, Daddy," she assured me as she took one hand off of the wheel to turn on the radio. Beyoncé was singing her song, "Run the World (Girls)."

"Who run this motherfucker?" Candi sang along with Beyoncé as she grooved to the music.

"Come on, baby. Sing it with me. Who run this motherfucker?" she asked and I gave her the answer.

"Girls."

"Who run this motherfucker?" she bellowed out again and I repeated the answer.

"Girls."

By the time the song had ended, Candi was dropping me off at the airport. I got out of the car to remove my luggage from the trunk.

"Okay, Daddy." Candi slammed the trunk closed, braided her long arms around my neck and kissed me passionately. "When will I see you again?"

"Soon, baby," I said, as I felt my dick growing strong again. I pulled her closer to me, so she could feel it.

"Oh no. You've already got my ass tender as hell. I'm going to need to soak in the tub," she admitted.

"I miss you already."

"You're going to miss your damn flight if you don't hurry. Go on. Call me when you get home."

I grabbed my luggage and walked into the airport. I turned back once to see if Candi was there, but she'd zipped off into the night.

I walked over to the kiosk to check in. I reached for my wallet, but it wasn't in my back pocket where it should've been.

"Oh shit," I said, patting myself down to see if I had it in another pocket. Popping my fingers, I said, "It must be in my other slacks that I packed up in luggage." I found a private corner where I laid my luggage flat, unzipped it and checked. I went through all of my slacks, but didn't find my wallet.

"Fuck!" I hissed as I thought back in my mind to the last time I'd seen it.

"I had it the night we went to the restaurant," I mumbled to myself. Then I woke up and was sick and then I went to the hospital. Then it hit me.

"Shit!" In my rush to pack, I realized that I'd left another pair of pants at the apartment, which was where my wallet was. Reaching for my cell phone, I called Candi.

"Hey, Daddy. You made it through security already?"

"Baby. Daddy has a problem," I announced.

"What's wrong?"

"I left another pair of slacks with my wallet at your place."

"You're kidding me?" she sounded disappointed.

"No, I'm not. I've looked through all of my things and I'm missing a pair of pants, the one with my wallet."

"Okay, let me think. Give me a minute while I figure something out. I'll call you right back."

I squatted back down and zipped up my luggage. I was going to miss my flight, but decided to ask a desk agent if there was a way I could get on the last flight out.

"Let me see," said the agent as she typed some information into the system.

"Okay. Take your time," I said, knowing that being nice would get me better results.

"The last flight back to Chicago is full. The best I could do is put you on standby. If not, you can catch the first flight out in the morning."

"Thank you," I said and stepped away. At least there was a slim chance I'd get out tonight. If not, I'd just have to stay another night with Candi, which I really didn't mind. I felt my cell phone vibrating.

"Hello?" I answered it.

"Are you okay? What the hell is going on with you?" It was Tameecia.

"It's a long story," I said, not wanting to deal with what awaited me when I did return home.

"Why haven't you called me? You had me all worried and shit. I thought your motherfucking ass was dying. When I talked to you, you sounded crazy as hell. And why in the hell are you sneaking around in Houston? I know you're not at a sales conference. I know you've been—"

I hung up on her. The last thing I wanted to hear was her mouth. I'd have to figure out how to deal with Tameecia later.

My phone buzzed again. This time I looked at the caller ID before I answered. It was Candi.

"Hey, baby," I greeted her.

"Okay, Daddy. Katina found your slacks and wallet. They were under the bed. She's going to drive out to the airport and give them to you. She's on her way now. Hopefully, she can get there before your flight leaves, but I'm not sure. Katina doesn't drive as fast as I do."

"It's okay, baby. I may be able to get out on the last flight. I'm going to have them place me on standby. But if not, one more night with you wouldn't be so bad, now would it?"

"Uhm, of course not, Daddy, but uhm, just let me know what happens either way," she said.

"Alright, I'll stand outside and wait for Katina to pull up," I said.

"Okay, I'll talk to you later," she said and ended the call.

It took Katina thirty minutes to arrive at the airport. When she did, she got out of her car and walked over to me. She'd folded my slacks and handed them to me.

"Thank you so much," I said.

"And here is your wallet, Quinn." When she said my real name, I knew she'd gone through it and looked at my identification.

# CHAPTER 29

*Codi*

K atina had been acting real salty with me lately. I wasn't sure what was wrong with her, I figured she was probably still hot over the way Larry showed his ass out at her place last weekend. But still, that was no reason for her to be trippin' with me the way she was.

When she slipped me the envelope with my money in it after work Thursday, I started to say something about all the 'tude she was throwing my way, but I decided against it. Julius and I had been talking about it quite a bit, too. The way she looked at me made me think about the conversation I'd just wrapped up with Julius before she came into the room.

"Baby, she's jealous of you," he said.

"Katina? Jealous of me?" I chuckled. He didn't know her the way I did. Katina was a serious man magnet. She never met a stranger she didn't know and people seemed to gravitate to her friendly personality. There was no way she could be jealous of me like *that*!

"Listen. I don't want you to let her come between us," Julius said. "Trust me. I've seen this kind of thing before. Lemme guess, she probably can't get Calvin to return her calls, huh?"

"I don't think she's talked to him in a minute," I said.

"See, think about it, baby. Here we are, kicking it strong, making plans for the future, our future together, and she sitting over there alone. Shit, I'd be hating on you and your man, too," he joked.

"Katina ain't like that," I defended.

"Maybe not before, while the two of you were both single, but, baby, now that you got a man? Huh! Mark my words. Watch what I tell you. Soon, she's gonna start telling you shit about me, trying to turn you against me and shit!"

I allowed what he said to roll around in my head. He had some valid points, she was bitter about Calvin. Katina wasn't used to men dumping her. But still, she had too many other irons in the fire to be worked up over one.

"Baby, Katina's not like that. My girl may have her issues, she's always chasing paper, but that's not her style, not by a long shot."

"You know what, Candi, I didn't wanna say nothing about this before, but now I should just go on and tell you. Just in case I'm right and some foul shit goes down between the two of you."

"What?" My ears perked up.

"Well, remember when I overslept and I was trippin' and shit, thinking I'd miss my plane?"

"Uh-huh," I said.

"Well, you remember it was Katina who woke us up, right?" he asked.

"Yeah."

"Well, when I got out of the bed, I was naked. Instead of walking out to give us privacy to get dressed, she stood in the doorway, staring at my shit. Her mouth was watering and her eyes had popped out of her head."

"What?" I was stunned by what he was trying to say.

"I know, babe. I didn't really want to bring it up, but you heard her when she made that little comment that she could see why you were screaming! That shit was way outta line, babe," he said.

I listened to what Julius was telling me, but there was no way

I'd let him get into my head the way he was trying to. Katina had her issues, but she wasn't checking after my man! That much I knew for sure.

"Listen, babe, she's coming, so I'm gonna call you back later, okay?"

"Cool" Julius said and hung up.

"You'll be here tomorrow, right?" Katina asked.

It wasn't the question, it was her tone, the way she'd been talking to me lately. It was like she spoke only when she had to and even then, she acted like it hurt her to say something to me.

"Katina, what's really going on?" I asked.

Her neck snaked and her face was twisted. "What do you mean 'what's really going on'?"

"Did I do something to you? I mean lately you've been walking around here acting like you can't stand to breathe the same air as me. I'm just wondering what the problem is and when are we gonna deal with it because I can't go on like this."

Katina blinked and blinked again, but she didn't say anything at first.

I didn't know what to expect as I stood waiting for her answer. I didn't know if she was about to go off on me or jump defensive and ignore what I was trying to tell her.

Suddenly, she burst into tears and literally broke down. I mean, like baby-bawling tears. I panicked. I didn't know what to do.

"Girl, my life is a mess! I don't know what I'm gonna do. I got so many issues I don't even know where to start," she boo-hooed.

I was stunned.

Katina was hungry for money, but otherwise her life looked pretty damn good to me. She was always dressed to the nines, her hair and nails were constantly on point and her business was going well. I didn't see a problem really.

I rushed over and gave her a hug. She was crying so hard and loud I had no choice but to let her get it out.

"It's gonna be okay. I'm sure it's not all that bad," I said.

"Oh, it's pretty damn bad," she said, sniffling.

When it finally seemed like she was able to talk, I tried to get it out of her.

"Girl, I'm sorry if I've been taking shit out on you. It's not you at all. It's just…" her chest was heaving up and down and she broke down again.

I sighed.

"Katina, what's going on?"

All kinds of crazy thoughts were running through my mind. What if she really was checking Julius? What if she was about to tell me she had gotten with him on the sly. I found it odd that he suddenly started trying to attack her and turn me against her. I wanted to be with the good doctor, but I knew enough about men to know they could do some trifling things.

She was sobbing so hard again that I couldn't get anything out of her. My patience was getting thin. I watched her crying for a little bit longer, then I just blurted it out.

"What's this really about? Are you mad about me and Dr. Cole?" I asked.

Katina suddenly stopped crying. She sniffled a few times, wiped her nose with the back of her hand, then frowned and looked at me confused.

"Huh?"

"Julius," I said.

"What about him?" she asked, still confused.

"Look, it's no secret that things didn't work out with you and Calvin. And, well, as you can see, things are really progressing with Julius and me," I said.

Katina's hands flew to her hips and she flinched back a bit with the frown on her face deepening even more.

"Things are progressing with you and *who*?" she asked, like she didn't hear what I had just said. Now that rubbed me the wrong way. My heart started racing and I felt my blood beginning to boil. Now she wasn't trying to be funny, was she? I rolled my eyes.

"So Julius was right. You are jealous of us! Just like he said. Another bitter, hateful, lonely-ass black female." I snickered. "You know, Katina, I expected to have people jealous of me for being with a doctor and all, but not *you*. We go way…"

Katina did a talk-to-the-hand motion that cut me off instantly. She got up and looked down at me. "Girl, please! *Doctor* my ass! I can't believe you're gonna let some dick come between us! How long have I known you? And how long have you known Julius?" Her previous vulnerability had all but vanished right before my eyes.

"Katina, you're the one who started throwing shade. I was trying to figure out what the problem was, but every time I mention Julius or you see us Skyping, it's like you get an attitude," I explained.

"Um, did it ever dawn on you that maybe I'm going through some shit that ain't got nothing to do with you and your damn side piece? You act like y'all got papers on each other or something. Newsflash, boo! While you checkin' me, you need to be checking the good *doctor* about who the hell Quinn is! And I tried Googling his ass. He probably ain't even no real damn doctor!" she hissed.

Now I was hot!

"Julius is a doctor," I defended.

"Oh yeah? What's his specialty? Where does he practice? Do you ever hear him talking about his patients? Does he ever talk about work? No! I'm not saying he is or he isn't. All I'm saying is, just like your shit ain't right, I don't think his is either."

"My shit ain't right? What's that supposed to mean?" I asked.

"Codi, we met these dudes on Facebook! We met them on the damn Internet! We don't know shit, except what they tell us! That's it. When I Googled Calvin, I did see where he played in the NBA, but I also saw where it says he's married with kids, so that's why I'm not trippin' over him! Shit, he's somebody else's husband! You of all people should get that. What trips me out about your boy is, just like I found a ton of shit on Calvin, I ain't found a damn thing on Dr. Cole, or Julius, or whoever the hell he claims to be!"

"That don't mean nothing," I said.

"You're right, it doesn't, but what I'm saying to you is, how you gon' let him slide between us? I don't give a rat's ass if he's a doctor or a bum, if he make your toes curl, if he pushing your back out, and he plays his position, then I'm happy for you! Plain and simple. You my girl. I don't want your sidepiece fucking up your home life, but shit that ain't my problem or my issue. I ain't thinking about you and your men! So don't ever come at me like that again!" she huffed.

I felt real bad. Katina and I had been through a whole lot, and never once had we ever crossed words over a man. She was breathing fire, and the more I thought about it, she had every right to be pissed.

"Katina, I'm sorry. I let Julius get all up in my head," I admitted.

She shook her head and looked at me with pity.

"Yeah, girl. Shit. I understand the power of good dick, but damn, *work* that dick, don't let it work *you*!"

At that, we both burst out laughing.

Once the laughing subsided, I looked at her, and said, "Okay, so I lost it for a minute, but seriously though, what's up with you? What's wrong?"

"Before we get to that, for the record let me say this. If he's Dr. Julius Apollo Cole, then why the hell does his driver's license say Quinn Hamilton?"

"What?" She told me that she had went through his wallet and saw his driver's license. She also said she found what looked like a check stub from a car dealership.

"Yeah, and remember, didn't Calvin say his cousin, Quinn?"

I really couldn't remember because we were all yelling at the same time when I had called Calvin. And he threw so many threats at us I could hardly keep up.

"I should've said something a long time ago, but, girl, I got my own issues. Speaking of which, I kept thinking I'd be able to handle it. Now this shit is so out of control I don't know what to do!"

I was still lost. I wanted to know what she was going through, but my mind couldn't stop thinking about Julius either.

"What is it?" I finally screamed.

Katina's eyes cast downward and she quieted down.

"Girl, what is it?" I asked.

"I owe this dude some money," she said softly.

"Okay, well, pay him. What's the problem?"

"No, not like that. I mean, I owe him big, and I don't know what he's gonna do if I don't pay."

"Like a loan shark?" I asked, still confused.

"Well sort of. It started out with the payday loans, then it morphed into this. Now dude is making threats and shit."

"Payday loans?"

"Yeah. Before I started making money with the business, I took out a few of them. A couple of three-thousand-dollar loans ballooned up to seven. Then it went from seven to ten."

I was beyond stunned, but the thunderous knock at the door made us both jump.

"Oh God! Who's there?" Katina screamed.

"Where the hell is Codi? This Larry!"

Katina and I looked at each other and started cracking up.

"Girl, go let that fool in before he put on another show for my neighbors," she said.

I walked over and pulled the door open for Larry. He came rushing in, bat in hand, and his wild, crazy eyes searching the room like he was looking for someone.

"Where he at? Where he at?" Larry yelled.

Katina and I looked at him, then at each other.

"Where is who?"

"I ain't no fool, Codi. I was talking to my boys about that shit that went down over here last weekend and them clowns called me all kinda suckas and shit! That dude wasn't gay. You fuckin' that fool, huh?"

Katina looked at him and frowned.

"Who? My brother, Julius?" She looked at me. "Codi, you didn't tell him Julius is playing for the *other* team?"

"I told his ass already that Julius don't want no fish!"

"You and your boys are off base with this one," Katina confirmed.

Larry, who was still all fired up, looked around again as if he might just see evidence of what he believed.

"If I find out you givin' my shit to somebody else, Codi," he warned.

"Larry, I ain't got time for no other man. You keep me on my toes as it is," I said.

"You damn straight I do," he said. He stuck his chest out a bit, then glanced toward the hallway and eased the bat down by his side. "And you know what, I'ma have to start waxin' that ass even more just to make sure you ain't thinkin' about lettin' some other fool grab your ass like that again. Let's go," he demanded.

"Okay, Larry. I'll be there," I said.

"No, now, girl. I mean it, dammit. Ain't no woman of mine gon' be hangin' around no gays. You might try to turn him straight!" Larry said.

I rolled my eyes at his ignorance.

"Look, we'll talk later," I told Katina.

She nodded.

I gave her a quick hug, whispered another apology in her ear and turned to leave.

As I followed Larry out of her house my mind was racing with all kinds of thoughts. Why hadn't she found anything on Dr. Cole when she Googled him? What kind of doctor was he anyway? And why was he intentionally trying to drive a wedge between Katina and me? And who was he really?

# CHAPTER 30

## *Quinn*

Silky and I were cruising down Interstate 55 toward St. Louis, Missouri. I needed to get out of the house because Tameecia had been making my life a living hell ever since I'd returned from Houston. Not that I expected her to act sanely once I got back, but she really needed to cut me some slack. When I returned home I found that my iPad had been smashed and my clothes were packed in a spare suitcase and sitting near the front door.

"There is your shit. Pick it up, turn around and walk right back out the fucking door." She was sitting on the sofa in the family room. Her arms were folded across her chest and she was hot with rage.

"No! Fuck that. You're not putting me out of my own damn house. I'm the bastard who pays the mortgage," I said, placing my luggage beside the one she'd packed for me.

"Why don't you go back to that bitch you were with, Quinn? You must have told her not to answer your video requests on your iPad because I've tried to connect with her several times," she hollered at me.

"You don't know what you're talking about. I'm not even going to go down that road with you. Besides, you don't have a clue as to where I've been or what I've gone through," I fired back.

"What the hell is going on out here?" Out of nowhere, Smokey Love walked into the room, wearing a leopard-print robe.

"What the fuck is he doing here?" I looked at Tameecia, then back at him.

"I'm sorry, baby boy. My bad. I see that I've walked into an Ike and Tina Turner moment. Pimp to pimp, playa to playa, handle your business. I was trying to make sure no one was breaking in the joint." Smokey Love did a 180-degree turn and marched back into LaQeeta's room.

"Don't worry about Smokey Love. I said he was welcome to come and visit LaQeeta as he pleased." Tameecia was being spiteful. She knew how much I hated that man being in my house. A castle that had two kings only led to someone getting their throat sliced opened in the middle of the night. I'd deal with the Smokey Love issue later.

"You have a right to be pissed off, and you should be."

"You're damn right I'm pissed off. You should've told me the damn truth. See that's why your ass got sick. God don't like ugly and he isn't too crazy about cute. What happened? You had a stroke or something?"

"Something like that. I was laid up most of the time I was there," I lied.

"See, Quinn, that's what I'm saying. You don't fucking listen. I kept telling you that you were pushing yourself too hard, and for what? Just to lose a few pounds? Look at where that landed you? In the hospital."

"At least now you realize that I was sick and wasn't fucking around," I said as I headed toward the kitchen. When I walked past her I tossed a copy of the hospital bill on her lap.

"What the hell? Why did you smash my iPad?" I yelled at her because I saw my primary means of communication with Candi destroyed.

"Why are you on those porno websites, watching nasty women

dance around? What? I'm not good enough for you or something?"

"You shouldn't have done this, Tameecia," I said, feeling my own temper swell.

"What was I supposed to think? Huh? Candi must look fan-fucking-tastick for you to log on all the time just to watch her shake her ass in front of a camera. You like prostitutes now?"

"Candi is not a prostitute," I defended.

"Newsflash, nucca. With a name like Candi, she can't help but be a prostitute. I certainly hope your ass didn't fly all the way to Houston just to drop your dick off in that nasty-ass pussy!"

"I told you. When I got there I got sick. I stayed in the hospital the entire fucking time."

"Why the hell did you go to Houston any damn way? What's the real deal, Quinn?" she asked.

"I just needed to get away. I needed to spend some time alone and reflect on my life."

"So you flew to Houston? What the hell? Why not Jamaica or the Bahamas? Those are places you go to reflect on your life, not Houston fucking Texas!"

"Well, that's where I chose to go because Southwest was running one of their cheap airline specials. It only cost me fifty-nine dollars each way."

"I see your black ass is cheap, too," she insulted me.

"Whatever," I said and walked into the bedroom. Tameecia pursued me.

"Oh, hell no. You're not sleeping in the same bed with me!"

"I don't want to," I snapped back as I grabbed an extra blanket and pillow from the closet. When I walked out of the room Tameecia slammed the bedroom door shut.

I pulled off of the highway to get some gas. I'd been driving for two hours and was in a small college town called Lincoln, Illinois. Once I filled up the tank I got back on the highway and headed in the direction of my house. As I drove along, my cell phone rang. I glanced at it and saw that it was Katina. I reluctantly answered.

"Hello," I said.

"What's up?" Katina was direct and to the point.

"Is something wrong?" I asked, thinking that something had perhaps happened to Candi.

"No. In fact, everything is going to be just fine," she said, laughing sinisterly. I didn't like the sound of her voice at all. "So Quinn, you really like Candi, don't you?"

"My name is Julius, my ID had old…"

"Baby, let's not bullshit each other. Candi and I met you and Calvin on the damn Internet. To be honest, I can't recall if we first made contact on my private page or via Facebook, but it doesn't matter. In my business I don't ask a bunch of questions, but you are somewhat of a mystery."

"What are you driving at, Katina?" I needed to know why she was calling me.

"I'm just saying, you could be anyone. For all I know, you could be an ex-convict who just finished doing hard time. Maybe that's why you're able to last so long and fuck Candi so well. Because let me tell you, you have the girl walking bowlegged now."

I wanted to chuckle, but I didn't. Katina wasn't the type of chick who'd call her girl's man just for the hell of it. That much I knew.

"Get to your point. I realize you're up to something," I said.

"You see, Julius, I was able to look up Calvin and actually see that he used to play in the NBA. I also found out that he's very married and has children. You, on the other hand, I haven't been able to find anything on. No matter how many different ways I plugged your name into my searches, nothing came up. Nothing for Dr. Julius Apollo Cole, Quinn Cole, Apollo, or Apollo Quinn."

"That doesn't prove a damn thing. Not everyone has all of their business on the Internet," I said.

"True, but I do have a copy of all of Quinn Hamilton's information. Quinn Hamilton lives at 1642 E. 57th Street in Chicago, Illinois. That type of information is worth something."

"Ha!" I laughed.

"Oh really," Katina said smoothly. "Well, I've been around the block a few times and I'm willing to bet that if you are Dr. Cole, or Quinn Hamilton, me showing up at this address, claiming to be pregnant with your baby, would probably cause a shitload of problems for you."

I remained silent. Since I didn't really know her I couldn't gauge if she was dead serious or just bullshitting.

"I want ten thousand dollars. You need to bring it with you when you come back to Houston next week. If you don't have my money you can expect to get a visit."

"You don't scare me, Katina," I said, calling her bluff.

"You have no idea what I can do with this private information of yours that I have. I'm actually being generous by asking for it. I have enough of your personal information to get a loan with a mean loan shark under your name. Now I don't care if you have to get the money from your rich cousin, Calvin, but one way or another, when you come back to Houston, you'd better have my money."

A few hours later, I was sitting on a barstool beside Calvin, laying everything out to him. I explained how Katina had gotten my ID, knew my real name, and had my home address.

"Fuck that bitch, man. If she comes anywhere near your crib, blow her motherfucking head off," Calvin suggested as he took a swig of his beer. "And another thing, you need to cut all ties with her and her friend, Candi."

"I happen to like Candi. We get along really well," I said. I didn't want my relationship with her to end.

"Come on, Quinn, be realistic, man. We don't know jack shit about either of those women. For all we know, Katina and Candi could be scam artists with a criminal record a mile long. Remember the shit that you're doing is supposed to be about playing a fantasy role. Dr. Julius Apollo Cole is fictitious. He's a figment of your imagination, someone you made up and placed into cyberspace for the purpose of meeting women, fucking them and moving the hell on. This shit was never about falling in love or meeting Mrs. Right. In fact, everything you've been doing has been about deception. You created Dr. Cole so no one would ever find him." Calvin and I both took another sip of our beers.

"So what do you think I should do?" I asked for his honest opinion.

"I say leave the shit alone and move on to the next chick."

Pausing for a moment, I said, "Yeah. I do have four more women who've inboxed me on Facebook who want to hook up with Dr. Cole."

"Then that's what you need to do. Find some new pussy to fuck." Calvin was very casual about using women for his own personal pleasure. At that moment, my cell phone buzzed.

"Who is that? Tameecia, stalking your ass?" Calvin chuckled. I looked at the screen and saw that it was Candi.

"Hang on a second, man. I'm gonna take this," I said, stepping away from the bar.

"Hello?" I answered.

"Hey, Big Daddy." By the tone of Candi's voice, I could tell she was smiling.

"Hey, baby," I greeted her.

"You have a birthday coming up," she said.

"Huh?" I was confused. My birthday wasn't for another several months.

"I got a Facebook notification that said your birthday is coming up."

Realizing that Dr. Cole had a birthday coming up, I laughed it off. "You're right. I do."

"How old will you be, Daddy?"

"Old enough to do it and young enough to get away with it."

"Ooo, I like the sound of that. I can't wait to see you next week. I'm going to give you the best birthday present in the world."

"Oh really." I smiled.

"Yes. Your face is going to be buried in it." She and I both laughed.

"So, Daddy, I have a question for you." She sounded so sweet.

"Yes, baby," I said.

"How come you never talk about your practice and what your patients are like?"

"I'm not a medical doctor," I said, realizing that Katina had apparently said something about my driver's license in order for Candi to begin asking questions.

"Oh." Candi seemed to be confused.

"I'm a professor. I work at a small community college. I teach."

"Oh, now I get it. Silly me. Thank you for explaining that to me, Daddy. There is one more thing."

"What's that, baby?"

"Uhm, I don't know how to ask this, so I'm just going to put it out there. Katina said she noticed your driver's license had your picture and the name of Quinn Hamilton on it. Is your name really Quinn?"

I froze. I forced my mind to think and come up with a believable lie.

"Why would she go through my belongings? Was she looking for gas money? Was she trying to rob me or something?" I asked. I wanted to put Candi on the defensive while I worked on a good lie.

"No, Daddy. It wasn't like that. I'm not sure how she noticed. Maybe it fell out or something," Candi said.

"Oh. Well, here is the thing, baby. Quinn Hamilton is my twin brother who passed away a few years ago. I kept his picture ID as a reminder of what he meant to me."

"How is he your twin? You have different last names?"

"Baby, listen and let me explain," I said.

"Sorry, Daddy."

"It's a painful story, but here is what happened. My father was an abusive man. He beat me, my brother and my mother."

"Oh no!" Candi gasped.

"Yeah, I know. That's why I got mad about the thing with your ex. I understand what it's like to be with someone who beats on you. Anyway, my mother died and my father beat my brother and me so much that the school system got involved. Next thing I knew, my brother and I were placed in foster homes. When we aged out of the system my brother started drinking and doing drugs. I ended up being placed with a good family. They helped me get through college. Anyway, to make a long story short, I decided that I didn't want to carry my biological father's last name anymore, so I changed my name and took the surname of the foster family that raised me."

"Oh, Daddy, I'm so sorry. I had no idea. I don't know what to say. I...I...I..."

Overjoyed that Candi fell for my line of bullshit, I said, "Don't worry about it, baby."

"What happened to your brother?" she asked.

"His lifestyle of drugs took him," I said.

"That's so sad, Daddy. When I see you I'm going to give you a big hug and then we're going to make sweet love."

"Is that what you called for?" I asked as I felt my dick getting hard. I couldn't wait to fuck her again. Although after that big-ass lie I'd just told, I was going to take Calvin's advice and cut all ties with Candi. But before I did that I wanted to fuck her once more before Dr. Cole unfriended her on Facebook and the webcam site and disappeared out of her life forever. I did, however, make a mental note to myself to get a fake ID that had my photo and the name Dr. Julius Apollo Cole.

# CHAPTER 31

*Codi*

The aroma of food tickled my nostrils and flirted with my senses the moment I approached the front door. I had to double back and check the number on the side of the house to make sure I wasn't at the wrong address.

"Yup, it's my house," I muttered under my breath. It smelled like someone had been doing some serious burning in my damn kitchen and my stomach was growling like a hungry bear on the prowl.

As I dug for the keys I felt my mouth begin to water. If the smell of good food wasn't enough, I heard laughter and some chattering. Who the hell was having a party at my damn house and why hadn't I been invited?

I stepped inside and noticed how clean the place was. Somebody had done some serious work. It smelled good and looked even better. My son was strapped to a high chair and he started giggling the moment our eyes met.

"Hello?" I called out, thinking Larry must've really lost his mind to be entertaining without me. I could tell this wasn't his ordinary get-together with the fellas.

It wasn't until I stepped all the way into the dining room and saw the scene with my own two eyes that I realized what was going on. Seated around my table was none other than Linda, decked out in her signature orange, Larry, and his ex-girlfriend, Darlisa!

Whatever was in my hands dropped and hit the floor with a thud.

Linda's head turned in my direction. The fork she had been using to shovel food into her mouth was suspended in the air only inches from her lips. Her eyes grew even wider. The others followed her stare and turned to look at me.

"Oh, damn. There you are," Larry said, sounding nervous.

"What the hell is going on here?"

"Look what all Mama did," he sang. "She came over early, cleaned the house and fixed us dinner," Larry said.

My icy glare traveled from him to his orange-loving mama.

"Hey, Codi. You remember Darlisa, right?"

"Your house is real nice," Darlisa said.

I wanted to spit on her and Linda. The bitch knew I remembered Darlisa's desperate behind.

"So this how we doing it now?" I turned my attention to Larry. He was stuffing his face like this scene was normal.

"What? Why you trippin'? Mama came and made all my favorites—ham hocks, pigs' feet, yams, and collard greens. Ooh! She even made hot water cornbread and red Kool-Aid," Larry said.

I could tell he was nervous. He wasn't even making sense, just running off like he had diarrhea of the mouth.

"You want me to fix you a plate?" Linda asked, talking with her mouth full.

I was still glaring at Larry, who was snatching anything he could to stuff his mouth.

"We was just talking about that social media stuff and how you can find just about anybody you looking for on that stuff," Linda said. She used her fork to stab at her food while she talked.

"Yeah. Mama was telling me some crazy stuff they got out there on the Internet," Larry chimed in.

"Sho nuff, crazy," Linda added. "Can you imagine some women even on there taking off their clothes for money!"

I felt my knees buckle a bit, but I wouldn't give that fat orange bitch the satisfaction. I knew damn well I didn't take off my clothes for money on the Internet, but I got her message loud and clear.

"Now that some foul shit right there!" Larry howled.

"You'd be surprised," Linda chimed in. "You know what they say—what's done in the dark will eventually come to light!"

I shot daggers at her with my eyes.

"When Linda called me and asked me to help her set up a webcam, so she could see her grandbaby, I was so happy to help her. I started my own web business a few years back," Darlisa said to me. "I'm thinking of starting a new line of DeeLish products."

I wondered why she thought I should give a fuck!

Linda had a smirk on her face.

"I can't tell you how many married folks catch their partners stepping out because of that Facebook! I was so glad when Pastor finally banned it at church!" Linda said.

"Your church banned Facebook?" Darlisa asked, like that was the most interesting thing she'd heard in years.

"Yes. We had way too many people catching up with old flames and finding new ones, so Pastor finally put his foot down. He even created these written agreements for couples to sign. It was one of the best ideas I'd heard in quite a while. No married folks got no business all on Facebook any doggone way!" she insisted.

I couldn't stand it anymore! I turned to Larry, hoping to talk to him without the others being all in our business. "Larry, I need to see you in the other room."

"Oh, that can wait 'til after dinner," Linda interjected. When I spun and glared at her, she retreated, but not enough. "I don't see why it can't wait 'til later, but oh well, Larry, baby. Don't let your food get too cold."

Once behind closed doors, I lit into him unmercifully.

"What kind of shit is this, Larry? I come home to find you, your mama, and your ex playing house in my own fucking house? What if I would've done some messed-up shit like that to you?" My neck was twisting and I was serving up major attitude, but I didn't give a damn!

Larry frowned. "I know you ain't trippin' off Mama and Darlisa. Girl, please. You know my mama don't mean no harm, and Darlisa, well, she ain't nothin' for you to worry about."

"I'm sick of your mama sticking her nose in business that's not hers!" I spat.

Larry looked distracted.

"First, she's trying to stir up mess over Katina's brother, then she starts telling you all kinds of questions you need to be asking me, and now this?"

His body was with me, but it was clear to me that his mind was still stuck on the food he left behind. Soon, I felt like the nagging wife who was bitching about a whole lot of nothing.

"Look, my food gettin' cold. You should be thankin' my mama for helpin' out around here. She didn't mean no harm," he repeated.

I threw my hands up in frustration.

"You done?" he asked.

"Yeah, I'm done."

I followed Larry out of the room, cursing his mother under my breath. When we got back to the impromptu dinner party, Linda and Darlisa were gone. They had left the table and were hovered over a laptop I'd never seen before. I was ready to put them both out until I overheard what was being said.

"So all we have to do is plug in the card number and 'Voilà'!" Darlisa said. "I'm not sure about her, but that girl she's tight with, oh, I know she's on there!"

"Well, you know what they say about birds of a feather," Linda mumbled.

They were busy banging on the keyboard.

"Larry, why don't you come on over here, son," Linda sang. "There's something I want you to see."

All of a sudden everything seemed to move in slow motion. Linda and Darlisa moved over so that Larry could slide between them to get a good view.

"What the fuck!" he screamed.

I rolled my eyes; the shit was about to hit the fan.

Linda's smirk had blossomed into a full-fledged grin. Bitch!

"So you and Katina on the Internet sellin' ass?" he cried, looking over his shoulder at me in horror.

"It's not what you think," I said.

Linda jumped in. "That's why I told you from the moment I laid eyes on her, she's too worldly for you—always has been, always will be."

"Linda, I want you out of my house!" I screamed. "Get your ass out of here!"

"You don't talk to my mama like that," Larry screamed at me.

"You know what? What was I thinking? You're right. She can stay. I'll go. I don't need this shit! It's always been three people in this marriage, and I'm sick of it!" I stormed into the bedroom, grabbed a bag, tossed some stuff in it, and walked over to snatch up my son.

But the way Linda was clutching him, I didn't have the energy to fight anymore.

Larry was still at the computer, cursing like a sailor. I glared at Linda, then walked out. All this time I was worried about Larry finding out about Julius, but never once did I think about him finding out about the website. It was all becoming too damn much.

Later that night, as I ran the entire story down to Katina, I realized something that hadn't dawned on me before. Since I was out of the house, I no longer had to worry about sneaking out to be with Julius. I felt the smile creep on my face.

Katina looked, and asked, "Um, not trying to make you feel bad, but how you gonna fix this shit?"

"I'm not gonna worry about it," I said.

Katina looked at me like I was crazy.

"Think about it. If I can stretch this thing out with Larry for at least two days, I'm in the clear for Julius." I grinned.

"That's right. When's he coming in?"

"Girl, tomorrow morning and I can't wait."

"Umph," was Katina's only response.

"Hey, enough about me. What's up with you, the situation?"

"Oh, it's working itself out."

My eyebrow rose slightly. "What do you mean 'it's working itself out'?'"

"Girl, you know me, always resourceful. I got something in the works," she said.

I was glad when her cell phone rang. I used that as an excuse and slipped to the back room and called Julius.

He didn't answer, but I didn't mind. In several hours my man would be right here by my side, and for a change, I wouldn't have to sleep next to him with one eye open.


I felt like I was on one of those old douching commercials with the woman running freely. That's how Julius and I ran to each other's open arms outside of Hobby Airport. We fell into a deep passionate kiss and I suddenly wished I could get us back to Katina's in less than sixty seconds flat.

We kissed again in the car.

"You hungry, Daddy?" I asked as we buckled up.

"I could eat something," he said.

"Let's go to my favorite restaurant."

"I wanna go anywhere you wanna take me."

When we pulled up in front of Pappasito's Cantina in Sugar Land I felt like I was finally living the life I'd envisioned when I decided to start a new life on Facebook.

Since things had taken off with Julius, I still checked in on Facebook, but I didn't take any of the men up on their offers. Trust and believe there were still tons of offers.

Lately I'd been thinking about making Julius my number one. Why should he be a sidepiece when Larry didn't want to do anything but listen to his nosy-ass mama?

We were seated in a secluded booth in the back of the large restaurant. I pretended like Julius was my husband and I was his wife. I couldn't remember the last time Larry and I had gone out to dinner.

Dinner to him was a bucket of the Colonel's cheapest chicken. This was the kind of life I deserved and Julius was obviously able to give it to me.

"So tell me, what subjects do you teach?" I asked.

He sipped his beer, swallowed hard, then sighed. "You know, baby, when I'm here with you, the last thing I wanna talk about is work. I mean, there's nothing real exciting about it, but if you must know, I teach several courses."

Everything about him seemed so smart. I was a lucky woman! If only he knew that it didn't matter what he said, as long as he talked, I would listen. I had suspected it before, but as I sat snuggled up under Julius inside my favorite restaurant, I knew for sure that I was falling in love.

It must've been plain to see, too, because soon the Mariachi trio came over to our table and serenaded us with a beautiful love song.

# CHAPTER 32

# Quinn

I awoke the next day with a dick that was harder than a calculus test. I was so happy to be sleeping with Candi. We were both naked and situated in the spooning position. I slipped my erection between the valley of her ass and pulled her close to me. I loved the feeling of my dick nestled between her ass cheeks. I inhaled the scent of her hair as my hand cupped her breasts and teased her nipples.

We'd made some serious love the night before. Not the fast, lustful shit. I'm talking about the slow, sensual type of love that touches your soul. It wasn't going to be easy for me to let such good pussy go, but I knew that by the end of my trip, my fantasy with Candi would be over. For now, I was going to enjoy every minute of it.

I told Candi that I'd made a hotel reservation at the Marriott Hotel off of the Gulf Freeway. I told her that I wanted us to have more privacy, but I really set up the hotel room to avoid Katina.

"Daddy, we can stay here, but I'll need to go back to get some fresh clothes. I didn't plan on us staying at a hotel," Candi said.

"I know, baby. You can run back in the morning," I said.

Candi began stirring in her sleep. I got the sense she was about to wake up and I was right. She stretched her limbs as far as they'd go and then repositioned herself to face me.

"Good morning," I whispered, being mindful of my morning breath.

Smiling, Candi said, "Good morning, Daddy." Candi touched the tip of my nose with her index finger as a gesture of affection. Turning over and then sitting upright, she said, "Come on. Get up. We're going to go have some breakfast and then head back to the apartment."

I dreaded the idea of going back to the apartment, but I wasn't about to tell her no. If Katina came at me sideways, I'd deal with her then. Besides, I'd already told Calvin that if I called and said Katina wanted to speak to him, he knew to say that he was getting the money together.

After we'd freshened up, Candi and I made our way down the hall toward the elevator.

"Did you like your birthday present I gave you last night?" Candi asked just as the elevator chimed. As she stepped inside I seized the opportunity and smacked her ass.

"Damn right I did," I said, feeling randy.

"Did you get the birthday card I sent to you?"

"Birthday card?" I needed her to clarify what she meant.

"Oh damn! It didn't get there in time."

"Get where?" I pressed her to tell me more.

"I had Katina give me your mailing address. I sent you a really nice and sexy birthday card and a computer printout of me in some sexy lingerie. I even sprayed it with my perfume, so you could look forward to seeing me," she said as we walked out of the hotel lobby.

*Fuck.* It was bad enough that I'd once again lied to get out of the house. I told Tameecia I had to see a medical specialist for a series of tests and I'd be gone for a few days. When she insisted on coming with me, I reminded her that she needed to be around to take the boys to school and help out with their homework.

She was very suspicious, but she decided to stay behind. If Candi's birthday card arrived while I was here, I was going to have one hell of a time explaining that away. I tried not to let her news sour my mood. I told myself that being with her was well worth the trouble.

Candi and I went to the breakfast club for a great meal, then we got back in her sedan and headed toward her apartment.

"So what do you want to do today?" she asked with a glow as bright as sunshine.

"Actually, you're going to be surprised."

"Really?"

"Yup. You know Beyoncé is in town tonight, right?"

"No you didn't!" She slapped her palm against the steering wheel.

"Yes, I did. I got us tickets to the concert."

Candi screamed loudly, and then said, "Oh, my God! I have to find something to wear."

"I'm sure whatever you find will be fine."

"All of my clothes are..." She didn't finish her sentence.

"What's wrong?"

"Oh nothing," she said and remained quiet as if something were bothering her.

"Are you sure?" I asked again to be certain.

"Uhm hmm," she answered as she pulled up in front of the apartment. "Come on, baby."

I got out of the car and walked directly behind her really close so that I could stare at her glorious ass and palm it as she walked. I was having a blast toying with her derriere. Then I heard, "Here this motherfucker go again!"

"Oh, God! It's Larry!" Candi said as she stopped dead in her tracks.

I looked up and saw the same big countrified motherfucker

walking out of the building with Katina. I stepped in front of Candi to protect her. There was no way I was going to let him get near her. Not on my watch!

"You need to take your sorry ass somewhere and leave Candi alone. What y'all had is over, man. You're an *ex*-boyfriend! Quit fucking stalking her!" I raised my voice and flexed up. I was ready for anything this big motherfucker would try.

"Ex-boyfriend!" Larry shouted. He looked either confused or mad. I couldn't tell.

"Larry, just calm down." Candi tried to ease the mounting tension. She glanced over at Katina as if she was hoping she'd help, but Katina's eyes were wide, as if she were watching an airplane take a nosedive toward earth.

"This motherfucker don't sound gay to me, Codi!" Larry's face turned red with fury.

"Why the fuck are you calling my woman Codi. Her name is Candi!" I yelled, sizing him up and itching for him to make a sudden move. At that moment, I heard tires screeching to a halt. All of us turned our attention to the street. Tameecia had jumped out of a sedan with LaQeeta in tow.

"Oh fuck! How in the hell did she find me!" As soon as the words left my mouth, I knew that the birthday card probably had Candi's return address on it.

"Yeah, that's right. I flew all the way down here to catch your dumb, cheating ass!" Tameecia's loud mouth was not welcomed. "Is this that Candi bitch you've been fucking around on me with? Is this the bitch who sent you this perfume-scented birthday card, talking about how she couldn't wait to see you again? Hold on." Tameecia unfolded a sheet of paper she removed from her back pocket. "Yeah. You the ho! And why the hell did she address the letter to Dr. Cole?"

"How in the hell did you even get here?" I barked at her.

"Smokey Love, nucca! He gave us the money to pay for the first flight down here!" LaQeeta answered my question.

"Yo' dumb asses got shit really twisted. Her name ain't no damn Candi. Her name is Codi and she's my goddamn wife!" Larry roared like a lion.

"Your wife!" I looked back at Candi.

"And you're my husband!" Tameecia added.

"Oh shit!" I heard Katina shout out as she placed both of her hands on her cheeks.

"So you been fuckin' my wife!" Larry hollered, as if he'd just been shot. "Codi, I told you that if I ever found out somebody was gettin' my stuff, I was gonna catch a case," Larry huffed at Codi.

"Baby, I can explain." Candi or Codi tried to once again ease the tension.

"What? You can explain? Just last night you were talking about us being together! Do you understand the risks I've taken to be with you?" I didn't think about what I was saying.

"So you were with her last night!" Tameecia snapped. "This bitch must really be stupid if she think you're anybody's doctor!"

"Oh, it's ass-kicking time!" LaQeeta pulled off her earrings and her shoes.

The next thing I knew, big-ass Larry charged toward me. He tackled me and we both tumbled to the ground. I ended up on my side. I was able to twist around and use his size against him. Larry landed flat on his back and I jumped on the opportunity to mount him and rain down several hammer fists to his face. All the while calling him a dumb motherfucker!

"Stop!" I heard Codi scream. "That's my husband!"

"Looks like your husband is getting his ass whipped. Just like I'm about to whip yours!" I heard Tameecia scream at the top of her voice. I stopped punching Larry long enough to watch Tameecia grab a fistful of Codi's hair and pull her face toward the ground while LaQeeta threw wild brutal punches that nailed Codi on the face.

"Damn it!" I heard Katina say as she charged in. She picked up a loose piece of asphalt and crushed it against Tameecia's skull. The eerie, hollow sound made me cringe. Tameecia let go of Codi's hair and then Codi and Katina began kicking LaQeeta's ass.

"Get off me, fool!" screamed Larry, who was still on his back. He threw a straight uppercut punch that landed under my chin.

"Son-of-a-bitch!" I howled out. The punch was powerful enough to give me double vision.

Larry pushed me off of him, got to his feet and began stomping me.

"Fuck you!" I said as I crawled to my knees and wrapped up his ankles.

Larry lost his balance and fell on his ass. He jarred loose one of his legs and began kicking my head and face. I released my grip, got to my feet and charged toward him. Larry tried to move out of my way, but once again stumbled because his jeans had come unfastened and were sliding off. I returned the favor of kicking him while he was down.

The next thing I knew flashing blue lights appeared out of nowhere and police charged in from all directions. A police officer hit me with a stun gun and stopped everything I was doing to Larry. I tumbled to the ground, twitching uncontrollably.

Another officer placed his knee on the side of my neck to hold me down while I was being handcuffed. I was hoisted onto my feet, marched over to a squad car, and placed in the backseat.

Larry was also arrested, along with LaQeeta, Katina, and Codi. Another officer was helping Tameecia to her feet. She was holding the side of her head. I could see blood running down the back of her hand. It was clear that Katina's blow had drawn blood. I closed my eyes, tilted my head back and exhaled.

"All of this bullshit because I wanted to live out my fantasy of being someone I was not," I whispered as I thought about the consequences of the lies I'd told and tried to twist into the truth. I asked myself if what I'd done was worth all of this drama. I didn't have an answer. At that moment, everything seemed dreamlike. Everything moved in slow motion and the only thing I could hear was the rapid thudding of my heartbeat. I had no idea what would happen now.

# CHAPTER 33

*Codi*

SIX MONTHS LATER

I dragged myself into the auditorium and took deep, labored breaths. All of the noise was making me nervous, but I had no choice. Some of the girls were popping gum, most were sectioned off into cliques, and that reminded me so much of my own school days.

As the teacher led me up to the auditorium stage, I took a seat where she directed me.

"Attention, young ladies," she spoke into the microphone.

Unfortunately, the chatter never quieted down.

"I said, attention, young ladies!" she repeated.

Still nothing.

"If you are *talking* you are not *listening*!" I jumped when the shrill of a whistle sounded through the speakers.

All of a sudden, a quiet blanketed the auditorium and all eyes focused forward and onto the stage.

"Now that's much better. Let's be the young ladies we are and show our guest that we are poised and we are disciplined and we know how to make the right choices! As part of our ongoing series on *choices*, we're pleased to introduce to you our speaker for this morning. Missus Codi Johnson is going to talk about how her addiction to social networking sites like Facebook, Twitter, and various websites nearly ruined her life."

As Ms. Culver told the girls about my background, my thoughts drifted to what I would say to these girls. As part of my probation and community service, I was required to go and speak to young people about the dangers of lingering on those sites.

I was convicted of assault and a series of other charges. It would have all ended with the fight outside Katina's house if Quinn's stupid wife hadn't shared our story with anyone who'd listen.

Thanks to her dumb ass, we were written up in the *Houston Chronicle* and featured on the local news. And, of course, that meant we were all the laughingstocks of our respective communities.

My business had been aired for everyone to see on TV and read about. The minute the officers asked her what happened, her dumb ass started telling how she suspected her husband had started cheating with someone he met on Facebook.

That led to jokes about us on the "Tom Joyner Morning Show," the "Steve Harvey Morning Show," and the *Tonight Show*. Basically, our story went viral, with mug shots included. One of Katina's neighbors even captured video of the incident with a cell phone camera and posted it on YouTube.

To avoid jail time, I had to agree to visit local schools and warn kids about the possible dangers lurking online. It was the best deal my attorney could work out. Katina was hot because she had to shut down the site once those nosy-ass reporters started digging up information. It had been one big, major mess.

I thanked God Larry didn't leave my ass. It was so funny. I wanted so desperately to get away from him, thinking Julius was the answer to my boredom and the spice my marriage needed, when all along, he, too, was living a lie.

When I heard Ms. Culver mention my name and look in my direction, I got up from my chair to the girls' rousing applause. I was speaking to students at Houston's new all girls' academy. I was nervous as all get-out, but I had no choice. It was either this or jail, and I wasn't made for nobody's jail!

"Hi, my name is Codi Johnson, and I am proud to say that I now have control of my life and my destiny, but six months ago, my addiction to Facebook and my desire to lead a double life nearly ruined my real life."

Whispers spread among the girls, but I definitely had their attention. I told them how it was so easy for me to assume another identity online and how that other identity became more exciting than my real life and how, soon, I had blurred the lines so much that things quickly spun out of control. I also shared how the person I met on Facebook was also living a lie. I told them how at first it seemed fun and exciting, but how it wasn't so much fun after I quickly got caught up.

I spared no details when I described how I had turned into a person who lied to the ones I loved, and how it became so hard to keep up with my lies and how things had quickly spun out of control.

"The ride in the back of that patrol car with my hands cuffed behind me had to be the longest I'd ever experienced," I said.

After I described for them how degrading it was to be arrested, fingerprinted, strip-searched, and shoved into a crowded holding cell with a bunch of filthy-looking people, I had everyone's undivided attention.

As I told the girls about my mistakes, I also thought about how lucky I really was. Things could've ended so differently for me. What if Quinn's wife had a gun? What if Larry had a gun? This story could've had a completely different ending.

By the time I wrapped up my speech and got to the question and answer part of my presentation, just about every hand in the room had shot up.

"Are you still on Facebook?"

"NO!"

"Did you sleep while in jail?"

"NO!"

I took my time and answered each and every question. Finally, Ms. Culver came up to the microphone and announced that we could only take two more questions.

After answering those questions the girls jumped to their feet and gave me another round of applause. I couldn't remember a time when I'd felt more proud.

"That was incredible," Ms. Culver said as we stood off to the side and watched the girls file out of the auditorium.

"I can't believe what you've gone through," she said. "All behind Facebook."

I couldn't believe it either.

Upon leaving the school my cell rang. It was Katina.

"Hey, girl, what's going on?" she asked.

"Just finishing my community service project. Where you at?"

"I was calling to see if you wanted to meet for lunch."

"Okay. Where?"

"I'm near the Galleria. Let's do the Cheesecake Factory," Katina suggested.

"Okay. I can be there in fifteen minutes," I said.

"See you then."

On my drive over to the Galleria I thought about Quinn. During our last court appearance I heard that Tameecia finally left him. He was still working at the used car dealership and, most surprisingly, I was stunned when I learned that he, too, was trying to escape his everyday life by reinventing himself on Facebook.

It came out in court that he had met a string of other women, of course tempting us all with his impressive title, which was fake!

I was just glad to finally close that chapter of my life. Larry wasn't perfect, but I finally resolved that neither was the next guy. At least I knew exactly what I was getting with Larry.

Of course, I arrived at the restaurant before Katina. Seated at our table, I looked up to see her approaching and the girl looked like a million bucks.

"Hey, girl. I'm glad we could meet today," she said.

"Me, too. It's been too long," I said sincerely.

"You doing okay?"

"I am. You look good."

"Yeah, well, you know since I turned state's evidence and decided to testify against my loan shark, things sort of turned around for me."

I nodded. Katina leaned in and dropped her voice to a whisper. "I wanted to talk to you about my new side hustle, girl…"

"Whoa! Hold up," I said, shaking my head, saying no. "I don't wanna hear it! I'm good!"

Katina started cracking up!

But I was serious as cardiac arrest!

# ABOUT THE AUTHORS

Many of *Pat Tucker*'s stories are ripped from the headlines and focus on socially conscious themes. Pat's work has generated tons of media coverage and has been featured on the nationally syndicated "Tom Joyner Morning Show," Essence.com, Yahoo Shine, Hello Beautiful, *Ebony* magazine, and a slew of local TV and radio stations. By day, Pat Tucker Wilson works as a radio news director in Houston, TX. By night, she is a talented writer with a knack for telling page-turning stories. A former television news reporter, she draws on her background to craft stories readers will love. With more than fifteen years of media experience, the award-winning broadcast journalist has worked as a reporter for ABC, NBC and Fox-affiliate TV stations and radio stations in California and Texas. Pat writes a weekly column, "Sexy Matters," for the *Houston Defender*, the city's oldest Black newspaper. The column focuses on all aspects of healthy relationships, including sex, love and dating. Pat's next novel is *Sideline Scandals*.

*Earl Sewell* earned his Bachelor's Degree in Fiction Writing and Radio Broadcasting from Columbia College in Chicago. Sewell has over twenty published works of fiction in various genres. His titles have enjoyed widespread success and have held steady positions on bestseller lists. He has been a guest lecturer at colleges and universities around the country and has been featured in numerous publications, such as *The Washington Post*, *School Library Journal*, *Jet* magazine, *Publishers Weekly*, *Upscale* magazine and *Black Expressions* magazine.

# READER'S DISCUSSION GUIDE

1. Think of the married people you know. How many of them do you think are truly happy?

2. Why do you think Codi was so convinced the grass would be greener on the other side, away from Larry, and living like Katina?

3. What do you think drew Quinn to Tameecia in the first place?

4. Would Quinn be as critical of Tameecia if he wasn't healthy?

5. What was the difference between Quinn's idolization of Calvin and Codi's of Katina?

6. Tameecia wanted to give her sons what Quinn called ghetto names. What are your thoughts about unique baby names?

7. How do you think Tameecia should have handled her sister when it was clear Quinn didn't want LaQueeta there?

8. Codi became enticed by Katina's fast money and she began to justify what her friend was doing. How realistic do you think that was?

9. Why do you think Larry treated Codi the way he did?

10. Do you think Quinn was going through a midlife crisis?

11. How realistic was it for two married people to pretend to be single on Facebook?

12. Why do you think Quinn tried to convince Codi that Katina could soon get jealous of their relationship?

13. When did Codi and Katina's relationship take a turn for the worse?

14. Did Larry suspect Codi was fooling around or was it the people around him who convinced him it was happening?

15. How realistic is it that people aren't who they seem on Facebook, or other online sites?

16. Why were these two people so willing to believe the lies when they knew they were also lying?